RIDICULOSITY
A DEPLOYMENT TO AFGHANISTAN

© 2016 Todd Campau
Cover Artwork © 2016 Brendan Yetter
First Print Limited Edition

The names have been changed to protect their dignity and honor. The stories contained in this book are based on actual events that occurred during the deployment.

ISBN: 978-0-9972979-0-4
Limited Edition First Print – 2016
Second Print – 2016
Third Print – 2016

Soldier Todd Publishing
SoldierTodd.com
Austin TX USA

For Chip, Shaniese, Woody, and Sister Mary Danger

AUTHOR'S NOTE

Ridiculosity – a Deployment to Afghanistan is based on email I sent to family and friends from late 2009 through fall 2010. It is a self-prescribed form of therapy for addressing lingering issues associated with the military deployment. All names and identifying information have been altered to conceal the identities of the characters described in the book. The opinions and characterizations contained herein are those of the author and in no way represent or reflect official positions of the U.S. Army Military Intelligence Corps, the Department of Defense, or the United States government.

FORWARD

I recently spent three years in Afghanistan, either as a deployed soldier or as a civilian contractor working for the military. We worked twelve to eighteen-hour days with little time off and were always on guard. Free time was precious – and even more so with our high tempo operations.

Friends and family asked about life overseas. I couldn't write a blog, nor did I have guaranteed access to the Internet. I didn't have time to answer each question, but I could and did start a series of e-mails, providing insight to our daily grind, the stupidity of the rules, our challenges, frustrations, and triumphs. At first, it was just descriptive epistles of my location and situation, but the e-mail quickly developed into vignettes of daily life. It was quite unlike the Hollywood version of war many people are familiar with.

Ridiculosity – a Deployment to Afghanistan is obviously based on a yearlong deployment. I led a team of five people tasked with collecting and analyzing data at a U.S. base in a volatile province along the Pakistani border. We became pretty tight and those friendships continue to this day. Well, most of them. Our work had a positive impact on the lives of soldiers and Afghans in our greater area, and I learned much from that year. Subsequent (future) work is based on my work as a civilian contractor in Kabul, where I served as a staff advisor and analyst to our section chief and department head on a NATO base.

I put the lessons from the military deployment described in this book to good use. You'll not read anything about operational issues, what we worked on, or the reports and analyses we published, but you will learn about the dysfunctional systems, unusual relationships, and the people who changed my life.

We know that the Army is a large organization composed of many smaller parts. It didn't surprise me that some of the soldiers I deployed with would resurface in my civilian adventures. I'll try to include stories of them when I can.

There are a lot of people in this book – because soldiers

throughout the battalion and beyond impacted our lives in some way. However, the main characters that created and fostered the Ridiculosity described here are mostly my team members – Chip, Sister Mary Danger, Woody and Shaniese. This book wouldn't be possible without them.

Most sections begin with an actual quote by the subjects involved. Yeah, soldiers often kept a Quote Board to record all the dumb or funny stuff said. Sometimes those quotes give insight to the subject; sometimes they're just funny or stupid. Either way, I hope you enjoy this voyeuristic look into my life in a war zone.

INTRODUCTION

If there ever was a government-sanctioned 'experiment' in social engineering it had to be the U.S. military. We're finally at a point where ethnic minorities, women, and gays are respected for their performance and contributions, instead of whatever 'group' they belong to. It's about time, too. Think about how much we gain, as a whole, when everyone's contributions are at least heard, if not adopted.

But social engineering cuts both ways. I experienced it on a personal level with two different groups. The first group was a serendipitous blend of soldiers, including two women, two gays, and two minorities. The second, more-homogenous group was the handpicked battalion staff. That entity was somewhat intentionally created so you can't really say the social engineering was 'by chance' like ours was.

The battalion staff accomplished their mission, but that journey was a nightmare compared to ours. Just ask anyone who served in Bagram. Note: our battalion HQ was located at Bagram Air Field, aka BAF.

Every unit that deployed overseas – whether active duty, National Guard, or reserves – must undergo multiple, sometimes redundant training sessions. Some was training they would've done anyway, while some was specific to the deployment. The fundamental purpose for all the training was twofold: to hone the skills needed on the battlefield and to get the smaller groups, which make up the collective organization, to understand their roles and how to work together. It was common to add or lose soldiers at the last minute. That's what happened to us and what made this pre-deployment training so important.

Our Battalion, like many units in the Army Reserves, wasn't fully staffed. Reservists from across the USA were sent to Texas to complete our roster. I got to meet and closely work with people in those fifteen months whom I would never have met. That alone was a very enriching experience. Some became friends, while others

3

became family.

Family - it's all about family, isn't it? Plenty of definitions exist for family. We're born into and/or raised in one – that's the literal sense. But your micro-family could be the guys on your sports team, the musicians in your band, maybe the office section you're assigned to, or the students in a study group. I suggest that each of us is a part of multiple families, some more tight-knit than others, but families nonetheless.

My military micro-family was formed during pre-deployment training and grew bonds so tight they survive today. That sometimes happens in the military and especially during a deployment. The experiences of life in a war zone will always bring people together, but the collective suffering and personal triumphs are what cement those bonds. While in Afghanistan, we missed the familiarity of home, but our deprivation paled in comparison to what some experienced.

I had to gel a disparate collection of personalities into a family, whether they liked each other or not. Chip was a challenge at first. A seasoned soldier set in his ways, he was smart and wanted to succeed. Thankfully, his work ethic rubbed off on the others. Woody, Shaniese, and Mary Danger would follow me into battle, if necessary. That wasn't going to happen but it was good to know I could rely on them. But had I earned their trust? I'd been absent during the majority of the collective training so they didn't know me from the next guy. Everyone kept saying they were lucky I was going to be their team leader – I was unaware of and frankly didn't consider my reputation in our unit. Our company commander fully trusted my judgment, having worked with me before, yet, was I worthy of it? I had deployed to Afghanistan and Iraq, but had never been to such a dangerous, kinetic area before.

Being entrusted with the lives of soldiers is a humbling responsibility. I was certainly aware of that responsibility, but not intimidated.

At our farewell gathering before getting on the plane, which would start the long journey to Afghanistan, Mary Danger's mom pulled me aside and made me promise to take care of her daughter. The anxiety of having no control over a rebellious child halfway

4

around the world was evident in her eyes. That was a touching gesture, one that I didn't take lightly. Danger was such a tough chick and would've been furious had she discovered I sent periodic e-mails to her mom about her stellar performance. Naturally, I left out all the ridiculosity the little demon started. Could I face this concerned, nervous mother again if I had to console her over Mary's death?

Deployments to a war zone are no joking matter, yet there was a time and place to let your hair down. Whereas I got to know my individual team members during our short pre-deployment training in Washington state, I had met and befriended Silas the previous summer when he and I suffered through a strenuous Army course together. Our personalities meshed perfectly and people commented that we were the two old guys from the Muppet Show (Statler & Waldorf) who sit in the balcony and heckle the actors. That's definitely a fitting comparison. Here's why, but first...

Friends suggested I front load a bit about myself. Meh, I figured y'all would come to your own impression after reading the book, but whatev, here's a piece from one of my soldiers. Sister Mary Danger wrote the following section. It gives a little insight to her, but more importantly, it gives you her initial impression of me. I emailed this early in the deployment.

RIDICULOSITY

*"Frum-**un**-dah district?*
I hope that's not where I think it is!"
I said, questioning the location of an attack.

THE BOSS MAN

When I told the team I'd e-mail my friends and family descriptions of each of them, I promised to send their descriptions of me – if they wanted to write something. Only one person wrote something, and here it is.

I am sure everybody who is reading this thinks they know Todd. But living with the man twenty-four hours a day, seven days a week…let's just say you pick up on every little thing. It has been one hell of a ride with Todd being the boss man. Here are just some of the stories about him.

We get a lot of care packages with mostly bags of nuts and chips. God forbid somebody opens up his bag of chips or nuts. Todd would not eat any because "everybody's hands have been on my nuts."

We must clean the office every Sunday per Todd's orders. Every Sunday he is amazed by how much dust can collect in a week…Hello, Pumpkin…we are in Afghanistan. What did he expect being in Afghanistan? And if there is one speck of dust left over, oh man, are we in for a rough week. I think Todd has flashbacks to being a medic. I can actually see him coming into the office one day with rubber gloves up to his elbows, scrubs, mask, and rubber boots armed with a mop saying, "All right, guys, let's have some pure, unadulterated fun!"

Speaking of which, Todd uses some big words. I am from Georgia, so my vocabulary is limited. Almost every sentence Todd says has a big word in it. I think I have opened up a dictionary more in the two months we have been here than I ever had in my life.

The other day, he thought he could get away with having a

quiet birthday. We figured out two days later that it was his birthday. Being here, we are kind of limited on resources, and the only thing we could find were Oreo cookies. We made a make-shift cake out of the Oreos and wrote a bunch of notes on paper and covered his desk complimenting his age. He wasn't too happy being reminded over and over how old he was. I think I got at least four text messages that night explaining how much he hated me.

Colonel Caution is a nickname we all use for Todd, and for good reason, too. He will buckle up, driving twenty kph (that equals to about twelve mph) in an up-armored vehicle with tinted windows. He says we have to buckle up because if we get pulled over we will get a ticket. The windows do not roll down and are tinted, so nobody can see in. I don't get his logic sometimes! Colonel Caution will yell at anyone for driving even one measly kilometer over the speed limit.

Speengeta is Pashtu for old man or (white beard). This is the definition of Todd. Todd is the oldest of the group, which means he should be the wisest. Todd regularly has senior moments, however. Speengeta is everybody's favorite word now. We all make sure to use that at least once in every sentence we speak to Todd. Every time we say that "S" word though, Todd gets mad. He gets this look on his face like he was about to strike a pose for the camera. It's his "pout-y" face.

When Todd really gets into typing he looks down and types really slow, like he is reading something on his lap. It's funny and he doesn't even realize he does it. He looks like Phil Collins playing the piano when he types.

Overall, Todd is a great boss and even better mentor. I think I would literally go insane if anybody else was my boss. Todd has very few menopausal times, which makes for a very great environment. He is my gym partner and thanks to him, I have gained ten pounds in muscle in about five weeks. Whenever there is an issue, Todd is the first to come up with a creative solution. I am glad I was deployed with him. I look up to him a lot…well, in a Speengeta way.

"Bro..." Don said
"Don't call me Bro!" I snapped.

"Buddy....?" he lightly tried, looking up for approval.
"No!" I hit back again.

"Jerk!" he laughed.

BE CAREFUL
WHAT YOU ASK FOR

During pre-deployment training, I worked with Silas and Don, who were sent to our battalion from a different unit. Silas and I were two of the five team leaders in our company, and Don supervised us all. Since Don, Silas, and I were about the same rank, we hung out together all the time. Don was a great guy – a high school calculus teacher from Salt Lake City with boundless energy. In his mid-fifties, 5'7", maybe 140 pounds, with a shaved head, and wild crazy eyes, it was weird that he had the most trusting, approachable demeanor.

He'd start a topic or sentence and then sometimes trail off, forgetting where he was going with it. I'd hate to road trip with him.

Silas, on the other hand, was born and raised in Holland to an American father and Dutch mother. A constant jokester, he lived in the D.C. area working some boring government job. Silas had the slightest of accents and most people would never guess he was foreign born. He loved to joke around and "poke the bear" so to speak. Both men were highly intelligent so we'd argue through all kinds of topics, each sure of the supremacy of his point.

The battalion spent four weeks training in Washington state where Silas, Don, and I shared a room. It was fun watching those two pick on each other and occasionally they'd gang up on me. Some of the junior-ranking soldiers would hang at our door just to hear what all the nonsense was about (we were loud). People develop a fun camaraderie when they share the same mundane experiences of pre-deployment training (or assclownery as we called it).

Across from our WWII era barracks was a jungle gym/ obstacle course thing. Teams of soldiers used it for physical training (PT), but no official, mass training or organized activity was ever forced on us. Gotta thank my company commander for that – he was a super cool guy who really "got it." And by that I mean he respected his subordinate leaders and expected them to do the right thing.

Silas, Don, and I were in the room one early evening after a day of training. Must've been on a Sunday cuz occasionally we had down time then. Don's energy level was that of a three-year-old – he'd go through major spurts of energy literally bouncing on the bunk beds and terrorizing Silas and me. Then he'd crash like a kid whose sugar-high wore off. One minute, he was talking a mile a minute – eyes all crazy-like, the next he was asleep on his bunk.

This time, Don was enthusiastically trying to get Silas and me to run over to the jungle gym and climb the knotted rope with him. Fuuuuck that, both Silas and I rolled our eyes.

"No, *you* go do it. Stay over there awhile. Play on each thing." I forcefully suggested.

Don kept badgering, but finally accepted us taking pictures of him climbing the rope from the elevated vantage point of the window in our room.

Don was that annoying kid who wouldn't go home, but his home was with us. So this was gonna be fun. While Don dashed out the door, down the stairs, and across the street to warm up, I convinced Silas to join me in pranking him.

"Dude, take a picture of my balls!" I whispered, bright eyed and excited.

"Your *what*? Silas giggled, shaking his head. No! I'm not taking a picture of your balls, dude!"

"Come on, dude! It'll be fun and get Don off our backs." I begged.

"No, dude, that's gross." Silas, paused, considering the genius of it.

This went on rapid fire for about ten seconds until Silas

agreed. I laid on my side and pulled my hairy peach basket between my legs so it rested on a hamstring, and Silas, grimacing and giggling, snapped shots from behind. Then I rolled onto my back and gathered them together in a tight fist for a couple shots.

By this time Don was yelling, wondering where the heck we were. He had already climbed the damn rope and was shouting, gleeful at his accomplishment!

"Climb the rope again from the bottom! *Come on*, we need some action shots!" Silas replied, muffling a laugh.

Damn, he was good. We got Don to descend and re-climb that stupid thirty-foot rope so that we could get action shots. Meanwhile, Silas kept snappin' pics of my agates in various positions mixed up with pictures of Don. I wanted some shots of my "brown eye" but Silas adamantly refused. He took a few last snaps of my soon-to-be infamous nutsack then a few more of Don.

Sweat glistening on his forehead, nearly out of breath from running back but grinning ear-to-ear like a kid opening up the best birthday present ever, Don returned to the room eager to see the digital proof of his mastery of the rope. He clicked through the last ones then screamed!

Silas and I fell off our bunks laughing.

All wild-eyed, Don sputtered through his laughter, "*You Guys!*" while a gaggle of soldiers crowded the door to see what was up.

Thankfully for Don, Silas refused to take happy snaps of my brown eye. That would've been gross – but balls, that's funny. Don began deleting "my precious" from his camera as some of the soldiers gathered around him, eager to share the latest ridiculosity.

At the end of training in Washington state, we were allowed a four-day pass in Seattle. Thank God – some normalcy before departure. We'd been at this training nonsense for months and would soon be deprived of the usual things for a year. A four-day sojourn would be a welcomed and needed respite.

Silas' wife joined him, Don's twenty-one-year-old daughter came to visit, and I went alone to the city for some mental down time. There were drunken nights at a sushi restaurant where one of our crew threw up on a waitress and later in the bathroom sink, and long walks through Seattle's neighborhoods, the light mist covering us. Later, I joined Silas and his wife at a live show: Puppetry of the Penis.

At the end of the four-day pass Don nearly jumped Silas and me when we met up on base. He and his daughter were at dinner one night. His daughter was going to buy a new camera (don't people use camera phones now?) but Don convinced her to take his – SIM card and all.

"*Dad? Oh my gosh!* Their family doesn't swear – must be a Mormon thing. What's this?" a look of confused horror on her face. Yup, there they were, in a mid-priced, sensible downtown Seattle restaurant that I'd never visited. On view during dessert – my hairy schweddy balls.

Don stutters and laughs telling that story even to this day. It was perfect and set the tone for the year. He and I became roommates during the deployment while Silas went to another base, but we definitely bonded over that experience and even better – it curbed Don's blanket trust in people. Well, at least in Silas and me.

THE DEPLOYMENT

In the fall, I was on my second deployment to Afghanistan and doing well. Our weather was better here than in Washington state, with highs in the 60's and lows in the 30's. We'd been on-site three weeks and it was surprising how much I'd grown into the position while discovering how much I needed to learn. My team was dedicated, fun to work with, inquisitive, and headstrong – all traits needed in this field. Our job was to talk to people, cajole them into telling us things like where weapons caches were located, who was financing the bad guys, and who was laying the IEDs in the roads, or making car bombs. I liked it.

We recently had our first rains but they didn't last long - one day of constant light rain, reminded me of Seattle. I didn't miss the states yet, but Seattle was on my mind, being the last major city we saw before deploying.

Yesterday a buddy of mine and I climbed to the highest point on base. A three-story, rickety, wooden catwalk was located in the middle of base near the base headquarters. Antennae and satellite dishes were on top. We slowly negotiated the narrow stairs to smoke cigars, taking in the 360° views. Our base was the biggest in the province, being the military HQ for three provinces. It had the area of five or six football fields.

We had walked in the shade of the mulberry trees lining one of the roads to get to the catwalk. I thought of the imposing mulberry tree in my neighbor's yard when I lived in the country as a young teen. That was so long ago.

A few small stands of eucalyptus trees dotted parts of our base in all directions; otherwise it was a dusty collection of roads and rock. I'd heard the US military destroyed the original orange and olive groves that grew here in order to build the base. Progress, ya know, anything to fight the Taliban.

Small, scraggly trees edged the outside of the imposing base fortifications, followed by irrigated yet dry-looking farm fields. Clumps of trees framed walled qalats (small private compounds) dotted throughout the fields. This scene extended to foothills of the snow-capped, majestic mountains of Pakistan, about thirty miles away. It was a rugged beauty, but one I wouldn't have much time to appreciate.

Yeah, the days were long. I was usually up by 6 a.m., in the office by 7 a.m., and done around 10 p.m. On Saturday, I vowed to e-mail my family and friends. Becoming enveloped in work to the detriment of one's sanity was easy. I made my team take time away from the office, and did so myself. I had so much to be thankful for - in light of the first two deployments. I wished everyone realized how lucky we actually were. 'It could always be worse,' that was my motto.

THE TEAM

Every army unit is composed of a group of individuals who together, made up the collective success or failure of the mission based on their strengths, weaknesses, age, experience, personalities, idiosyncrasies, and ability to get along. My team was no different. We hailed from across the U.S. (Texas, Maryland, Nebraska, California, and Georgia). I'd like to think we were successful because of my astute leadership, but I wasn't dumb. I created the environment in which we could succeed and my teammates worked their hearts out – some more than others.

My company commander had a list of names from which to form teams. Some of those names were organic members of our organization while others were newly assigned soldiers. He and I go way back, so he knew my leadership style. However, he was blind to the new soldiers sent to our unit – they were just names. He selected my team and thrust them upon me when I returned from specialized training with Silas. Thank God that was the case because I wouldn't have initially chosen to work with some of them for whatever reason.

I long wanted to give you a snapshot of our team and finally decided to reveal the inner machinations of a, dare I say, "kick-ass" group of soldiers. I told the team I'd update my friends/family with information about them. I gave each team member an alias – and to be fair, I offered them the chance to give their personal opinions of me.

I must say that I was proud of our diversity. The Army is multi-cultural – and our team really represented multiculturalism more than any other. Of five core members, only one was your stereotypical white American male. Our diversity included one Asian, one African-American, two gays – a homo and a muncher, and the stereotypical white dude. Such differences enhanced our success instead of detracted from it because we leveraged the strongest parts in each of us. Here's the team, starting with Chip.

RIDICULOSITY

"Good thing Mexicans didn't invent fire, or else we would've never had any." Chip sneered, ragging on his Mexican friend, Marc.

CHIP

Chip, my assistant, was half Asian, but was atypical in the sense that he was a monster of a man – approximately 6'2" tall, and 235 lbs. He had a great laugh when he chose to put it out there and often greeted his contemporaries with "What's up, fuckface?" or "Hello, faggot."

Chip played that whole "abrasive" thing well, especially with his friends, and I had to shut it down at first to prevent cuss word-sparring. He liked to give the impression he was in a bad mood and would verbally push you to see if you'd back down. Chip ragged hard on his ethnic friends – especially Mexicans – which was quite ironic and funny considering they made fun of him in a bad Asian accent (Chip had no accent).

It took me a while to get used to him, but now I wouldn't want anyone else as my second in command.

"All I hear is *Oui, Oui, Oui*," Chip said, referencing my French heritage.

Although he had ten years in the army, this was Chip's first deployment in our career field, having re-trained from another job. That military background, his thirty-four years of life experience, his mixed family, and his time living in both Japan and California, made him great for this job. Chip could get in anyone's head if in the right mood, but he could be an ornery fuck.

One of his nicknames was Eeyore – you know the donkey from Winnie the Pooh? That was one of my favorite books as a kid, although Eeyore was never my favorite character – who ever heard of a blue donkey? I more identified with Pooh, maybe because I was an overweight kid......Ah, sorry, back to Chip. He was Eeyore because of his occasional drab, down responses to questions.

One of Chip's traits that we picked on him for was his habit of looking intently at you, brown eyes ablaze, as he described something important – raising his eyebrows up and down for emphasis. It was like they were attached to electrodes. We've laughed at him enough times that he consciously tried to keep a motionless forehead, but his concentration to stay still was so obvious, that we made fun of him anyway. Making fun of Chip was an art form that Mary Danger perfected.

Since being in Afghanistan and getting to know my expectations, Chip exponentially picked up his game. He became the workhorse of the team – talking to the most people, QC-ing reports, taking care of the junior soldiers, and letting me do my job of providing direction, liaising with outside agencies, fighting battles, protecting our interests, and developing an environment in which we could flourish. Chip was a sergeant and I gave him free rein to do sergeant business. Danger, another coworker, once called Chip the Mom and me the Dad. Chip didn't like it but we all laughed.

I'm always railing on Mary Danger for the mistakes in her reports.

"Life is full of mistakes..." Sister Mary said while grinning at me.
"...and then Mary was born." Chip chimed in without looking up from his computer.

THE GREAT ESCAPE, PART 1

Cabin fever - it affects everyone. During the workday (especially near the end), don't you just want to be outside in the sun, on the slopes, on your bike? Anywhere but the office. During class lectures, the hardest time to pay attention is near the end of the period, right? Driving home from a long distance trip is always great but the last couple of miles home can't come soon enough. You just want a change, and "back home" we have the option of making changes to some degree, but when you're deployed that option is gone. You're powerless to change your situation and that powerlessness intensifies the cabin fever mentality. Some people went so stir crazy, they took huge risks just to experience something different. The excitement of breaking the rules heightened the thrill of the illicit experience – especially later in the deployment. Just ask Chip and Sister Mary Danger.

Maybe I didn't give these guys enough freedom or time off during the deployment but we had lots of work to do. Maybe they wanted to rebel against authority, like many young people do. Mary was twenty-two and Chip was used to being his own boss. Maybe it was because our interpreters spoke the language and itched to get off base as well. Who knows?

On our way home from Afghanistan, I discovered that Chip, Danger, and Mahmud used to sneak off base in our vehicle more often than I ever thought possible. The first time was halfway through the deployment. They chickened out, driving only about

RIDICULOSITY

500 meters on the pothole-filled dirt road that led to the town bazaar, before turning around and scampering back.

Understand this: There was no safety net off base – no OnStar assistance, no Good Samaritan law, no tow trucks or local mechanic shop to tow your broke-down vehicle. However, there were Taliban sentinels watching the gate reporting who and what came and went. There were burkha-clad women walking dirty little children on the roadsides. There were whining crotch rockets zooming helter-skelter around people. There were bicycles laden with goods, hay, vegetables, wood, or carrying three to four passengers slowly weaving around the potholes. There were no traffic rules off base. Might made right. So if Chip et al. crashed, blew a tire, got into a firefight, hit a pedestrian, or were kidnapped – they were on their own. Ratchets up the excitement factor, doesn't it? I see why they got scared the first time.

The kids 'escaped' a few more times and brazenly traveled further away from base with each adventure. They wore civilian clothes, used our non-descript civilian truck, hid their weapons, and didn't stare at anyone. The plan was that Mahmud would do any talking if necessary so they thought they'd be 'safe' but his accent was from northern Afghanistan and we were in the east. It would've been obvious that he wasn't local, like a redneck from Texas trying to pass himself off as a local New Yorker. Afghans were extremely xenophobic when it comes to their own ethnic groups. If you weren't from their village or valley, you were suspicious. Chip and Danger doubtfully considered this snag. Thank Christ nothing ever happened – we would've been crucified.

"Do you think they have a smoking sensation class here?" Callie hopefully asked, meaning smoking-cessation classes.

CALLIE, AKA SISTER MARY DANGER

She'll kill me for using this nickname, but Callie was a riot to have around. She dropped out of a Georgia college after two years and decided to join the army after working as a sous chef for a while. I guess the swimming scholarship and academics didn't sit well with her abundant energy and smoking habit. Oh, yeah, Callie smoked like a longshoreman. Wait. Is that even a profession anymore? I've heard the saying and understand it well enough, but I've never met a longshoreman.

Anyway, Cal loved her cancer sticks – and I ragged on her almost daily. "I'm gonna quit when I get back." She lied to herself and the rest of us, squinting through smoke while standing in the sun outside the office, cigarette slowly burning between her cracked, unmanicured, skinny fingers. Nothing I said seemed to register.

I made a bet with her over something and she lost. The wager – one day of not smoking. And I got to pick the day. Being the benevolent (and manipulative) boss that I was, I promised Cal I'd give her that smoking day back if she enrolled in and completed a college course during the deployment. She was so addicted to cancer (my term for smoking) that she'd forego one day of abstinence for weeks of classes. That was a good deal because it got her mind back in the "school" game – to which I wanted her to return after the deployment. Besides, she already promised me she was gonna quit smoking before the deployment ended so it was a win for both of us.

I had a couple nicknames for Callie including Betty Sous, Mary Mumbles, Scrappy Doo, Betty Badass, and one she came up with herself – Mary Danger. Because Cal went to a Catholic high school, I called her Sister Mary Danger – or a derivative of it.

Danger soaking wet was about a buck ten (that's 110 lbs.) and a complete tomboy. "I wanna go out on mission and kill Taliban." she'd mumble without moving her lips – I swear that girl has a future in ventriloquism. We joked that Mary'd be the first in our unit to get a confirmed enemy kill – but certainly there'd be someone else who'd garner that distinction, thank God.

If you've ever seen the original Alien movie – the character that best described Sister Mary Danger was Vasquez – the tough, badass chick who wanted to shoot first and ask questions later. Well, kind of... Danger also reminded me of those Rosie the Riveter posters from WWII, especially when she showed off her impressive guns.

Like Chip, Danger was a hard worker. She had a bit of an attitude but one of the best work ethics I've come across in a young soldier (Mary was a twenty-two-year-old Specialist – SPC). She was up in the morning to hit the gym and dragged me there more often than I wanted. She was one of the first in the office, usually the first to clean the meeting tents (we conducted meetings in the tents), the first to clean our vehicles, first to volunteer for whatever I needed done, and the last to depart at the end of the day. Unfortunately, she had the most unproductive and challenging group of people with whom we met. But she turned that into a positive by helping the rest of the team.

In spite two years of college, Danger had a remarkably narrow vocabulary and blamed the Georgia public school system. She tried growing it by hitting the crossword puzzles that came in care packages. Mary would only attempt the level one puzzles, but we got her to level three a few times. She even admitted that she learned a lot of new words since working with me (I edited her reports).

"Yeah, like *'hello'*, *'please'*, and *'thank you!'*" I smiled.

A bug-eyed, shocked look on her face at my response, for once, she was speechless as we all howled with laughter. One of her favorite pastimes was to make fun of me – usually the more outrageous the better. She was good at it.

"Do you realize what little work I'd get done if I had a mirror?" Devon yelped, when I tried putting a gift mirror on his desk.

DEVON, AKA WOODY

From Baltimore, Devon was twenty-four, possibly of Greek, Italian, Jewish, or other Mediterranean descent. With his hair grown out and a full beard, he passed and was often mistaken for an Afghan. Sometimes he smelled like an Afghan, so that lent credence to people thinking he was local. There's another chapter coming on "Life with an Afghan."

Devon reminded me of one of those Borscht-belt comedians – like Groucho Marx. The way he talked was almost stage-like at times, as if performing. He was quiet, brainy, read books on psychology, and loved learning new words from the dictionary. Sudoku was a hobby. He often mumbled when answering questions – for which we all yelled at him. He chewed his nails down to the nub and even the skin around some of them – maybe the guy was perpetually hungry.

He got really animated when passionate about something and you had a different opinion (or just wanted to fuck with him and take the opposing side – Mary Danger often did). He had this trite habit of raising one eyebrow whenever someone aimed a camera at him so most photos of Devon depict this one-eyebrow-raised, hairy Afghan-looking dude. You had to catch him off guard to see the real Devon.

Devon had a hundred nicknames and seemed to acquire them daily. The guy did so many dumb, funny things it was easy to find a name for him. 'Woody' was a derivative of Hollywood. Why? Well, the guy couldn't help but look at his reflection in any reflective surface - store windows, mirrors, polished metal, etc., hence, Hollywood – he called himself that. Well, I considered the name too sexy so I dubbed him Woody. But it wasn't his first nickname.

"Come on Devon, we're gonna get BBQ." I informed him one night during pre-deployment training in San Antonio.

"Chief, we can leave base?" he questioned, wide-eyed.

"Dude, really? Where'd you get this guy?" Silas asked, pointing a thumb at Woody. "You're with the Chiefs kid." Silas joked, and winked to keep me from laughing as we squirreled Woody off base for dinner. No, we weren't supposed to leave base, but ya think that stopped us?

I learned he'd be on my team and I wanted to get to know him. We made small talk, but it was mostly me and Silas joking.

"What's your middle name Devon?" Silas asked. It was actually Kurt, but we heard Curly instead. "No, no, I said *Kurt!*" he protested in vain. We started calling him Curly in spite of his protests. Ironically, Woody later told me that his nickname as a kid was Curly – it was fitting because the guy was covered with thick, black curly hair – I mean you could braid the hair on his legs. He was self-conscious about it and thank God we had to wear pants. Otherwise, I would've probably called him Chewbacca.

I dubbed him Lurch and Grinder the day he learned how to drive a stick shift. One of our vehicles was a standard pick-up. I had to teach Mary Danger and Woody how to drive. Sister Mary stalled out four times before we even moved a foot. Lurch, aka, Grinder, aka Woody, ground the gears a few times and we lurched forward at each stop. Praise Jesus, there were no hills on base.

Woody had a self-professed, bad work ethic. If the kid had applied himself – he'd have mopped up. He worked as a bartender at a bowling alley back in B'more so he had that "I can talk to anyone" thing going for him. The drawback was his contemplative and introverted nature. During music appreciation (more on that later), Woody'd stand up and jam on the air guitar, or start this goofy dance. He fed off the attention and laughs. However, he didn't want to go to the Sunday night BBQs where we'd interact with our counterparts, which was great for networking. I almost had to physically drag him there.

Woody forgot when to show up for work (I think I finally fixed that problem), he forgot to take his phone on a mission once, he

24

forgets where he put his clothes, he left stuff everywhere, etc. He was the typical guy – forgetful of unimportant (to him) things yet functional in life.

Eating and food. Did ya ever have a kid brother who made a complete mess every time he ate? He always took too long to prepare his sandwich or cheeseburger or salad. No one wanted to sit by him because wherever he sat there'd be food everywhere and usually on him, too.

Woody was oblivious to the fact that he wore half his meal. Add the thick, hairy beard to the feeding mix and it didn't make for a pretty sight. If it weren't for us making fun of him, the guy would've walked around with enough crap in his beard to feed a small Afghan family. I made a conscious effort to comb my beard after every meal thanks to Woody. He was fundamentally a good kid with a decent disposition and attitude and I was thankful to have him on the team.

RIDICULOSITY

"You Sir, are Hitler to our Western Europe!" Woody announced, fists on his hips, the first time I told them to clean the office.

"You should feel violated then, because didn't Hitler like, invade everybody?" I stated matter-of-factly.

SLEEPING BEAUTY GETS A WAKE UP

Ah Woody, in retrospect I grew to appreciate that kid more than I thought possible. He was hard working, intelligent, witty, had a good sense of humor, etc. Yet he was also messy, disorganized, and incorrigible in some respects.

In spite of the structure and guidance on both our responsibilities and mission, the team had enough flexibility to do their jobs, exercise, take classes, watch movies, goof off, or do whatever they wanted. My only absolutes were they must get their work done first and come into work on time. No one missed their report deadlines or took our mission lightly, but Woody had a habit of showing up late.

That wasn't gonna fly. First, I asked Chip to deal with him because Chip is my assistant team leader. Here's the sticky part – he and Woody were roommates. Imagine if you and your section lead lived in the same apartment and you were always late for work. The lead might not care, but the manager cared – a lot. That somewhat represented our situation. Chip was okay with Woody being ten to twenty minutes late, but I wouldn't stand for it. I don't think it had anything to do with the arbitrary 8 a.m. start time. We could begin the day whenever we wanted, actually. I didn't even mind the disrespectful innuendo of missing the beginning of the day. What irked me the most with Woody's perpetual tardiness was that it displayed a lack of discipline. To me, discipline and the military had to go hand-in-hand, especially in a war zone.

RIDICULOSITY

Sure, Woody was young and his association with the military was short, but if he were to be successful (in my mind), he needed to instill a sense of discipline in every aspect of his young life, not just his job. Woody was determined to attend a four-year university when we returned. I even reviewed his application essays during the deployment. So hopefully, my mania about him being on time transcended the year in Afghanistan and carried over to attending classes, especially the ones he'd be forced to take early in the morning.

What to do, what to do? Chip didn't want to deal with the "problem" but I insisted he at least verbally counsel Woody, explaining that it was easier to drag his zombie-like body to the office on time than to deal with me. Poor Woody, I gave him one chance to fail after that counseling. Then, I brought down the hammer. I didn't want to, but he forced my hand, and I've got big hands.

Between our row of single-story, beige office buildings and the olive grove was a long, rock-covered parking lot. However, the rocks weren't evenly spaced. And some areas didn't have rocks at all. A few piles of dirt mounds with rocks abutted the grove. If Woody needed some help getting to work on time, spreading rocks might do the trick. But it wasn't gonna be that simple.

I showed Chip the area and what I wanted done, explaining in minute detail how Woody needed to first collect all the trash including any cigarette butts, papers, water bottles, or anything else that wasn't naturally there. I overlooked the rocks, they were supposed to be there. Next he had to sift through the piles of dirt for all rocks bigger than a tennis ball and pile them in one area. Filling in the low spaces or "pot holes" was the following task. Finally, he was to use a shovel, rake, or any other device he could find to evenly spread all remaining rocks.

Woody didn't strike me as an outdoor person so this should be annoying at the very least. Just in case I read him wrong, I made him wear what we call "Full Battle Rattle", which meant helmet, protective vest, gas mask slung at the hip, and his M-4. Sounds shitty, right? Well, to add insult to injury, he had to do this extra-curricular, non-judicial corrective training on his half day off and

28

start at 7 a.m., instead of noon. I was there to ensure they didn't fuck around. Yeah, I said they. I made Chip supervise, at least until 9 a.m. when I took over. Woody was miserable. It was a sunny, balmy 75 degrees.

Chip grumbled and no doubt cursed me under his breath. But he only had to sit around in the shade, smoke cigarettes, and wait for me to relieve him two hours later. I almost felt sorry for Woody at 9 a.m. He wasn't moving very fast but he had made progress. The area was cleared of trash and most of the big rocks were in a pile. He was working on the potholes then had only to level the remaining mounds of dirt and rock. I figured he'd be done by 11 a.m. – a full hour before he would've normally been in the office.

At 10:30 a.m. my boss came over to ask what was going on. He let us run our teams and didn't interfere. He was impressed by Woody's work and jokingly suggested he'd like to borrow him for another project. I chuckled but Woody stood there motionless, mouth agape. I could tell he was pissed and shocked even if I couldn't see his eyes through the dark sunglasses.

I gotta hand it to him. Soldiers must follow lawful orders even when the orders may not make sense to them. Woody could've protested, done a half-ass job, loitered around, etc., but he didn't. Everyone was at least mildly impressed with his efforts, but probably because they were sympathetic to his plight. The fact that he did a good job was a testament to his character and sense of duty. The punishment ensured Woody was never late for work again. In fact, he was usually ten minutes early and cheery.

This type of counseling would never fly in a civilian company. What recourse does a boss have for the terminally late employee? Performance-counseling statement? Docking pay? What if the employee is salaried? Termination? Isn't that too severe? How does one remedy a tardiness problem? Guess I'll have to try that myself to see how my boss reacts, or maybe I could just ask him. But that wouldn't be as much fun.

RIDICULOSITY

"You got a frosty…not quite a milkshake...the eighty-nine cent kind." Shaniese offered, as Mary Danger mumbled the Milkshake song while stumbling into the office one morning.

"It's more like an ice chip." I added over my shoulder.

SHANIESE

Shaniese, the last person to join our team, was originally part of another team but transferred to us toward the end of the training cycle in Washington state. Her original team went to a COP (Combat Outpost), which didn't support women. I.E., the COP had no separate shower, toilet, etc., facilities for women. I'm glad we got Shaniese because she had a fresh, naïve, outlook on the army, our job, and Afghans.

Shaniese spent time in college, but not as much as Mary Danger. She was twenty-one, originally from Nebraska but lived in Norman, Oklahoma, and talked a mile a minute when excited. A former high school basketball star with a smile that lit up her entire face, she was a total dude magnet.

One night the team finished dinner at the DFAC (Dining Facility) and was leaving when this tall guy in PT clothes literally came running after Shaniese, throwing his game, trying to get her phone number or e-mail.

I was holding the door and watched Cool Breeze pour on the smooth talk. She and I smiled at each other (her beaming). Breeze was embarrassed as he saw me with the door, but Shaniese motioned that it was okay so we left her to be wooed by the most recent war-zone Casanova.

Shaniese was very attached to her family and called them daily, sometimes more than once. I'm unfamiliar with phone plans available to deployed soldiers, but I did ask my carrier about overseas rates. It wasn't pretty. It charged at least $4.99 a minute to call home from Afghanistan. I don't know what phone plan Shaniese had, but if it was like my old carrier, that girl was gonna be broke.

Shaniese was from the country and man, that girl sounded *country*. It was quite endearing even if we had to ask her to repeat what she said, usually just to tease her.

"Shaniese, rummage through those shelves and see what we can archive and what we can shred, will ya?" I asked one morning. It was early in the deployment and the previous team had left disorganized crap everywhere.

A couple hours later, "Chief, what do you want me to do with these fowls?" – meaning files. I repeated "*Fowls*? I didn't know we had chickens up in here?" (I know, it was a lame joke and you really had to hear it to appreciate it. We laughed, including Shaniese.) She freely admitted to sounding too country.

If she was known for anything in the battalion, it was for combatives training in California. Combatives was basically hand-to-hand combat every soldier must undergo as a part of validation to deploy. Poor Shaniese was paired with the battalion commander (BC) – an opponent everyone dreaded because of the possible, imagined repercussions if you happened to win.

To put her match in perspective, Shaniese was paired with one of the few people who had universally united the more than 200 Battalion Soldiers. How? The BC was a stay-at-home mom who had never deployed to a war zone in spite of her years of service. She was an insecure, misogynistic, emotionally immature, closet racist with a Jekyll & Hyde complex. It was fair to say most everyone hated her.

To be honest, I didn't witness their match (I was at a different school with Silas), but people described it to me in such vivid detail that I could see it as if I lived it. Twenty-one-year-old Shaniese was stuck doing hand-to-hand combat with the forty-five-year-old "leader" of the entire battalion because they're relatively close in size. Every time the BC tried a move, Shaniese blocked it. Whenever forced to take the passive role during a re-set, Shaniese quickly took the upper hand.

The pivotal moment of their match happened as the women were standing, the BC behind Shaniese, in a vain attempt to force the young girl to the floor. Shaniese easily grabbed ahold of the BC's arms, quickly bent over, and flipped that contemptuous woman onto her back. The BC made this ungodly scream of terror and incredulity as she went from vertical to horizontal in a flash, while one hundred soldiers looked on, some cheering. People still talk about that match...with a smile.

Surprisingly, Shaniese knew and sang along with some of my music (more on that later). Her Gramma loved and played Motown music, so Shaniese was very familiar with all those classic artists. I grew up listening to Motown and played it in the office on my iPod. Only she and I knew who performed those tunes, so I guess when I played Motown, it prolly reminded Shaniese of times at Gramma's house. That might've been a great memory for her, but the last thing I wanted to do was equate spending time with the boss to spending time with Gramma.

RIDICULOSITY

"Do all Asian people know Ti-Known-Do?" Mary Danger smiled and mischievously asked Chip (spelled [to her] phonetically meaning Tai Kwon Do)

"You dirty whore." Chip chuckled under his breath.

GETTIN' MY LEARNIN' ON

We work hard, but don't get much time to play so "playing hard" is out of the question. No matter, I intended to keep the team engaged during the deployment. Some smart, driven people worked for me and they were open to taking college classes during the Afghan trip, if possible. Well, Woody and Shaniese were excited. Mary Danger took some convincing. I definitely made it possible and even encouraged their efforts. Why sit around playing video games or watching DVDs all night when you can apply your critical-thinking skills to something other than the day job, right?

"I got to study for the first day of school, or else I'll *fail* the class!" Woody exclaimed with a panicked, nervous look, opening his textbook a week before class started. I loved Woody's enthusiasm and dedication. The kid took three college courses during the deployment and still put in a full day's work on the job. He was probably too smart for his own good because he was often socially awkward. But he'll grow into that nerdy, distant intellectualism thanks to his profound love of learning. He sent off college applications during the deployment and was accepted to Penn or something like that. Smart kid.

Shaniese planned to be a nurse when finished with the military. She wanted to join the Army as a combat medic but that field was already full. Everyone wanted to be a medic when she joined. She was smart, so they offered her something in the intelligence field. She would be better at the job when her writing and critical-thinking skills improved, but her heart wasn't in it.

Shaniese did the smart thing and signed up for a class she

needed for her major, like biology or something. She had to take a year off from college to deploy, so enabling her to continue her education even just a little bit, was a success for us both. It also kept her head in the "college game", hopefully making it easier to adjust next semester.

Sister Mary Danger, help me, Lord. I really did love that kid, but wanted to strangle her sometimes. Danger protested against doing *anything* extra to further her education. I think she had a deep-seeded fear of failure, but I wasn't about to let her fail or postpone classes. Whereas Woody started reading his textbook well before the first day of class, Mary was happy to skate by, blissfully content with simply passing. If I didn't always remind her to go to class, she'd have gladly skipped. Mary thought the easiest class would be the ones with the fewest requirements and homework. What class could that be?

I don't exactly remember the name, but it involved watching movies and writing a two-page critique afterward. Can you believe it? The only class Sister Mary considered taking involved sitting on her butt and watching DVDs, typical Danger! Thankfully these weren't inane, mindless movies. They were cinematic classics with a deep message and theme. She was supposed to prove she understood those themes in her papers. Well, Danger spent more time looking up the Cliff's Notes versions for answers and themes than actually trying to understand what was going on. Yeah, her critical thinking needed lots of help, but at least she tried.

Her favorite movie was "Apopalips [sic] Now" – I love her. I think she related to the war aspect because of our deployment. She probably thought she experienced the same thing as the characters did, or maybe she wanted to. Again, at least I got her to take a class, any class. You should've seen her excitement when it was over. Danger had earned a B and was exuberant with pride. Woody would've hung himself.

"I am literally the redheaded stepchild they treat me like!" – Josh said, complaining about his boss again.

JOSH

Josh was an honorary member of our team, I felt sorry for the dude. The poor guy was yanked from his original team and floated around Bagram for a bit before finally being sent to our base. Josh partly worked for me but partly worked for the commander and partly worked for another group, which had a less strenuous work pace. He never felt like he belonged anywhere until very recently when he volunteered to replace a guy who redeployed home much earlier than anticipated. Josh's new boss was Don – my rope-climbing roommate.

With pale skin, flame-red hair, and a slightly darker red beard, he was dubbed many things including: Ginger, Flamer, Powder (his skin tone), Duracell (the coppertop battery), and Red. But Josh was dared to do something during pre-deployment training and hence, we call him Firecrotch.

"I bet the drapes don't match the carpet." one jackass soldier taunted Josh about his pubes in a crowd of guys. "You probably don't even have a bush, if ya can't grow a man-sized beard." he continued. This came from a dude genetically incapable of growing facial hair, except for eyebrows – and those were pretty thin.

"Yes, it does!" Josh snapped, his flame red hair framing his deep red blushing face, pissed that jackass would pick on him in front of everyone.

"Prove it then!" All eyes upon the defiant Josh, waiting to see what he'd do.

Much to everyone's surprise, Josh yanked down his pants and showed his curly, bright, red bush – to much whooping and hollerin'. Now the Firecrotch name lives in infamy.

Josh was smart, soft spoken, occasionally snarky and fun to

RIDICULOSITY

have around, and of course, there was that crotch – just don't dare the guy in public.

INCOMING VS. OUTGOING AND REACTIONS

Artillery is one phenomenon we experienced in Afghanistan most people can't understand stateside. Typically around sunset, sunrise, or the middle of the night, the artillery battery on our base would shoot off rounds. The artillery battery was responsible for providing coverage and support to a large portion of our province, thus at any time during the day or night one could hear the sounds of out-going artillery.

Soldiers at far off locations called for artillery support when under attack, when they had positive identification of insurgent locations, and/or when they needed illumination at night. Although the blast of out-going artillery was always shocking and unexpected, I thought of it as the sound of salvation – who knows what the soldiers requesting artillery were going through. Thus, artillery – the sound and feeling of freedom. And by feeling, I do mean feeling.

Outgoing artillery was characterized by a series of huge blasts. Since we were located on the same end of the base as the artillery battery, we really got to experience outgoing. Blasts typically shook the building, rattled the metal window coverings, and always made you jump. If you were outside, the blasts literally shook your chest cavity. You know what I mean? Have you ever watched a movie with loud, surround-sound, digital, Dolby, THX stereo and your whole body convulsed when explosions go off or something crashes? Well, imagine that tenfold, with no visual warning. It was enough to make you crap your pants. Well, not me, at least not yet.

Woody and Josh were in the office late one night playing Xbox. You'd think they'd want something other than a war game, but nope, it was a shoot 'em up thing and they were intently focused on some killing mission. I had just left work and was walking back to my hooch when the attack siren sounded so I ran back to the office. Those two were so engrossed in the loud game that they never heard the siren. I barged in the office and started yelling at them just as the outgoing artillery boom went off, breaking their concentration – it was fucking classic. What an entrance, what an effect! I love my job.

Incoming was a totally different experience. It was not as loud, but the psychological affect was much more damaging because you could die from incoming – hardly the sound and feeling of freedom. Ironically, today we experienced incoming. That didn't happen very often on my base, thank God, but we heard this one land nearby and yeah, there is a kind of whistling noise followed by the boom of the explosion. About thirty seconds later the base alarm siren went off and continued sounding for twenty-five minutes. We had only one round come in – a mortar launched by someone on a nearby hill. Thankfully, no one was hurt. Two of my team were inside the office and two were driving to the front gate when the shell landed. The two driving parked the vehicle, jumped out, and ran to a nearby bunker, then called me to say they were okay. One of the first things we do during an attack is get and report the status of the team. The entire crisis lasted only twenty-five minutes, then we went about our business. Mission first, remember?

We had mortar rounds dropped on us last night. Everyone expected the spring offensive to hit full force once the winter snows melted. About 1 a.m., a couple of muffled explosions sounded nearby. No one was injured. But as usual, the alarm sounded, we got a quick accountability of everyone, sent it to the commander, and then went about our business – which for me was back to bed. Everyone except Carmen was in his room. It was anyone's guess where she was at 1 a.m. but five bucks says she had her heels to Jesus and was saying, "Oh, God." I'm sure it had nothing to do with the incoming artillery. Lucky girl. More on her later.

"It's like a retard telling a retard, 'You're retarded'!" I sputtered, about the battalion leadership team.

THE DYNAMIC DUO

The Army's military intelligence field is one in which women have significant representation. I've no idea of the actual percentage, but believe me, it's something that would make any feminist very happy. And it should be. Gender, ethnic background, etc., should play no role in deciding assignments in the intelligence field. Women are kept from some fields in the military because of a chauvinistic, arcane idea about not having our baby incubators in harm's way (on the battle field). Well, in a war zone, with mortars and indirect fire (pot shots taken by Taliban) occurring at bases everywhere, the distinction of serving in a support role versus combat role is blurred. But I don't want to get off track. I'd like to give you some insight into my battalion leadership, just so you get an idea of what is at the helm of this organization. Thankfully the obstacles continuously placed before us didn't overwhelmingly hinder the professionalism of our soldiers.

But a little ground work before we begin. In general, a battalion staff consists of the senior officer: Battalion Commander (BC), the senior sergeant: Command Sergeant Major (CSM), the next senior officer: Executive Officer (XO), and staff sections that include -- personnel, intelligence, operations, supply, communications, and the chaplain. Each section head may argue that he or she is more important to the mission than the others, but honestly each one is vital to the health of the collective whole. I mean, out of your five fingers, would you say one is more important or vital than another? Of course you wouldn't.

The role of the commander is to provide direction and vision. The CSM is a liaison between the enlisted troops (the majority of the force) and the senior leadership. He or she provides guidance

41

to the commander and should have a "finger on the pulse" of battalion morale. The XO runs the staff (like the Chief Operating Officer at a civilian company) and helps implement the command direction and intent. Well, that's how it should work in a normal unit. Ours was the exception.

This is the second instance of the social engineering I mentioned earlier. A battalion commander often has choices when filling vacant staff positions. Sometimes he chooses his staff, or inherits staff members, and sometimes candidates are forced upon him – that's what happened in our case.

To be frank, our higher headquarters in Washington, D.C. *royally* screwed us. The battalion commander should've been replaced, but that didn't happen. One can only speculate why, and you'll get different opinions from each person you ask. Here's mine.

"We are living it. Living this intelligence operations thing we are in." the BC blankly said at the end of a nightly staff meeting.

The commander of our battalion was a woman, big deal, right? Well, in the grand scheme of things, it really was. She had been in charge for two years, her basic command/leadership commitment was up, and it was time to go. Instead, the national organization promoted her and sent her to Afghanistan. But their biggest failure was sending a female senior enlisted adviser (the Command Sergeant Major) with us. That might have been palatable to the soldiers (male and female) if either was competent. Sadly, neither was.

One thing spoke volumes – the BC's futile attempts at rejecting the CSM as her senior enlisted advisor. The national HQ forced both women on us. The national HQ didn't grasp the importance of having a male soldier in a senior leadership position. Thankfully, we were blessed with a very competent and war-tested executive officer, another female. Can you see where I'm going with this?

I think it deserves mentioning that a female was the director of the national organization in Washington D. C., and the leader of the unit between the national organization and our battalion was
42

also a woman. I'm no misogynist. I appreciate women in positions of senior leadership – that is, competent women, but WTF were they thinking – Grrrl Power?

The military is overwhelmingly male. Thus, one would expect there to be a guy in at least one of the main leadership roles and/or staff sections in the unit, right? Well, there wasn't. Our battalion was run by a coven of female officers otherwise known as the Spice Girls. Shelly came up with that name – a brilliant woman. Shelly was funny, professional, whip-smart, accomplished (she's an actuary in the civilian sector) and unfortunately, didn't deploy with us. She transferred from our battalion before the deployment – but not just because she could, because the BC didn't like her.

"You should make *me* look good….wait, I mean make the battalion look good." Molly snapped at her subordinates.

Here's what we had at the top: Molly – the BC, a blonde, Caucasian stay-at-home, control freak, helicopter mom awarded the command of the battalion and tenaciously clinging to it in spite of all hints to leave. She was insecure, had zero people skills, was focused on her career and rank, had no concept of leadership, was a closet misogynist/homophobe, and felt the only good Army officer was a male West Point graduate – just like her husband.

"*You!* Shut yo' mouth!" Rhonda bellowed at someone yet again during a nightly staff meeting.

Rhonda - the CSM, an African-American, cigar-smoking cop from New England who was grossly overweight, horribly inept and didn't know how to fire or clean her 9 mm pistol.

Magda – the executive officer, a Latina with a previous deployment to Iraq, probably one of the most organized and efficient officers with whom I've ever served.

Shelly – the fiery-red head, brainy, witty, incredibly efficient, personable, and the one who departed before the nonsense got too far out of control.

Ana – a quiet, devious Latina whose department often

screwed up and whom everyone despised.

And finally Carrie – a Latina, the quietly efficient, steady, patient, and long-suffering pillar of strength of her section. She progressively lost more hair as the deployment chaos continued. I'm pretty sure it all grew back after we got home – albeit with a few grey strands.

Can you see why they were known as the Spice Girls? Male army reserve soldiers across the U.S. clamored to deploy with us (not knowing what they would've gotten into) but the BC decided to fill her staff with women. I'm no woman-hater, but *damn!* Even my female peers loudly complained of the lack of male leadership at the battalion staff level. We even met with and appealed to representatives of the national organization who came to visit just before we left the U.S. Nothing changed.

Early in the pre-deployment training, after the staff was picked, Shelly and Magda joked about which Spice Girl they'd be. "I'm Ginger Spice!" Shelly announced with pride, way before the deployment began. Duh honey, you're the redhead. I called her Saucy Spice – to her face. Too demure and humble to accept being Posh Spice – Magda became Brainy Spice. "I can live with that." she said, beaming.

"So who's gonna be Scary Spice?" I intoned. Neither offered an answer, nor wanted to be considered 'scary.'

Carrie became Sporty Spice – because of the group, she was in the best shape. Ana wasn't around to pick a name. "She's definitely Annoying Spice, or Devious Spice." I joked. Laughter aside, it was fitting because ya never knew what Ana was up to or capable of.

That left Rhonda. "What about the Sergeant Major?" I mischievously grinned, eyebrow cocked. Again, neither of them had an answer, waiting bright eyed for me to continue. Maybe they secretly respected her?

"Fudge Puddin Spice!" I barked. We all burst out laughing. "No, wait, wait! More like Turd Spice!" More laughter, even through Magda's disapproving look. I'm certain Shelly peed herself right there cuz she ran out of the office.

Ah, but the difficult one to name was the commander. A

hushed silence cloaked the room as if someone had mentioned Voldemort's name. How could one succinctly capture the essence of that woman? Her aura suppressed the sun.

Baby Spice was appropriate due to her maturity level, but inappropriate 'cuz when one thinks of babies, images of something cute and harmless comes to mind. Molly had been nicknamed "Combat Barbie;" possibly cute, but not harmless. Frantic Spice, Hysterical Spice, Exhausted Spice? No, none of those worked. Ranting Temper-Tantrum Spice was too long. Monster Spice sounded about right. If there had been an ounce of humor in that woman, the Spice Girl name game might've provoked more laughter.

Granted, three men were on battalion staff, but none had a visible leadership role. Molly replaced one poor bungling worm of an officer because of his continuous failure to live up to her hysterical demands. Oh, and she didn't like his appearance, compelling him to get manicures each week, iron his uniform, and be physically inspected by Rhonda. That had to be humiliating. Uh, we're in a war zone, honey. To be honest, he was a goof, but his crime was that he obviously displayed an ineptitude Molly recognized in herself.

The soldiers came up with a few names for Molly and Rhonda: Pollyanna and Prudence, Dizzy and Wheezy, A Salt with a deadly Peppah, the Gruesome Twosome, Those Two, the Curse, that Woman and her Shadow, Shag and Sumo, and a few more that I can't repeat (soldiers can be creatively vicious). Suffice to say, it was a frustrating 15-month training and deployment cycle for everyone in the battalion with those two 'leading' the way.

RIDICULOSITY

"I get inspired everyday by our soldiers, not necessarily by the leadership, but I do by our soldiers." Molly stated to a group of high-ranking visiting dignitaries in front of her staff and leadership team.

Molly hollered while considering a nickname for our battalion: "Helios?! Prometheus?! Dragon Slayer?? No! No! No! These won't work! These are stupid! Back to the drawing board Slayer! Who came up with these?!?"
"Intellectuals. People that read books." A Lieutenant sarcastically remarked under his breath.

BIG PICTURE - ENABLING THE MISSION

I don't want you to think everything was bad under Molly's tenure. Public speaking is a key way to instill trust and confidence in you and your leadership. Unfortunately she didn't have "the gift" of any display of self-confidence. She always looked put upon, exhausted, or bored. Maybe she was overwhelmed with the pressure of the job, and the self-imposed pressure she created. But she did make one good, key, forward-thinking decision.

Remember the month-long pre-deployment training at Ft. Lewis in Washington state where we lived in "historic" WWII housing. By "historic" the Ft. Lewis leadership meant our WWII housing was dilapidated and condemned – at least by HUD standards – but it couldn't be torn down. I bet the federal government wouldn't have housed detainees or refugees there, but it was good enough for the military.

We could and did go to the Post Exchange (PX) or other on-base facilities every once in a while – it was a great treat and a short adventure to which everyone looked forward. I mean, those few short trips to the PX were our only mini escapes, having been deprived of any and all normal adult decision-making for months.

RIDICULOSITY

My whole team went to the PX one Saturday and quickly broke apart. Shaniese and her girl, Lolo, went to the food court. Chip found his smoking buddies and hit the tobacco section with Mary Danger in tow. Woody naturally vegged in the book/magazine section and I went with Silas to electronics. It was a typical shopping experience, browsing the shelves, picking up items and putting them back, finding unnecessary things to buy because you could – not because you needed them. How many times do you find something at Wal-Mart you didn't intend to buy but picked up anyway?

So I'm browsing an aisle in electronics and hear someone making a loud commotion the next aisle over. Normally, I'd ignore it, not caring or wanting to get involved in the commotion, but this time I wandered to the end of the aisle and peered around the corner – just in case it was someone in the battalion acting stupid. And there he was, standing white-faced and stiffly at Attention, Woody.

I knew the kid well enough to realize he wouldn't do anything egregiously wrong and since he was my responsibility I walked up to the soldier doing the yelling. Turns out it was the senior enlisted advisor for the entire base. Some rabid Command Sergeant Major barking about Woody's quickly developing beard.

Because we collected info from Afghans – the more we distanced ourselves from uniform-wearing military members, the easier it was to pry information from locals. Soldiers in uniform went to Afghan villages and did "bad things" according to them. Locals really hesitated to speak with uniformed personnel, so if we wore civilian clothes and had a beard, it put them more at ease and greatly facilitated the information flow.

Molly took the advice of enough professionals and allowed the men who'd be talking with locals (me, Woody, Chip and others) to get a month-long start on the beard growing process. That meant we were growing our beards while in uniform in the states and in transit to Afghanistan. Anyone who knows the military understands that men absolutely must shave when in uniform – and yet here was Woody getting chewed out by the most senior enlisted man on base because he followed Molly's directive.

Poor Woody, he's very respectful and probably would've

soiled himself had the verbal barrage continued.

"Sergeant Major, this is my soldier. Can I help you?" I said. Woody continued to stand there, immobile. The CSM launched into me, though with a shade more respect, even though I was sporting a beard similar to Woody's which probably pissed him off just as much. Ya see, he could and did chew on Woody because of Woody's junior status. Although I technically outranked the CSM, I'm not stupid. I recognized his position, power, and reasons for foaming at the mouth and calmly stated the reasons for our facial hair.

"Our Battalion Commander allowed the exception to policy due to our impending intelligence collection mission in Afghanistan." I calmly stated, simple as that. I could've been real snarky and told him to take it up with Molly, but a soldier doesn't get to his level of sergeant major without some clout and power. It was smart to let him know I understood his point, to stroke his ego, and listen to him. Army general orders about grooming aside, this megalomaniac needed to vent and I took traumatized Woody's place.

"Specialist, go report to Sergeant X, I will speak with you later." I firmly yet gently told him.

We went around and around for a bit speaking over each other, me explaining the rationale behind the growth, him not backing down from his rock-solid circular reasoning.

"Colonel Molly X is our battalion commander. We are on north fort in the old, decrepit WWII buildings for another couple of days if you want to speak with her." I finally said. The adjective "decrepit" probably added fuel to his fire, but I intentionally wanted to piss him off, the asshole. He was pissing me off for acting like a puerile fuckwit.

Molly was what we called a "full bird" colonel. Her rank was higher than the typical battalion commander's and actually one step below a General. I think that might've swayed the rabid CSM's position, because he seemed to let it go. I was able to save Woody, placate a megalomaniac, and hopefully diffuse a potential embarrassing situation, if I didn't F it up with the decrepit comment.

Molly was absolutely terrified of negative press or any action that would reflect poorly on the organization. She perceived negative attention as a direct reflection on her nonexistent leadership. When something went wrong, her first instinct was to blame us, not to investigate or learn the actual facts. So if the base CSM had complained to his boss, Molly might've shit herself. And we know what rolls downhill... so there could've gone the beards, to the detriment of the overall mission. Short-sighted adherence to the rules without considering the impact on the big picture is common among military leaders. Molly learned of a caveat to that rule, drafted, signed, and distributed official memorandums to all affected men, and figured she was covered, which she was. We were lucky we didn't have a myopic "relic" like this guy as our senior enlisted advisor.

I had to give Molly props for that decision. Not everyone in the battalion was allowed to grow facial hair and wear civilian clothes, but for those whose mission involved regular interaction with Afghans, the luxury of not shaving or wearing a uniform was a massive morale boost, and by extension, a relief to the entire battalion. It would've been nice if she had "let go" and treated us like adults the entire time, but that wasn't in her DNA, and complete control was hard to give up.

The local military commander we supported in Afghanistan didn't allow his soldiers the benefit of beards and civilian clothes. He didn't grasp the bigger picture and thus his soldiers had a more challenging time collecting information. I felt sorry for them, and at the same time, thankful for Molly. She might've been crazy, insecure, and disliked by most everyone in the unit, but she was our lunatic and looked out for us and the mission in her own way.

"Listen up soldiers. Do not drink water after 7 p.m., just don't do it. If we all just don't drink water after 7 p.m. no one will have to go to the bathroom at night and no one will get raped." Molly announced at the microphone during one of her first appearances in front of the entire Battalion before deploying (stunned silence followed).

THE SETTING

You might want to know a little bit about where we were stationed and how we lived. Each location was unique, some had much greater deprivations than others, while some had great amenities. Here's a short run down of my Afghanistan. It was nice, but no camping trip.

Bases

"It's like they dropped us in the middle of nowhere, put a fence around us, and told us to *stay!*" Sister Mary Danger whined about being stuck on base.

It was all a matter of perspective. Soldiers were based at different types of installations in Afghanistan. Some installations, like Bagram Air Field (BAF), were monstrous in size (relatively speaking) with accompanying ridiculous rules and regulations. People complained that being on BAF was akin to being stationed in the U.S. because the rules were similar or worse to those stateside.

Commanders and their sergeants major were more concerned with what type of boots you wore or if your reflective belt was worn across your body right to left versus left to right. They lost sight of the bigger picture: we were at war, and the Taliban didn't care what we looked like. Their goal was to kill infidels. Sometimes I wished the insurgents would've started with the myopically focused enforcers of inane, morale-busting rules. Thankfully, I was spared the idiocy of BAF.

My base was smaller, more neighborhoodly (if that's a term), and much more manageable. Yeah, there were dumb rules, but there were dumb rules everywhere. The leadership wasn't oppressive. I was on a Forward Operating Base (FOB). This FOB supported many units and had amenities not available on smaller facilities. A few professional football cheerleaders, a comedienne, and some D-list celebrities recently visited to entertain the troops. You didn't get USO-like entertainment at smaller installations. We had shower trailers, latrine trailers, a gym, large dining facility, PX, an education center, Morale Welfare & Recreation (MWR) building, coffee shop, etc. Heck, there was even a hair salon and local bazaar at which local Afghans hocked substandard products to eager, shopping-deprived soldiers and civilians.

Sister Mary Danger, Shaniese, Woody, and I would get a chance to travel off base on official business. Because of our remote location near the Pakistani border, it was always a dicey crapshoot on what might happen off base, but cooperation between my unit and others could only contribute to the greater safety of the entire province. I always hesitated to let the team support missions for other units, but they eagerly wanted a change of pace from our mundane existence and sometimes I gave it to them. More on that later.

Perspective

I never complained about my FOB. It was basically a small city, large enough to support fixed and rotary wing aircraft. That meant both planes and helicopters landed there. The U.S. post office was located near the finance center, the combat hospital tucked around a corner from it and down a dusty road. I empathized with my comrades at the smaller FOBs or worse – the COPs. A COP (Combat Out Post) was the smallest of installations. They were usually smaller than half a football field and could tightly house up to 150 Soldiers and/or civilians. One of my friends and colleagues was stationed at such a COP. There were only seventy-five people at his location.

I used a "proper" shower, whereas he used baby wipes. I sat on an actual toilet, while he crapped in the sawed off portion of an oil drum that had a board placed on it. You could sit, but many preferred to squat. I used a urinal, but he peed into a tube that stuck out of the ground at an angle. I lived in a proper room, with a door and window, and a roommate. It was one of eight rooms in our building. My friend slept in a connex with five other guys. A connex was basically the metallic-box structure of a semi-truck, which sat on a flat bed. You know, the kind you see on the highways in the states. Yeah, six stinky guys lived in that smallish connex with all their gear and funk. It wasn't a pleasant situation, but one steeped in memories, both old and yet to be made. So, I never complained about my location. I knew I was lucky.

Light Discipline

One trait that many installations shared was blackout conditions. That meant during night hours, after the sun set, the only authorized illumination was moonlight or small flashlights. We were supposed to use red-, green-, or blue-colored flashlights but I'll be damned if many people didn't walk around with bright-white flashlights. Hello! Target! Aim here!

The blackout policy was in place to prevent the enemy from identifying our locations of night activity and directing fire accordingly. Did it work? Who knows, I didn't get an opportunity to ask the local Taliban living near the base. They tended to shy away from casual conversation with Americans.

Stars

Some nights it was so dark that you literally couldn't see your hand in front of your face. When no moon shown and the clouds covered the stars, it was impossible to navigate without some kind of artificial light. Ah, the stars. That deserved a separate chapter, but a few words for now. The stars – on a cloudless night – you could see how the Milky Way got its name. They overwhelmed.

RIDICULOSITY

The bright shiny stars were obviously closer, captured in the light of 'cosmic dust.' Big ones, little ones, huge waves twinkled across the black night sky in various patterns or no pattern at all.

Because of the lack of ambient light, nothing dimmed the stars' brightness. I imagined it was what the ancients saw way, way back. I understood how the Arabs were able to navigate in the desert, or the Greeks sail the Mediterranean.

Once you've mapped the constellations, everything is relative to them.

"Abandon hope, all ye who enter here..." I answered Woody's question about the tattoo inscribed on Sister Mary's lower abdomen, right above her chocha.

TATTOOS AND ARMY CULTURE

Ya know, I almost felt naked sometimes. I know that sounds weird, given that we were required to wear uniforms. And thank God for that. I would've probably had nightmares and needed years of therapy if I had seen some of these people naked. But that's not what I'm getting at. Whether doing PT, going to or from work, at work, or off duty, we wore some kind of uniform. Then, it was the ACU, soon to be replaced by the multi cams. If doing PT, we wore shorts, athletic shoes, and a T-shirt. It was during PT times that I felt most naked.

The army has always been a culture unto itself, with unique bonding mechanisms, hierarchy protocols, telltale haircuts, and definite fads. Clothing fads come and go, but the uniform remains the same. Nowadays, especially among the younger generation and even some career soldiers (not-so-younger generations), tattoos are *de rigueur*. And this was why I felt naked.

My dad has a tattoo he got in the '50s while in the Navy. It's a faded anchor displayed on his forearm. It looks good, even today. My granddad had a tattoo he got while in WWII, but his brother-in-law Sy, didn't have one. Sy was an officer, they didn't get tattoos. So I guess the tradition of ink runs in my family. Hell, Sister Mary Danger sported script-like sayings all over her body. Maybe it's a generational thing. Tattoos have been around the military forever it seems, but to this extent? I don't think so.

I've got a few tattoos, but neither was visible when I wore clothes, which was ninety-nine percent of the time. However, I had the uncomfortable sensation of feeling almost naked around soldiers, especially in the gym.

For those uneducated in the tattoo culture, a sleeve is a mural or set of tattoos on one's arm extending upward from the wrist or downward from the shoulder. The Army sanctioned them during the height of the Iraq crisis, acquiescing to the inevitable fact that if you wanted to fill the ranks, yer gonna have to take what you can get. And quite often what you got was people with a tattoo fetish.

So, the sleeve is/was a huge "fad" tattoo location for a couple of years. It's passé to have just one or two tattoos on the shoulder, arm area, etc. The days of the simple armband tattoo are long gone (they were big in the '90s). Now you'll see intricate sleeve tattoos extending up the arm and across the shoulder and sometimes the back. My buddy, Mark, has one that wraps his upper back and one side of his chest, enveloping the shoulder and extending down his upper arm. He wants more. Jesus, what some guys spent on tattoos could be a down payment on a house. So, that's the sleeve. But I noticed a few new places for tattoos.

The calf and shin were the new "sleeve" locations for mural tattoos. You'd see gothic crosses, a snake intertwined with a skull, creeping flames, intricate medieval arches, names/logos, etc., on guys now. Oh, don't let me forget the leg band, similar to the armband, obviously just lower. But what do we call these murals on the calf/shin areas? Pant legs? If a mural on the arm is a sleeve, doesn't it make sense to call the ones on the legs, pant legs? They're really not pants, right? They're more like knee-high socks, the kind kids wore in gym class in the '70s. So, knee-highs, that's what I called 'em.

But wait! There was more – the back. On Army women, back tattoos were generally located at either the base of the neck or at the base of the spine. Those at the spine were commonly referred to as the "tramp stamp." I wish I could take credit for that one because it's funny, but the tramp-stamp moniker has been around for a while. That tattoo often revealed itself when the shirt became untucked, or when the clothes didn't actually fit properly and parts of the abdomen and/or hips were exposed. For guys, full back tattoos were becoming more popular.

Colin, a dude who lived in a nearby building, had a full back tattoo. I wouldn't have noticed it if we didn't share the same shower building. And yeah, I couldn't help but notice it as the thing was huge, covered his back, and was primarily bright blue. If I had something that gaudy on my body, I wouldn't want to be constantly reminded of it either. Keeping tattoo artists in business, one crazy mural at a time, right?

I noticed the calf has already given way to another more baffling location (at least to me). And that is the neck. Oh yeah, you're gonna love this. There were so many it's almost too hard to describe. I wish this was an "audio" book, but then people would complain because I've been accused of talking too fast. A coworker told me once he needed to sit down when I talked because he got dizzy at the rate of my speech. I just laughed. Anyway, the neck.

For the love of your mother, why would anyone want to get a neck tattoo? Even if you wore collared shirts all the time (I'm sure most of these cretins didn't own one collared shirt, except for their military uniform), the tattoo was visible when you move. I had lots of favorites, but one that certainly didn't make that list was the word *Psycho*. Yeah, you read that correctly. I saw three guys and one chick with the word Psycho tattooed across the back of the neck. Why advertise that you're a lunatic? It was already apparent that you were a dumbass for getting a neck tattoo. Did the free advertisement add to your street cred? What kind of creature did you intend to attract? What will the kids and grandkids say years from now when that Psycho tattoo is wrinkled and saggy, yet still visible? (Yeah, these creatures seem to be prolific breeders whose spawn starts off in the world "in the hole" so to speak). Baffling, I tell ya.

And finally, the one that really inspired me to write – the pistol. That's right, a tattoo of a pistol, usually on the neck, just below the ear, pointing toward the face. Symbology? A potential suicide? Someone with a pistol-whipping fetish? Whatever the case, a pistol tattoo on the neck was disturbing to everyone except the tattoo artist. To him, it was income.

I saw stars, teardrops, arrows, hearts, and other names (besides Psycho) all on the neck. I hope that area doesn't become the new mural site. What would you call it? A muffler, turtleneck, pearl necklace? (No, that's something entirely different.) How about a noose? Cuz ya sure killed yer chances of getting a job outside of the army with that thing on your neck. Real classy! Neck tattoos made me feel dirty, like I wanted to bathe or consult a priest. And I'm not even Catholic.

I guess tattoos are supposed to be cool, but if you looked like everyone else, weren't you just a conformist? How did these identically placed tattoos mean anything unique? Mine are individual tattoos, tell no "story", and are definitely not faddish. I waited until my thirties to get my first tat. I'd seen something similar on someone years before, but waited to finally design and get my unique stain. The second came along a few years later and was actually something I toyed with before deciding on the first one. So, I put much thought into what I wanted, waited, thought about it more, waited, and finally got my permanent ink.

Many of the soldiers I saw on base would've surely looked different had they waited awhile before putting the needles to their skins. But then again would it have mattered? Tattoos seem to be a constant and everlasting part of our Army culture.

MAN-SCAPING
(IN A WAR ZONE)

Everyone should be familiar with or at least heard of the practice (carried out mostly by women) of trimming or shaving the pubic region. There is an entire array of practices from the simple "hedge trimming," which is keeping the lawn bushes presentable in a semi-natural state, to what I call the "deep cut" where most of the hair is trimmed down to less than a quarter inch in length, to the "high and tight" akin to the male haircut of the same name but with nearly all of the pubic hair shaved away with only a small patch surrounding the most vital parts, to finally, the "Brazilian," which sounds barbaric – the full waxing of all hair around the genitalia. I shudder to think how women can deal with (or want to for that matter) hot waxing their poonanny. Hot wax is for candles and nipples, enough said.

Some guys do a version of this trimming process, but we call it "man-scaping." Except for the waxing part, I know guys practice all the variations. I've yet to meet a man who's "man enough" to put hot wax on his stick – unless it was for some kinky sex. And quite honestly, even though it'd be like a car wreck you're drawn to but don't want to see, I can't imagine hearing about it, let alone trying it.

Jack is a guy you'll learn about later, but his antics fit here. Jack was a real metrosexual – meaning he overly cared about his looks and went to great lengths to keep his nose hair, toenails, and manbush neatly in check. Jeremy deployed with my company and was pretty much the same way. I caught him shaving off the entire carpet in the shower during pre-deployment training in Washington state. I guess I could see doing it there, but keeping that bush trimmed while deployed seemed too much to deal with. However, there was one area (besides the face/neck), that should regularly feel the scrape of a razor and which most men ignore – and that's the butt crack. Please let me explain.

Ah, the butt crack – a greatly misunderstood, maligned, and

59

neglected part of our anatomy. But why should it be? It's the "seam" if you will that keeps the two orbs of our ass together without which, our butts might bobble around uncontrollably. We've all seen those "bubbly butts" that look as if they'd jiggle right off the owner if it weren't for the pants in which they were tightly tucked. But I don't want to discuss size so much as hair, especially butt crack hair.

You may be wondering what's with my fascination with "down there" hair. It's not so much a fascination as an interest in hygiene. Some guys have hairy butt cheeks. That's not the hair I'm talking about – I'm not concerned with butt carpet. Thankfully I'm not afflicted much by it. Butt cheek hair sucks, because in the summer, when wearing jeans outside and you're hot and sweaty and sitting down or readjusting your seat - trying to get comfortable, sometimes the butt cheek hair will tug on my drawers and it can be annoying. So, I'm not talking about that. I'm talking about the fluff, fuzz or forest (depending on the guy) located between the balls and around the sphincter, or as I more commonly say – the coo-yahns and the pucker (or brown eye). That area is of special interest.

Now I wasn't keen on shaving the hair off my agates. The skin on my peach basket was too wrinkly, it would've taken too much time to trim the hair, and no one besides me would've cared or paid any attention to those poor underutilized marbles anyway. But the brown eye, well, that's a different story altogether. I mentioned hygiene earlier. The more hair one has in one's armpit, the more one might be prone to sweat and smell, right? Yeah, there are products for armpits, but have you ever encountered one for crotch sweat? I haven't.

But sweating wasn't the main reason why I shaved my crack hair. Well, why I'd prefer to shave it. God, this is getting personal. Maybe I should file this away under WTMI (Way Too Much Information) and end this section entirely. I rarely embarrass myself because I have very little shame, but I think I'm approaching the line. Mom, stop reading, please! For the rest of you, proceed with caution.

The reason I very gently and lightly ran a razor over my trembling pucker once every couple of months was because I wanted to save money. WTF did I just write? Yeah, to save money.

60

Here's the deal – the more "eyelashes," per se, one has around the brown eye the more "stuff" gets stuck in it. Now, I could write an entire dissertation on the amounts, type, and constitution of, well, you know what I mean – that urgently works its way out of my body at times. Needless to say, what one eats has a direct effect on how much toilet paper one uses. Understand? If you have fewer "eyelashes" around the brown eye, you might use less toilet paper and thus, save money. The tertiary benefit is fewer unwanted and unexpected "cling-ons."

Cling-ons, dingleberrys, crackles – they're all the same- unwanted bits of toilet paper stuck in the twisted butt crack hair surrounding the brown eye. I always use toilet paper until it comes back mostly white, then I take a wet wipe and swab the area again, just in case there's some crackle or smudge-like substance lurking around. No one wants a crusty crotch. I learned that practice on my first deployment to Afghanistan. Oh, that reminds me….

Have you ever watched a dog take a dump? It's funny and gross at the same time. I think dogs have this genetic ability to push out their rump/anus area so that very little gets stuck on their butt hair. If there is "cling-age" dogs can always lift a leg and lick themselves clean. I know, revolting, ain't it? Think about that the next time some dog tries to lick your face. Some really hairy dogs, like sheepdogs or some shepherd breeds, get "crusticles" around their back end. For some reason that's what eventually comes to mind when I see or meet a really hairy guy who doesn't seem the "manscaping" type. *Don't ask me why!* Sometimes I don't want to visualize the things that pop into my head – they just pop, and I just laugh, and sometimes throw up in my mouth.

Now, back to shaving. Before we left the States, I thought I'd be clever and thoroughly get rid of every hair in my nether region. How? Why Nair, of course! I mean, who wouldn't Nair their ass crack instead of taking the chance of severing an artery with a razor in the pursuit of saving money and avoiding crusticles? Hello – me! Okay, so there aren't arteries on the pucker, but come on! I'm much more comfortable with some stinky smelling crème on my back end than a razor. Thus, I bought some Nair at a nearby drug store, went to my room the night before we departed Seattle, and prepared to lather and rinse.

I read the directions well – *don't let crème stay on longer than five minutes, test a region first, don't rub with a cloth*, blah, blah, blah. Whatever. I wanted to be as smooth as baby skin. Let me tell ya, I had every intention of following the directions. I placed my watch on the bathroom counter, disrobed, lathered up, and waited. The shower was ready because I wanted to get all the smell off, just in case I "got lucky" on my last night in Seattle. What happened instead was that I burned my balls.

Oh yeah, Murphy's Law came into play in full force yet again (we have an intimate relationship, Murphy and I). I hadn't even washed the extra Nair off my hands when my cell phone rang and of course, I answered it. There was some crisis, which I've long forgotten, that needed my immediate attention. I did my best to deal with it and in the process went over the recommended time limit. I think I finally hung up after seven and a half minutes. Nothing hurt at the time I showered, washed, and rinsed so I thought I survived. However, while getting dressed to meet my friends in the hotel restaurant, my crotch suddenly felt like it caught fire. I freaked out.

I raced to the bathroom where the light was brightest only to stare in horror at my flame-red peach basket! What the Hell? I had chemically scorched my junk! Oh, I was hair-free all right, but I might've taken a layer of skin off with it. Ice? No way, besides I didn't want to put on clothes, trek down the hall to the ice machine and return. Cold water? Uh, no, it didn't seem like a good idea. So I used the blow dryer on my nutsack. In retrospect, I was a fuckin' retard.

I finally settled on applying liberal amounts of Neosporin ointment all over the affected area. Eventually the pain subsided but the red color persisted. How does one explain to a potential "mate" the sunburned coloring of one's junk? It's like I went sunbathing in a crotch-less full-body suit – in cloudy Seattle of all places. I felt like a dumbass. And no, I didn't get lucky that night – nor did I pay for it.

After the immediate pain went away, I got dressed, met Silas, et al, and bought a round of drinks as penance for being late. At least I had a whistle-clean brown eye, or in my case, a red eye.

I guess you could say I had a bloodshot eye. Anyway, that was my last experience with Nair. Now, I didn't swear off it altogether, but since there was no bathroom or shower privacy in Afghanistan, and no Nair for that matter, I resorted to the occasional swipe with the razor. I certainly wasn't going to let a simple scorching incident prevent me from de-hairing my vitals. It wasn't so much of an economic benefit. I didn't pay for the pathetic, see-through toilet paper we used. It was more that I didn't want all that hair. You could say I was on the continuous quest for a crust-free butt.

RIDICULOSITY

"Every time you open your mouth, you show your ignorance!" Mitchell haughtily snapped at Sister Mary Danger.

THAT'S NOT MY NAME!

Chip wasn't the only Asian soldier cross-leveled to our unit. He and Mitchell came to us from the same California-based unit and never really got along until late in the deployment. Don't know why, maybe it was an Asian thing, but it was weird. You'd think people from one organization sent to another would bond, but not Chip. He didn't respect or like Mitchell and it was obvious. Chip worked for me and Mitchell worked for Don (remember my rope-climbing roommate), which meant they saw each other and had to work together. Both contributed to the success of the overall mission and eventually became friends.

Mitchell wasn't her real name – yeah, I said her. Don't know why she chose it, but Mitchell was the guy's name this woman wanted when she came to the U.S. Her real name was probably Hong Bang or something naturally un-American. But, Mitchell? Come on.

I asked "Why not Michelle, Melissa, Melinda, *anything* but a guy's name?" Nope, she insisted on Mitchell, so we called her that, rolling our eyes every time someone called the office, expecting a man.

"Does size matter?" Mitchell naively asked about the length of her report.

Mitchell was motherly in that Asian Tigress way, but she was hard, too. She rarely showed much emotion, but would pull me aside asking for advice on how to deal with her irascible young troops. Turns out, they didn't respect her either. That must've sucked. I listened, empathized, and offered advice that she'd sometimes take, but Mitchell (never Mitch) had a mind of her own. Since Chip gave her a hard time, the younger soldiers did too. That insidious, underling disrespect wasn't initially obvious to the leadership – or else we would've talked to them about the importance of teamwork and getting along.

That reminds me, why do non-U.S. born citizens of Asian descent never understand the full scope of their chosen names? You'd be stunned to know how many Korean-born wives of soldiers and airmen chose the English name Sue. I served in a unit where three guys had Korean-born wives, all named Sue. It must mean good luck or something positive. But don't call 'em Susan, Suzy, or Suzanne. Nope, just Sue. Once I tried to playfully chide a fellow college friend by imperiously calling her *Patricia!* The implication was lost on her. She was Patty and nothing else. Then there is my good friend and former coworker, Katherine. Never Kate, Katie, or Kathy. Maybe in their cultures, diminutives of proper names don't exist. Who knows… Anyway, back to Mitchell.

Whenever she needed a break from her office she'd walk down to ours to see what was going on. Chip joked that Mitchell, being an Asian woman, was probably good at massage. I immediately pointed to my shoulders and insisted she prove it. Dude, she was great! Henceforth, whenever poor Mitchell walked into our office I'd point to my neck and make her at least give a cursory rub of my shoulders and neck. She'd always have a sharp retort for anyone who tried to give her shit. Like the time when everyone else in the office pointed to their shoulders each imploring her for a massage she tersely stated "You guys pass me around like a *slut!*" turned and walked out, head held high in the air.

Loved that woman, even though she left me without a happy ending.

*"Don't use words you don't know!" I shouted at Mary.
"How 'bout Fuck You!" She responded, eyes ablaze
with snark.*

WHAT'S IN A NAME?

Unlike in the civilian world where people work, shop, play, go to school, and mill about in complete anonymity, the vast majority of us in the military had our last names prominently displayed on our chests above the shirt pocket. There were exceptions. Some people wore "sterile" uniforms, meaning there were no markings of rank, name, or unit affiliation of any kind on display. Some people wore civilian clothes, like us. Well, I owed much to those regular Joes, their uniform nametags on display for everyone to see.

Stateside, when we hit the gym, go to work, school, or church, we know and greet one another by our first names. It's what we do, our cultural norm, unless of course, someone has a title, like Pastor, Doctor, or Coach. In my civilian job back home I greet people by their first names, if I know them. In the military, it's usually rank and last name. I found entertainment in the ridiculous when I came across a last name with which a soldier had to suffer with his entire life. I kept a small notebook and pen on me at all times to jot down those crazy names and other random thoughts.

These are real names of actual people on my base. The other day I walked into the chow hall and Achilles was doing head count. That was the thankless task of counting the people who entered. What a noble name for such a mundane chore. No, he wasn't dressed in some gladiator outfit and didn't have a sword or helmet. He had a crossword puzzle book and by the looks of it wasn't doing too well. Maybe he should take up sword fighting.

Glasscock – he was a real toolbag and I don't mean that in the good sense. He had the face of a ferret and beady eyes (like Frank Burns from M.A.S.H.) and always had this ridiculous eager yet smug expression. People said he tried to act like a tough-guy ranger and wanted to be associated with them but in reality, he sat on his ever-expanding ass behind a desk and made bad decisions. My team suffered from of one of those bad decisions. He's a douche. Twathead would be a more appropriate name than Glasscock.

Lieutenant Kirk was a skinny dude with an earnest face. I bet he was anxiously awaiting promotion to Captain. Too bad there weren't any extra Starships in need of a Captain around here. He was probably in charge of nothing more glamorous than a fleet of dump trucks or shit suckers, if that. What? You've never heard of the shit-sucker trucks?

The shit-sucker truck, or SST, was basically a medium-sized pickup with a huge cylindrical tank in the "truck bed" portion, if you will. The tank lay horizontal and was attached to a motor of some kind. Various hoses were attached to the tank at different points. The Afghan drivers (and cleaners) went around to the port-a-johns on base and "sucked" the shit outta the port-a-john receptacle. Hence, the name, SST. A cleaner used another hose to spray water all over the inside and outside of the port-a-john. It was very necessary because our locally employed Afghan friends had the most bizarre method of crapping.

Afghans didn't sit on the toilet seat to take a dooker. Instead, they climbed on the seat and squatted over the hole, which left the seats soiled with mud and often crap (Afghans are notoriously bad aimers). There were specific port-a-johns for local nationals, U.S., etc., but for those who couldn't even read their own language, you couldn't expect them to read ours. I was so thankful for my proper latrine building. Afghans were only allowed in to clean. Back to funny names...

The DFAC was the best place to see people. I saw Butcher and Baker together (but no Candlestick maker); Knight, Day, and Weeks; Penny and Nickels; Love, Healer – wouldn't it have been great if he was a medic -- Poison (no shit, hope he's not a cook), Threat, Gross (he looked like a vampire), Peacock, Lavender, a man with last name Tiffany (poor bastard – ya know he was teased mercilessly as a kid), another guy named Darling – that would've sucked too, and three of my favorites -- Cockey, Sick, and Poleskin. Sick had better not be a doctor. Cockey is actually a cool guy. And what hell would it've been growing up with the name Poleskin? There was also the time when I sat across from a table of soldiers, four of whom had last names beginning with the letter "Z." Only in the military.

Maybe they formed an exclusive club or something. A whole new batch of soldiers just arrived to replace the units returning home. Don't worry; I'll update this section accordingly.

RIDICULOSITY

STRANGE ART

Soldiers arrived and departed Afghanistan regularly. You'd see someone in the chow hall for months then all of a sudden he'd be gone. You never noticed the absence right away, it usually took a few days or a week, if you realized it at all. One clue was the presence of new people. That signaled a change in personnel. The same held true for contractors.

On my base, the percentage of soldiers to contractors was about sixty to forty. There were a lot of civilians around here. They rotated back home, like the military. The main contracting company at my location was FLUOR. It hired U.S. civilians for the very critical jobs -- Macedonians mostly for the laundry and chow hall, and local Afghans for the most menial labor. Former soldiers who became civilian contractors for the government staffed some military positions.

Layla noticed a new civilian in the chow hall the other day. You should've seen her excitement. She had a serious boyfriend working on a different base who was a member of our battalion, so I wondered why she was so fascinated by this new guy, knowing how dedicated she was to the BF. Well, when she finally pointed him out it was obvious. The guy had tattoos. I mentioned tattoos earlier but this guy redefined what it meant to have tattoos.

He had tattoos on his face. That's right, his face. It was beyond repulsive, like Darth Maul had escaped the Star Wars set to visit Afghanistan. Tribal-looking ink extended from the bridge of his nose to his ears. The tattoos, shaped like tribal knives, were positioned right under his cheekbones. Similar tribal-looking tattoos were on the front, back, and sides of his neck, but they didn't connect. Each was distinct. And don't forget the tattoo on his chin, from which sprouted a six-inch long braid – a misplaced soul patch on a man who looked like he ate human souls for breakfast. I couldn't bring myself to look at his arms, hands, or any other part, nor did I want to. Update: I saw his arms today and as expected, ugly, dirty-looking, faded tattoos – not a sleeve per se, but a dreadful waste of money nonetheless.

Was I wrong to think this guy had "questionable" judgment? Was it un-Christian to think he looked the type to sacrifice kittens on a headstone in a cemetery? Should I not have been morbidly fascinated by his entire persona, wanting to hear his voice and hear what he said? Whenever I saw him, which wasn't often, the voices of different villains, each chilling and sinister, came to mind. Moreover, who the hell in his right mind hired a guy like this? That perplexed me more than anything else. The word "Psycho" and a pistol tattoo on the neck could be discretely hidden by hair. Without a thick layer of pasty makeup and dim lighting there was no way to hide the obvious graffiti covering Darth Maul's skull.

Shouldn't showing up to a job interview looking like an extra from Apocalypto or Lord Of The Rings be an automatic disqualifier? Yes, parts of Afghan society were Stone Age and some were Bronze Age, but we weren't here to scare democracy into them. Hopefully this guy wasn't required to leave base, because I don't think Obama would want 'Tattoo' representing our U.S. contribution – and everything there was perception.

Unfortunately, the damage was already done. Local Afghan workers came on base daily. All of the chow-hall workers had already seen Freakazoid and no doubt stared in disbelief. Afghans blatantly stared. But back to the hiring manager.

WTF? Inkface must've been a friend of the guy who hired him. How else could one explain this circus sideshow attraction in Afghanistan? It wasn't like Barnum & Bailey were touring this shithole. He must've been given a "pass" from the hiring manager and by the time he was at the processing center awaiting transfer to this war zone it was too late to rethink or annul his contract. Made me wonder why KBR Engineering Company lost the contract to FLUOR. KBR didn't have people with tattooed faces on the payroll, at least not here. Was this really the best we had to offer?

*"Move, Afghan, **move!**" I loudly grumbled, dashing to the latrine.*

A SYMBIOTIC RELATIONSHIP: MY COLON AND THE AFGHAN CLEANING CREW

Warning – mildly offensive material follows. Proceed with caution.

There seemed to be a symbiotic relationship between my colon and the Afghan cleaning crew that serviced our latrine. And I wasn't the only one. You know how when a couple of women live together their menstrual cycles naturally sync? I never understood why, but it happens. Ladies, can you offer an explanation? Well, it seemed the three guys in our office began to "cycle" together, too. But by that I mean we had to crap at the same time. And when would that be? Exactly when the crew had the latrines closed for cleaning. How the hell did that happen?

For whatever reason, no matter what time I went to bed, time I woke up, what I ate for dinner, or the amount of coffee I drank, no matter how hydrated I was or whether I'd been to the gym, my colon needed to empty between 9:30 – 10 a.m., when the latrine closed. Woody and Chip suffered the same indignity and we joked about it.

Recently, I tried waddling to the closest port-a-john at the street corner with a "baby in the birth canal" the last time the latrine was closed. It wasn't a pretty experience. By the time I got to the port-a-john, my butt and legs were dripping with sweat. Have you ever smelled butt sweat from holding in a "deuce" for too long? You don't want to. I finally reached my destination only to find the SST cleaning it! *Mother of God, I'm gonna die!* Never again!

RIDICULOSITY

My body wouldn't wait for the SST to finish so I started waddling back. Over the approximately 300 meters between my building and the port-a-john, I was in agony. Do you suffer from the phenomenon of the closer you get to a bathroom, the worse you have to go? I do all the time, and if I have to drop a deuce, my butthole starts puckerin' the closer I get to the commode. If it's a power crunch, I can forget holding it until my skin reaches the toilet. My colon involuntarily clear-outs with force during the act of undoing my pants and sitting. I've had issues...but thankfully, not recently.

Anyway, I got over halfway back to the "closed for cleaning" latrine, intent on busting in and stinking the place up, when my brown eye started "turtling" (turtling is the horrible action of something trying to poke out – heaven forbid, succeeding – from your anus before you're prepared). *Why me, God?* This isn't gonna end well. I had two alternatives -- keep walking and shit myself or stand there, legs twisted like a pretzel, beads of sweat peppering my forehead, pants slowly becoming darker in the crotch due to the profuse ass-sweat soaking through my trousers, trying to look nonchalant like this was natural, while I waited for the urge to purge to pass. Could this get any worse? Yes.

While standing in place, staring at a bunch of cigarette butts, the image of the latrine (only a hundred meters away) teasing me, three young soldiers came around the corner, cigarettes out, ready to smoke. I had emergency stopped in their smoking area. *Really?*

After an awkward moment of silence (three guys in uniform quietly studying a bearded stranger in civilian clothes with a pained look on his face who had inadvertently invaded their holy smoking sanctuary), I looked at them and jokingly said, "Can I bum a smoke?" (Those who know me know how much I hate smoking). What else could I say? "Excuse me for invading your space, I'm trying not to shit my pants."

No one really wanted to move, but eventually I got a cancer stick, lit up, and successfully untwisted my legs without the dreaded filling-of-my-shorts that I so hauntingly expected. I concocted some lame excuse for standing there about counting the butts on the ground. I don't know what planet they were from but the dumbasses
74

believed me. We chit-chatted for a bit, them joking about getting "smoked" by their platoon sergeant (disciplined through excessive push-ups, sit-ups, etc.), me trying to feign interest, all the while my butthole clenching tighter and tighter, cringing at the possibility that the wet sweaty sensation in my shorts was more than just butt sweat. It's happened before.

I threw down half the cigarette, said, "Thanks for the smoke, nice meeting ya, I gotta hit the shitter," (just saying that word made my colon involuntarily contract in pain). I dashed to the latrine, my legs locked together from hip to knee, moving only from the knee down (I learned that trick long ago). Squish, squish, was all I could think as I rushed to my destination. I didn't know how, but I made it. But have you ever tried to climb stairs, even one stair, with your knees tied together in unholy matrimony? Take it from me, don't do it. Yet I successfully scaled the four stairs.

Oh yeah, you guessed it, that pucker throbbing intensified with each step to the door. Wouldn't it have been a kick in the balls if those little Afghan cleaning bastards still had the place closed? They didn't, but two of the four stalls were taken – probably by Woody and Chip. I didn't care. I skooched into the nearest one, didn't even do the obligatory wipe of the toilet seat. I fumbled with my zipper (having undone my belt and pulled off my pistol holster on the way to the porcelain throne), simultaneously pulling down my pants, and sitting down.

Sure enough, ole' turtlehead launched out of its cloister with a roar, making its presence known. I must've let out a moan or something because I heard giggling. Maybe it was the jaw-clenched chorus of *"Shit, shit, shit!"* I repeated upon entering, that caused the giggling.

I won't describe what came outta me. It was inhuman and what I had done to my colon was inhumane – fitting I'd say. Best-case scenario – I was okay after the panic subsided and I didn't crap myself. Worst-case scenario: my pants were soiled and I had bits of intestine dangling underneath, resting atop the pile of hell that surely had accumulated below. This is what it must feel like to have the fist of an NFL lineman yanked outta your ass.

I was out of breath, feeling like I had just anally given birth to seventeen-pound Siamese twins. You'd expect the toilet to clog – it did. You'd expect there to be blood – there wasn't. The backs of my legs were wet down to my knees, but by the grace of Jesus and some seriously strong sphincter muscles, my nuthuggers were only sweaty, not shitty. After what seemed like a lifetime, I cleaned up, returned to my room to change drawers (I didn't want to develop a rash), then returned to work. I never learned if Chip and Woody were the ones enjoying my pain from the adjoining stalls, and I never told anyone about that near accident.

One might ask, "Hey dumbass, why didn't you go to the bathroom sooner?" Well, my tired old carcass doesn't always give me fair warning. Sometimes I have no more than a minute to get to a toilet. I've had to leave meetings or risk soiling myself. And no, I'm not suffering from some disease – I've been this way my entire life. This, unfortunately, is normal for me.

UPDATE ON NAMES

Remember awhile back when I told you of the unique and unusual names I encountered on base? Remember I mentioned a new military unit was soon to arrive, bringing another complete set of funny names? This section contains some newbies and people with whom I served. Others, well, they're just funny army last names.

Karr, Parr, Carr, and Harr. Who could make that up? Karr and Parr served on the same base as me. Carr and Harr served on different bases. It'd be cool to see them get together and have dinner one day. Fat chance of that happening.

We had lots of "pair names" like Eagle and Pigeon (the noble and the nuisance), Clark and Kent, Barnes & Noble, Pitcher and Thrower (no catcher in the bunch, at least no one who admitted to it), Sears & Roebuck; Pope, Priest and Pagan (there's Christian too, but no infidel, however, there is a Savage), King and Bishop (even with Knight it's not a complete chess set), Person, Child, and Ladd; England and Ireland (Scotland and Wales anyone?); Teach and Tutor (the education pair); Elmer, Guido, Pepe (each of which would've sucked growing up); Cupp and Glass; Frost and Snow; and Steel and Edge.

Then there were a bunch of goofy names. Budge, Oaf, Olli, Starr, Lax, Householder, Morehead, Handy, Clingfrost, Fair, Wisdom, Flook, Killingbush, Place, Cone, Lima, Wang, Almond, Lakes, McClung, Tumbling, and Seller.

Last, but not least, we had a name from a previous e-mail (Lavender) that must be added to the group I dubbed "The Crayolas." No kidding, a black guy named White, a white guy named Brown, (but you'll never see an Asian named Red or a Native American named Yellow), plus Green, Black, Golden, and Gray. Typical names but a bit stale. Why isn't there a Lilac, Chartreuse, Mauve or Ecru? We might've had an entire L.L Bean catalogue collection going there.

RIDICULOSITY

"PLUS 1"

We had a couple personnel additions during the deployment. It was common for soldiers to move around, but our company seemed a "correctional institute" for problem children. We gained a real needy one who absorbed drama wherever it occurred. Earthquake in Chile – her Gramma was affected. Problems in Haiti – a friend deployed there. Riots in some neighborhood – sister was visiting and trapped in the crossfire. Dude! Give it a rest! I can see why she wasn't wanted anywhere else, too much drama. She was quite the distraction but fun in retrospect – she even talked to herself. I mean, who doesn't appreciate a mental meltdown? Real Housewives, anyone? But, we did receive some additions that were value-adds, not detractors in Red, Layla, and Theo.

Poor Red. She wasn't the most personable of women, but competent at her job (which was talking to people). Red was stuck in Bagram suffering under Molly's frenetic leadership and unfortunately, got on Molly's bad side. That was a death sentence for anyone. Red should've gone out of her way to smile and say "Hello, Good Morning!" and "Can I get you anything, Ma'am?" But she didn't. Being somewhat reserved and introverted, Red kept to herself, which drove Molly insane; the insecure woman needed to be liked by everyone to feel good about herself.

Stout, from hearty German stock, it didn't help that Red could never fit Molly's stereotype for the ideal female soldier. With muscular legs, puffy arms and cankles, Red would've been a perfect female rugby player – but she didn't like sports. However, Red was an avid LARPer. Ever heard of that? Live Action Role Playing.

Wearing a Renaissance-period, dark blue and gold brocade dress with matching flowing veil, Red attended Renaissance Festivals around the country, re-enacting the life of a seventeenth century lady. Well, at her size, she'd more likely work the fields pulling a plow instead of sipping tea and playing the mandolin. Not everyone had horses back then, nor mandolins. Chip didn't like her,

79

but then again he didn't like many people, or so he said. But Red was good to have around. Layla was the antithesis of Red, and Chip liked her.

Layla, what a great chick. She was the type of woman everyone was instantly drawn to but hesitant to approach. It was probably her calm, cool, collected demeanor or maybe her intimidating height, like six feet. Maybe it was her nonchalant smoking, good looks, sarcasm, or the fact she looked you directly in the eye when speaking. Layla transferred to our base about midway through the deployment to help fill a staffing deficit, and lived with Mary Danger. Those two got along pretty well and it was entertaining to see Danger eventually come under Layla's girly influence. None of us ever expected that.

Layla had been dating Mark, a fellow soldier at another base. Thank Christ those two weren't stationed at the same location. That was never a good idea, with the potential for distraction ever present. Layla and Mark used the crappy Afghan cell phones multiple times a day, and you'd often see her tall, lanky body squatted down in the shade, deep in conversation with Mark, cigarette in one hand, cell phone at the ear. I became a mentor of sorts, seeing so much potential in her and discussing how to deal with the curveballs life throws at us. Like Red, Layla was a great value-add.

Theo also came to us midway through the deployment. Theo hadn't been a problem child at his previous location, but he wasn't being used effectively so my boss put him to work with Red & Layla in the understaffed section. Theo had ink-black skin and a natural scowl. It was just how his face is formed. Most people expected him to be an aggressive asshole, but he was often a soft-spoken, articulate, quiet man, intense in his work and a loner. Theo was dealing with some issues back home he was powerless to do anything about while deployed and that made him contemplative, and distracted. Ya gotta keep an eye on the quiet ones, ya never know what will set them off. Chip was ambivalent to Theo and tolerated him. Why is it so hard for people to get along?

Red, Layla, and Theo worked together but only Layla hung with us. Probably because she roomed with Mary Danger, and while Danger gave Layla shit for being a girly-girl, I bet Danger secretly wanted to dress up. It'd be like cross-dressing. Plus, Layla regularly joined Chip and Danger out back to smoke. If skin cancer didn't do them in, lung cancer might.

RIDICULOSITY

*"**Irreplaceable**? That's a big word!" counting syllables on her fingers she added wide-eyed, "I can't even count that high!" I had called her irreplaceable.*

PIMPIN' MARY

If there's one thing I hate, it's asking one of my soldiers to do something I wouldn't do myself. I always pitched in when cleaning the office, servicing the vehicles, moving equipment, etc., but sometimes ya can't help but leverage your assets to get something you need.

Carmen could and would use her feminine charms to obtain anything on base. She'd coyly tilt her head down and look at you with those beautiful brown eyes. Plus, she radiated pheromones like a cat in heat. Carmen was effective.

Well, our team needed something from another unit on base but no professional liaison, bartering, or sweet-talking helped, and I didn't have Carmen at my disposal. I tried going through the formal channels, then my boss used his connections. Nothing. I tried the "help us for the greater good of the general mission" argument. Nothing. But during an all-hands meeting, it hit me.

Being a woman, Mary Danger got plenty of attention. One of the civilian workers in the office from which I needed help eagerly stared at Sister Mary, showing obvious interest. Sure, Mary had the ratio thing going for her man vs. women, but this civilian worker was also a chick. Bingo! I decided to leverage my assets and pimp out Sister Mary Danger. It made me think of something our chaplain said, "Shall we open our hymnals now?" Chaplain Stein commented on a movie scene where two girls lick an Eskimo pie while seducing a guy.

Don't freak out. It's not like I wanted Mother Theresa to pull up her frock and chant some satanic verses. We needed Danger to go on the charm offensive in order to greatly further our mission.

Chip had tried talking up Renee, the chubby civilian, to no avail. I tried, but she wanted even less to do with me. Yet Danger had that tough-chick persona, remember? Well, Renee was the exact opposite. Mary's "butch" was the perfect complement to Renee's "lipstick." And although she protested because it "is against my morals!" we got Sister Mary to pull a page from Carmen's book, work her (cough) 'charms,' to metaphorically lie down with the devil and secure what we needed. Oh, and a bag of Hershey's Kisses helped – Renee ate them like Tic Tacs.

Unfortunately, Mary's dangerous liaison had some unintended consequences. The entire team now had a chubby sidekick who always wanted to hang out. Renee tried befriending all of us.

"That fat whore is dead to me" an unsurprising response from Chip. He was butthurt from her original rejection and ignored Renee. I was nice enough, feeling both grateful for her help and guilty for pimping our dear Sister. Woody and Shaniese were initially oblivious, until Renee's behavior became too strange for even those naïve kids to ignore.

At first it was funny (at least to us, Sister Mary claimed she hated me), then it slowly turned annoying, then downright threatening. I don't know what "girl magic" Danger worked on Renee to secure what we needed but Renee was smitten and wasn't going away quietly. She began eating meals with us in the chow hall, appearing at the gym whenever we were there (never figured out how she learned of our erratic lifting schedule), then literally stalking Mary. I'd never seen such desperation before and was at a loss for what to do.

Thankfully, we dodged a bullet. The interest in Sister Mary evaporated as quickly as the infatuation had erupted. Renee went on R&R and rekindled a romance back home, whetting the fire in her loins.

"That's bullshit! How can she do this?" Mary blurted out, barging into the office indignantly. Renee had creeped Mary's Facebook page and sent a snarky message about "…it being over" between them. Danger was pissed for a couple reasons, probably because she subconsciously looked forward to "girl drama" with

84

Renee after R&R. Danger lived for the drama.

"WTF? You're safe, calm down, she's not going to bother us anymore." I exclaimed. Unfortunately, that also meant we'd probably not get any future support from Renee's office. Well, maybe not. There was always Mitchell.

RIDICULOSITY

THE OIL-CHANGE FIASCO

In spite of the number of years U.S. forces have been in Afghanistan, I learned we were losing the war on common sense – one civilian contract at a time. Get this, I used and was responsible for two civilian vehicles: an armored pickup truck and a regular pickup truck. One was dispatched from and serviced by U.S. civilian contractors on my base. The other technically belonged to a company based in Kabul. We rented it from them or something like that. I never looked into the nebulous contractual relationship our organization had with the company, I didn't care and it wouldn't have mattered if I did. That was my boss' job. Turned out that when the vehicles needed servicing, problems arose.

I was in a war zone. I didn't care where the food came from, just feed my soldiers. I didn't care where the bullets came from, just supply us with ammo. I didn't care who pumped the fuel, just fill my tank. By extension, when the tire on my armored truck got a flat, I took it to our motor-pool yard, run and staffed by contractors. But they wouldn't touch it because it wasn't a vehicle under their contract. It didn't matter that I had my own spare tire. It didn't matter that one of my soldiers volunteered to jack up the heavy armored vehicle and change the tire herself (love you, Sister Mary). The contractor wouldn't allow us to use their yard, jack, or other equipment because my vehicle wasn't allowed servicing. Are you fuckin' kidding me?

"I'm in a goddamn war zone trying to keep your lame Fobbit-ass safe from outside attack and you won't change my tire because 'by contract' you can't account for the man hours required to do the work?" I exploded at the jackass contractor. What kind of nonsense was that? Why did we have contractors at all if they weren't able to work on anything that needed servicing? It's not like there was a line of Afghan civilians and Taliban members waiting for new brake pads or five-point inspection. We've been contractually losing the war, kids.

Enter my buddy Nick, poor fucker.

RIDICULOSITY

"Fuckin' idiots at BAF said I have to get the oil changed on this piece of shit, or else they won't pay for the contract anymore and I'll lose the vehicle. What the Fuck?" he grumbled one night at chow. We were discussing the problems I encountered getting my tire changed. Nick used a Suburban-type vehicle too. He called the motor pool to see if they'll perform the oil change for him (where's Jiffy Lube when ya need one?). Nope, vehicle wasn't on their books. Nick contacted his boss in Bagram for guidance, who in turn, contacted the rental company.

Two weeks passed before I saw him at chow again. Wondered if he got the oil changed. The solution: the company flew a mechanic from Bagram to do the oil change, but get this... by regulation the work had to be inspected and supervised by someone of authority, so the company flew a manager from Kabul to watch the mechanic do the oil change. Brilliant and efficient use of American taxpayer dollars wasn't it? Yeah, but that's not even the most outrageous part.

"You won't fuckin believe this," Nick heatedly told me at chow when I asked him the details. His vocabulary mirrored that of Mary Danger's. Maybe they were both from Georgia? No idea. Because neither the mechanic nor the manager had an office or representative on our base, they weren't allowed to use the contractor's motor pool to perform the oil change. Sound familiar, are you laughing yet?

Here's the kicker – the three of them (Nick, the mechanic, and the manager) were compelled to drive out the main gate and pull over on the side of the road in front of the base to do the oil change, letting the discarded oil drain onto the roadside. Can you say environmental pollution, kidnapping, drive-by shooting, car-bomb attack? Some stupid rule and ridiculous rule-enforcers put the lives of three men in danger all because of a stipulation in a contract about an oil change, where it could be done, and who was allowed to do it.

Ladies and Gentlemen, you cannot expect order and efficiency out of idiocy and stubbornness. We are our own worst enemies!

THE CONCEPT OF TIME

A couple months had passed since we'd been in the country and yet it seemed like no time at all and time immemorial. The concept of time had become so foreign that I often looked at the calendar to see what day and/or date it was. If not for the date stamp I put on my daily reports, I had no idea of the date. The weather was the only real way to distinguish months. It was strange. You knew it was winter because the precious daylight evaporated before you realized it, and it was a bit colder. Summer meant more than heat, it meant being able to see outside after dinner at the chow hall.

I had a good idea what time to get up – my bladder let me know. I knew what time it was during the day when I had to go to the latrine, otherwise the hours seemed to pass without notice. There were no kids to drop off at school, no classes to attend at college or the gym, no running group with which to meet up, no pool league, no movie times, no baseball games, basically no concept of time. The work 'week' was continuous.

Oh, I tried to give the team time off and yeah, it usually fell on a Sunday, but we were always open for business because one never knew when the locals would want to meet. The locals, actually all Muslims, took Friday as their Sabbath. And although there were fewer local workers on base come Friday, we always went to the office no matter what. But time, by itself, was like air – it was present but you didn't notice it.

If it weren't for the occasional growl from my gullet, I'd have not known when to eat. Work never stopped, there was always something to do or something that popped on the radar. I was usually in the office by 7 a.m., sometimes earlier, and out by 10 p.m., sometimes later. For some reason we always had meetings at 8:30 p.m. with reps from the units we supported. Why couldn't they meet at a respectable time? I'd never been a night person so I bet the guys at the meetings thought I was a real asshole because I didn't say much except how we could speed up the meeting or

89

make it more efficient (I hated meetings with no focus and people aimlessly rambling on).

I figured my teammates senses also dulled. To combat this prison mentality, I instituted a few mind games. No, I didn't institutionalize the process of messing with their heads – that's an informal art form in which all of us partook. We had morning Jeopardy! trivia questions, thanks to the day calendar I found at the PX. The PX was good for more than just Corn Nuts and Whoppers.

Yes, morning Jeopardy! become a ritual, with Mary Danger or Woody always reminding me – they were so competitive. Just like categories on the show, each day had an assigned category and value amount. Usually the categories lasted four-five days then we got another category for Double Jeopardy! and a single question for Final Jeopardy! – you've seen the show, right?

To make it interesting and get the team's buy-in, I made it a competition. I replaced the money value with a point value. I didn't take away their points when they were wrong (you should've heard the protests when I suggested it) and Final Jeopardy! was only worth 500 points. I read the question twice and everyone wrote an answer on a piece of paper to hand in. No cheating. I collected the bits of paper; repeated the question then read their answers. Correct answers won the corresponding point total.

If everyone was correct, everyone got that number of points. At the end of the competition, which was at the end of the deployment, I promised the winner a prize. Initially I had no idea what to give them. Then I decided on some pre-paid gift cards – everyone got something. We loved Jeopardy! and it jump-started the logical thinking process early in the morning. Woody destroyed everyone and poor Mary, with her "Georgia public-school education" was always in last place. But we had fun nevertheless.

Jeopardy! wasn't the only thing we did to dull the mindless passage of time. I also instituted music appreciation. Nothing brings people together like music, and in the interest of team building, I started this exercise long ago to jog their minds and educate them. What is music appreciation? It was delightfully frustrating – for them.

"Is that China music?" Mary Danger derisively asked Chip

90

about a song on his iPod.

"You dilty whole!" Chip laughed his response in a bad Asian accent.

Music appreciation – I had over 9,000 songs on my iPod and a set of speakers I used each morning and sometimes throughout the day. I set the iPod to shuffle and asked the team to guess the artist. With genres like classic rock, pop, classical, grunge, R&B, country, Motown, jazz, and vocal, it really made us think. We started this early in the deployment, and yet we never heard the same song twice, amazing if you ask me.

Recently, Woody took a turn with his iPod. It was fun to challenge myself with a totally different collection of stuff. Woody was much younger than I, thus it wasn't surprising that our musical taste differed greatly. My buddy, Tom, used his music library a few times when he worked with us. Now that was fun – he had a lot of songs from my recent and far past. Suffice to say, everyone loved music appreciation, even without the competitive aspect.

The last thing I hoped to do to combat the incessant boredom was spontaneous – "Dance Offs." Shaniese gave me that idea one day when I caught her jamming to her music while typing a report. She was doing some serious chair dancing and neck bobbing. We quietly crept up behind her and when she finally noticed our smiling faces, she burst out laughing, a deep gut laugh that got us all laughing. She was the inspiration for the dance offs.

Each of us would take our MP3/iPod with headphones and listen to whatever music got us moving. It'd be like we're all jamming in our own music bubbles, yet together. I could see Woody and Shaniese joining me, but Mary Danger and Chip were too uptight to let loose that way. That was unfortunate for them, and probably why they wouldn't do karaoke with Woody and me. What? I didn't tell you about karaoke? I guess ya got another e-mail to look forward to.

RIDICULOSITY

NAVIGATION BY CRACKS OF LIGHT

Many things went hand-in-hand on base, two of which made life challenging – the gravel that covered much of where we worked, lived, ate, and walked, and the fact that we were a "blackout base." This place was constructed on and around an orchard. Because of the lack of rock, hard surface, and the omnipresent dirt/soil, the military used gravel as ground cover in most locations. It was ideal during rainy season, which usually fell in the colder months. So, instead of trekking to the bathroom, shower, chow hall, or office in mud, we walked on gravel. There was an obvious plus, but a sinister minus.

Have you ever walked on sandy beaches/dunes? Know how after a while your calves get sore? Well, that's what walking on gravel was like. Ya pretty much got used to it after a week. But unlike a beach, the gravel wasn't uniform in size or composition, meaning there was gravel of various sizes everywhere and it was common to stumble over an outsized rock among the more consistent gravel. That sucked, cuz it usually happened to me while talking to someone or in front of a group of people. I wobbled and cursed. They laughed and made fun of me. It happened to everyone. It was our norm.

Now, if walking on gravel was a bit challenging during the day, it completely sucked at night. Those outsized rocks became downright obstacles in the dark. Blackout conditions, remember? No, we couldn't have regular lights – no porch lights, no street lights, no light through windows, no vehicle headlights, no normal illumination of any kind. It sucked. We could have flashlights, but the light had to be colored – blue, green, or preferably red. But even if you were shining your flashlight directly on the ground you couldn't see the difference in rock size or contour.

And what about night vision? I was often challenged by the complete darkness that enveloped this place upon leaving a well-lit building or room. For example, only during the summer months did we enjoy daylight after dinner chow. Early in the deployment we'd head to dinner at dusk – it got dark around 5 p.m. So we'd exit the chow hall into complete darkness, going from well lit to utter blackness. It was nearly impossible to navigate when we first arrived because we hadn't yet learned our way around. Flashlights were a must. Later, as we got accustomed to the inky blackness it wasn't as bad, but it still wasn't easy.

I came up with a game – well, it was more like a survival mechanism. When leaving the office at night, completely exhausted after an eighteen hour day, I turned off the inside lights – the hum of the computers and dull glow from their screens was my only company. Then I opened the door to the outside and stepped into the awaiting darkness, completely enveloping myself in its opaque fold. It usually took ten to fifteen seconds for my eyes to adjust to the lack of illumination. If the moon was out, I was lucky, but times when the moon was absent were the most fun. You honestly couldn't see two feet in front of you. I didn't use a flashlight. Instead, I lived the navigation game.

The navigation game was born one dark night when I left the office and remembered that both my flashlights where in the hooch – my destination. I had walked that distance between the hooch and the office everyday so I knew what to expect. I used the familiar cracks of lights emanating from underneath or on the sides of doors, windows, etc., of the buildings and rooms I passed en route to my own. It was easy, because I knew how many cracks to count and when I should see them. If one was mysteriously missing, that probably meant something was blocking the light's path.

I didn't realize the meaning of not seeing those cracks of lights until I ran into the back of a pick-up truck one night. We had just arrived on base and I hadn't come up with my navigation game yet. I left the office one dark night, heading back to my room. I heard some people talking ahead but thought nothing of it. The quiet voices got steadily louder and then *thunk!* I ran into the back of their truck. They stopped talking as I gathered my wits, and moved around it. I also started laughing. If I had witnessed someone hit a truck, I probably would've laughed out loud. I mean
94

come on, that had to be funny, right? That was the last time I ran into anything at night.

I became a pro at night navigation. When passing a building and someone opened a door, the smart thing to do (in order to preserve your night vision) was look the opposite way. Tiny lights became beacons by which one could get one's bearings. Eventually I knew where most things were located so walking around in complete darkness was pretty easy. Driving, however was another story altogether.

Blackout conditions were extremely dangerous when driving. All vehicle headlights were supposed to be covered and/or muted. People painted them tan, red, blue, or simply used duct tape to get the vehicles in compliance. The lights on both our trucks were covered over and pretty dark – by order of the base commander. The windows were tinted on both vehicles, but we could roll down the windows on the pickup, which greatly helped when night driving (the headlights on neither vehicle emitted much light). However, the windows on the up-armored truck didn't roll down, so driving that one was always a crap shoot.

One night we came out of the chow hall in pitch black and my eyes hadn't adjusted yet. It was cold outside and none of us wanted to wait to regain our night vision. We made our way to the vehicle, climbed aboard the up-armored truck, me behind the wheel. I usually drove to dinner. I started the truck, turned on the lights, put it in reverse, and inched backward. Woody sees some dimly lit figure walk across the front of the vehicle and position himself next to my door as I'm backing up. We quickly put on our seatbelts, me expecting this figure to be an MP, checking seatbelts – they did that often. I opened the door to see what the ghostly figure wanted.

It was him – the most senior man on base. Mind you, this driving incident happened long before I officially met him so thankfully he didn't recognize me. "Yes Sir, what can I do for you?" I asked, although I thought of being a total smart ass and offering him a ride somewhere.

"Can you turn your lights down?" He more commanded, than said.

RIDICULOSITY

I was dumbfounded! I couldn't see now – with my lights on, why would I want to turn them off? "Sir, I can turn them *off.*" I responded half-jokingly.

"Okay, thanks," he said and walked away. Are you fuckin' kidding me... Off? Why would I turn them off? I wouldn't be able to see anything if they were off. Well, he was the man, so I turned them off and inched forward.

Everyone inside the cab squawked. I was scared, honestly. I mean, my eyes hadn't quite adjusted, my feeble lights were now off, I couldn't see anything and was moving forward.

Woody, the voice of reason and panic quickly whispered, "Chief, you can't see anything. Why don't you turn them back on?" It didn't take much convincing.

We had moved maybe ten feet when I turned the lights back on. I didn't care whether that lunatic was running behind, yelling. He wasn't, well, not that I could see. We got back to the office and vowed to never use that vehicle again at night. Ya know, I bet it was the base commander's goal to make driving at night so dangerous and such a hassle that people stopped.

Not only were headlights forbidden at night, the speed limits were changed from twenty kph/ten kph (day vs. night travel) to ten kph/five kph. Dude! You could walk faster than that at night. Hell, I was driving ten kph one day and a dude *ran* by me. I felt so emasculated. Thankfully the old speed limits were adopted again in some places, but jeez... what was that guy thinking? Ya get used to mindless rules from small-minded individuals, but that one was absurd!

"A fly just landed on my head!" Woody said. "I wish it landed on your head, then I could've seen right to it."

WOODY AND ME

We always had a contentious relationship, Woody and I. He viewed me as a hypocritical know-it-all, and I initially thought of him as a coddled, young, spoiled boor. He did some cool things in his twenty-four years, like drive motorcycles cross-country with his dad from Monterey to Baltimore. Who wouldn't want the solitary, yet bonding experience of spending a week or more with your father? It made me think of Easy Rider – the Peter Fonda film from the '70s. I've never seen it, but now I'm compelled to. I was unsure if Woody had issues with authority or just me. I liked the kid but he could be a pain in the ass, and like all my other team members, Woody liked to pick on me.

"Chief, what's the mission?" Woody asked the morning we saddled up for a trip to the provincial capital.

"Allah Akbar al Haji said he has info about the attack on the police station from last week. He probably just wants money, as usual." I casually offered while gearin' up and grabbin' a carton of Marlboro reds – Haji was one of our regulars and would do backflips for American cancer sticks.

We were gone most the day, leaving around 9am and returning after dark. The mission was somewhat fruitful, considering we made some good contacts, and returned without getting attacked, which was always a plus, but we were more bored than anything after the long day away from base. Oh, and as expected, Haji had nothing of importance for us, but ya never knew what morsel of info might've helped with other cases. We hadn't hiked anywhere and we mostly traveled with infantrymen escorts, so I couldn't say it was really that dangerous of a mission. But ya' had to remain on guard because ya never knew when you'd get hit. I'd

97

trust Woody in a firefight, but I'd worry about him shitting himself. Nobody wants to travel in a hot, snug MRAP with someone who crapped his pants.

A requirement when going on mission was staying in contact with HQ. I texted Chip just before we departed base to let my boss know we left and would return later. The mission was already approved, but everyone needed to know your movements, just in case. Because of the horrendous phone service in country, we'd text each other before departure. Woody's phone was acting up so I messaged with mine. We texted when we arrived at the town center and again when we departed for the return to base. Upon arriving 'home', we had to inform HQ we had returned. Woody's phone was still jacked so I had to text.

If you like messing with someone's head, isn't it great when that person is your boss? I think that was Woody's deal. He wasn't as bad as Mary Danger, but he totally loved to poke me in the ribs then run, when he could get away with it.

The walk back to HQ was about twenty-five minutes. Most people might say, "What's twenty-five minutes? They'll know you're back when you pop in to say hi."

Well, two things were wrong with that. First, it was ingrained in our heads to notify the command of our exact return, probably because of the basket case of a Battalion Commander we have. Second, what if something distracted us and we didn't call? Something like a mortar attack, or visiting friends/coworkers we hadn't seen in forever, or we totally forgot? The right thing was to report and be done with it. Thus, I commenced texting.

The moon was a mere sliver of light, which offered nothing to guide us. It was pitch black and there was no illumination – we hadn't brought flashlights. The light from the cell phone screen was like a pair of high beams right in my face. Power generators hummed in the distance, and thankfully the omnipresent smell of the poo ponds was only a faint wisp, but my night vision was gone.

"Chief, stop bumping into me!" Woody carped. I couldn't help but bob and weave on the bumpy gravel road.

"Well, hold my arm then to guide me." I suggested – well ordered him. Is this what a blind dude experiences?

98

Thank God it was dark cuz I probably looked like a complete shit sandwich – helmet on cock-eyed, heavy flak jacket hanging open on my torso, first aid kit bouncing off my ass – it was attached to my web gear. The long gun swayed haphazardly from my right shoulder and the pistol held up one side of the flak jacket, intent ook on my dimly illuminated face. It was going slowly because of the shitty phones. Then, fuckin' Woody.

His night vision was perfect, cuz he didn't have that bright ight in his mug. I was at his mercy. It seemed to be going okay.

"Dude, *stop* with the potholes, will ya?" The little bastard giggled and apologized each time I stumbled. 'Seriously, am I gonna twist my ankle?' I wondered.

Seemed my protests had an effect because the ground got much smoother, Woody was quietly leading me. I was almost done with the last text (had to send two), but gradually going downhill. I didn't think anything of it because bases are uneven like that, but then it got steeper and I stumbled, falling to my knees.

"*Woody! What the fuck!*" I yelled as he scrambled out of reach, heartily laughing at my expense. That little bastard had nonchalantly led me into the ditch! "You fucker!" I fell on my ass and still couldn't see anything, so the experience was funny, but frustrating. I laughed inside but wanted to strangle the bastard, and mock-yelled at him the rest of the way back.

Woody didn't have much to worry about as far as retribution. Some leaders physically lash out to assert their dominance or authority over their crew. Sure, it was wrong, and too much of it could get you in trouble. But in some hyper-masculine organizations a bit of 'judicial' wrestling was a primal method of getting your point across and confirming dominance. I just yelled at Woody all night and told everyone what he did the next day at breakfast. That served two purposes – to rib and give props to Woody for cleverly harassing me, but also to let the team know I wasn't a complete ogre. However, an unexpected result was that I sensed those tiny, broken cogs in Mary Danger's head churning, trying to think up yet another way to fuck with me.

RIDICULOSITY

THE LOWEST BIDDER

The U.S. government, for all its wasteful spending, has a process by which the winner of any contract to provide the government with a product or service must be the lowest bidder on the contract. It's a common excuse for mismatched clothing, poorly made boots, way-too-fragile equipment, and shoddy products that the lowest bidder got the award. Just think – your loved ones go to war, the shuttle launches into space, submarines dive to insane depths, all thanks to the lowest bidder. It's scary, but that's how our government and its contracting process work.

Three cursed things came to mind that I attributed to the lowest bidder.

#1 – plastic utensils. First, plastic utensils were a colossal waste of money. I understood the benefit – no need to install and service industrial-size dishwashing machines or employ people to work them or pump water to utilize them (in a country in a perpetual state of drought). Also, the problem of theft and repurchase was made obsolete if one always disposed of one's utensils. But for crying out loud, where was the comparative cost-benefit analysis of plastic versus stainless steel? Everything was disposable including utensils, plates, bowls, Styrofoam coffee cups, etc. Over the course of X number of years, don't you think it would cost less if we re-used our utensils and such? Let's not even bring up the subject of trash disposal or burning. If all the trash from all the chow halls was burned on a daily basis, there'd have been a constant haze stretching from one end of the province to the other.

So, the utensils. We had two kinds – the sucky ones and the decent ones. When I first arrived we only had the sucky ones. They sucked because they were almost dangerous to use. They came with a sad little napkin in a cellophane wrapper. The fork tines would often break if your meal was especially well cooked, grizzly, or crunchy or if you tried using them on undercooked vegetables. Just as often, the fork would break at the point where the handle part met the "fork" part. The knives were a joke and incapable of

101

cutting anything. I can't tell you how many times someone would be cutting meat or chicken and the knife would literally break apart. The handle and the blade portion snapped, sometimes flying across the table. Plus they were as dull as chemistry class. I bet you more people were injured than fed when we used the sucky stuff.

The decent ones were light years better than the old ones. I never saw anything snap in half or shoot across a table, unless someone threw it. I assumed that someone of very high rank had a fork tine break off in a piece of chicken and stab him in the cheek as he chewed. Now that would've prompted the change in vendor for sure.

#2 – shower curtains. The curtains by themselves were relatively okay. Perspective, remember? At least we had proper showers and weren't using baby wipes, for which I was eternally grateful. The curtains had to be replaced often because the ghetto hooks used to hold them up ripped the pre-made curtain holes. Either end of the curtain was usually unattached to the bar because the pre-made hole was torn. Subsequent "man-made" holes were also torn. So, we had a space at either end of the three-foot shower curtain where the curtain didn't touch the sidewall and three of five hooks held up the sad curtain.

It might've been manageable if the curtains were cut to fit the shower stall openings. I didn't get it. We had these white plastic shower curtains that some "genius" cut too narrow to completely enclose the shower. WTF? They hung too the floor, but the width was always short because the moron in charge of hanging them couldn't seem to fathom the concept of privacy. Because of the two-inch gap at either side of the curtain/wall space, water fell from the shower and pooled on the floor. It was always a challenge when changing into or out of your clothes. Success was measured by the fact you avoided dropping your pant leg into the ever-present water when disrobing. I wore shorts to the shower even in the winter. That way, there was less material to keep from getting wet.

#3 – toilet paper, my biggest gripe. We are the most powerful nation on the planet and yet our military uses the most pathetic toilet paper on earth. (Well, that's if you don't count the time I used newspaper in a Moscow public toilet, or the sand that many people in Arab countries use... don't ask.) Thank you, Lowest Bidder. Again, perspective – at least we had rolls of it and there was a "proper" toilet on which to sit. My buddies on small COPs used cut off metal barrels with a wooden "toilet seat" on top. When full, they had to literally burn their crap. If you've never smelled burning feces – and I hope none of you ever has – it's almost beyond description. But this is about the lame toilet paper we used – sorry for the distraction.

I kid you not when I say the toilet paper was literally see-through. I tested it one day, magazine in one hand, swatch of TP in the other. Unbelievable. It ripped as you pulled it from the roll. It tore so that you ended up with a fist full of thin TP samples of various lengths. I can't remember why my hands were wet one time as I grabbed some TP to do the obligatory wipe of the toilet seat. The stuff dissolved in my fingers. Tissue paper used to wrap clothing in a gift box was much sturdier than our TP. And you needed at least five layers of it when you blew your nose. I can't remember how many times I was in a hurry to blow my nose and just grabbed enough TP for two layers – ending up with wet, slimy fingers... I'm at a loss to explain why except for – the Lowest Bidder.

RIDICULOSITY

DID SOMEONE SAY KARAOKE?

How many of y'all have gone to a bar with your friends, got drunk, and sang karaoke? A little liquid courage is required when belting out tunes, right? Who wants to get up in front of a crowd of friends and strangers totally sober and sing so bad that dogs yelp in pain? I didn't, and neither did Mary Danger.

Well, it happened nearly on a weekly basis at our location. Maybe because no one cared what others thought – we were in a war zone dammit and someone's assessment of my lack of singing ability was no big deal. Alcohol was verboten (Muslim country, war zone, U.S. rules, etc.). I was certain anyone would sound better with a few beers in my belly, but that wasn't an option. Oh, I'm not saying everyone was completely sober. I'm just saying that I was.

We got wind of karaoke night one day when leaving the gym. A dude Woody knew from the finance office invited him along and told him to bring friends. Naturally that meant us. Like I said, Danger wouldn't sing without a few beers so I doubt she'll ever get up on stage. But the entire team meandered over to the big tent after dinner one night. No one knew what to expect and it was poorly attended, but we had fun.

This wasn't my first go around with war-zone karaoke. In 2003, I deployed to Baghdad and was lucky enough to end up at a relatively safe location. Soldiers from different units worked the same mission and I met "The Sisters." That's what everyone called them, one indistinguishable entity, like conjoined twins even though they were a few years apart. I forgot their names but remember they served in the Cali National Guard and brought the coolest karaoke device.

Their set up was basically a mic with interchangeable computer chips. Each chip contained like 5,000 songs. About half of the songs were in English and twenty-five percent each in Spanish and Tagalog. It was Cali after all -- guess Filipinos love karaoke. Maybe all Asian cultures do. Let me tell ya, our small tight-knit group learned to love it, too. I'm sure some it was the wild abandon of singing at the top of our lungs to the collection of new friends. Remember, this was very early in the Iraq war redux. Bigger! Longer! More costly than the first! We were still giddy with excitement at the newness of being in Mesopotamia, the cradle of civilization. But I digress, that's a completely different chapter in my life. Back to the Baghdad karaoke story.

I joined the crew after they'd already been established, so as the newcomer I was a little anxious. I didn't need to be. I was a karaoke virgin, soon to have my trembling vocal hymen busted by an understanding group. Uh, that sounded like a karaoke gangbang, didn't it? Oh well, it wasn't, but each of our songs climaxed in applause. If only that happened every time I climax…

I'll always remember a few things from that time. First, the karaoke machine actually scored how well you sang the song. In that debut performance I scored a ninety-seven percent, higher than anyone thus far. And I picked something really obscure that no one had expected, including me. Who would've thought Chitty Chitty Bang Bang was the perfect song?

The second thing was the support we gave each other no matter how good or weak the experience was. One dude only did the song "Wild Thing" by the Animals. He mostly talked the lyrics but at least he performed. Two coworkers sang "Summer Lovin'" from the Grease soundtrack, and we had a few rockers who always gave their heavy metal best. One night on a dare I butchered a Tagalog song called "Panaginip." Not until years later did I discover it was a beautiful soft lullaby, quite unlike the Japanese acid-rock version I did.

My most vivid memory from Baghdad karaoke was the reaction we got from the prisoners. Wait, that might not be the most PC term. I think they're called detainees. Anyway, those poor bastards weren't going anywhere. As we fumbled through our songs taking delight in one another's bravery, the poor Iraqis literally howled in derision. Such support. The rudimentary detention facility at which we served was located caddy-corner across the dirt road from our karaoke tent.

This was *really* early in the conflict, well before buildings, beds, even proper toilets were established. The Iraqis unfortunate enough to spend time with us were housed at one big, fenced-in, open area. They sat on their blankets atop pallets in groups of twenty or so. The only protection from the elements was tents, the sides of which were rolled up during the blazing summer months to let air circulate. It wasn't much better than what we had, but at least we could sing karaoke. And sing we did. Soldiers and karaoke, I guess some things never change. On to Afghanistan.

Woody was one of the first to jump on stage that night, belting out "Stacey's Mom" and dancing while we laughed and clapped our approval. A few others sang. Then it was my turn, Mary Danger practically pushing me up the stairs to the stage. Yeah, there was a stage. The tent was enormous and used for other purposes, like when a USO tour visited or someone had to give a large, official briefing, etc. I was nervous, even though the place was mostly empty. I think it would've been easier if more people had been there. Not that I cared much what people said/did but more catcalls or applause is better than less, right?

"You Sexy Thing" by Hot Chocolate was my tune. Man, what a great choice. The team had never seen me cut up before. Figured since I can't sing and have no swag I'd be as loud as possible and throw in some bad dance moves. Oh yeah, I laid down some smooth gyrations, hip thrusts, neck bobs, and the rest. Then I burst out laughing at the end, jumping down the stairs and back to my astonished and laughing team. The guy who followed me, Commando, was even more memorable…

We had a group of Afghan commandos training and working with the Rangers at our base. The commandos would go on night raids with the Rangers and usually take the lead on missions, especially when they breached Afghan compounds or had to interact with village elders. One dude was pretty Americanized, had big, longish black hair parted down the middle like someone from "That '70s Show", and sported a thick porn-worthy mustache. Everyone called him Commando. He spoke English pretty well and was very friendly. Commando took the stage after me.

Maybe the idea of performing in front of a crowd excited him. He sang "Celebration" by Kool & the Gang, but Commando needed help. He only knew the hook "Celebrate good times Come On!" and

107

could sing only that, but ya had to give the guy mad props for trying. A couple of female US soldiers climbed up on stage with him to sing backup and dance. Yeah, he was dancing a lot. It was hilarious but I was torn between laughing *at* him or laughing with him. It took big balls to "karaoke" in a foreign language in front of a bunch of strangers. So yeah, I was laughing *with* him, and everyone else.

That was a great night of team building for us, even if only Woody and I performed and Danger made fun of my smooth dance moves for weeks. Maybe we can get Shaniese, Danger, and Chip on stage before redeployment, but if not, at least they might come to watch and mock us, making fun of our efforts while secretly wishing they had the stones to join in our ridiculosity.

*"It's like a **rave**!" Sister Mary exclaimed in awe as lightning flashed across the night sky.*

FREAKISH WEATHER

We had some really freakish weather recently, which I'd never experienced anywhere before in my life. One of our interpreters worked at our base more than three years and said he never saw anything like it. It must've been because of the geography. Our base was located in a "bowl," similar to Denver, but much smaller. High mountains encircled us, so high in fact that snow didn't completely melt away until early June. Those impenetrable barriers/protectors of dirt had a huge impact on local weather patterns. So over the past two weeks at approximately 5 p.m. and extending well past sunset, we've had some incredible lightning shows.

It was weird, the sky was bright enough, but you saw neither clouds nor sun. The surrounding mountains were blanketed in purple, dark blue, or even grey clouds through which shot jagged, irregular bolts of lightning as the sun set. The weird thing was the silence, a really strange phenomenon. One could say it was because the mountains were too far off in the distance and the peals of thunder dissipated before reaching us. Well, I figured that explained the quiet – until last night.

On Sundays a group gathered at one of the Morale, Welfare & Recreation buildings to smoke cigars. We were the Rocket City Cigar Club. This base used to be called Rocket City but thankfully things had quieted down. Anyway, the club met at 6 p.m.

"Hurry up, I don't wanna get wet." Mary said matter-of-factly. Fair enough, she'd look like a scrawny, wet alley cat if soaked. We hurried from the office to the truck to the MWR building.

Our crew arrived a bit early because we wanted to avoid getting caught in the rain. Dark ominous clouds had settled over the distant mountains tonight, as they had for at least ten days now, their fog-like tentacles menacingly extended toward our base as if to say, "I'm coming for you."

The intense weather show was proving to be more of a draw than the camaraderie of cigars. Silent flashes of lightening blinded us for an hour. More and more people gathered in the open, dirt courtyard, spellbound by the supernatural surrealism.

Gusting wind created dirt-devil tornados, pushing the revelers to the minor protection of the corrugated porch awnings. We cigar chompers were forced to share our tiny sanctuary with others. Nightfall had crept upon us without anyone noticing.

The team stood in silence under the awning, our backs against the building; the only noise was the wind. Coming quicker and quicker, the lightening flashes spawned dancing silhouettes in the courtyard. Eyes ablaze like seeing fireworks for the first time – Woody and Mary stood awestruck. Chip's normal scowl was replaced by an excited intensity. Our cigars carelessly burned, unnoticed, forgotten.

Tips of those cloud tentacles appeared overhead, having slowly snaked across the mountain behind us. Lightening abruptly interrupted the unknown darkness. The windstorm raged, unleashing the fury of Allah on us invading infidels. It was unholy!

"It's like the hurricanes back home." Mary mumbled, trying to seem non-plussed. Tree branches whipped in every direction; the wind owned the night. Time and again darkness instantly evaporated as lightning bolts broadly stretched across the dark sky overhead. Mother Nature's circus was in full force – but the most bizarre thing – not one clap of thunder the entire time – it was like a color, silent movie. I still can't understand how that was possible. It wasn't like the United States had the market cornered on thunder and noise, despite the copious amount of bluster in Washington, D.C.

We enjoyed this wind-driven silent lightning storm with mounting expectation until the rain hit. Around 7:45 p.m. the first urgent drops began to fall. A deluge quickly ensued, soaking any and everything not under cover. Woody and Mary laughed at people mad-dashing for any protection, even Chip smiled, then

110

burst out laughing as a fat soldier slipped and fell. The rain was cold and loud – our overhead cover was a tin roof. Then, the hail. We yelled! We whooped! I was overjoyed, the loud crescendo of my last Metallica concert paled in comparison to this natural, full-blown symphony.

Small BB-sized pellets of hail pelted everything for about ten minutes and then the rain increased with a fury. Gushing rivulets of water turned the dirt courtyard to a mud pit. Sheets of rain reached back to us deep under the awning.

Dude it was like, early May. Temps should've been in the mid-80s already and yet we were treated to the mildest summer I'd ever experienced in Afghanistan. The intense rain quickly passed but continued off and on 'til about 9 p.m., at which time we departed the cigar club, our energy spent.

I wanted to chill a bit longer to witness the finality of the storm but Mary was cold and the others had become bored so we left. We promised to come back next Sunday.

I wish I hadn't returned to the office because after everyone left, the phone started ringing like crazy and I worked until midnight. So much for my lazy, relaxing Sunday. But I wouldn't have traded Mother Nature's intimate show for anything in the world.

RIDICULOSITY

EAU DE TOILETTE

I grew up in the city before my mom married my stepdad, and we moved to his house in the country. It was a rough adjustment for a twelve-year-old, but nothing was more "in your face" than the plumbing. We lived midway down a dead-end road in farm country. Our water came from a well and our wastewater emptied into a septic tank. Have y'all ever smelled a septic tank in need of cleaning or replacement? Gag-nasty. The stank water floated to the ground surface, stagnating, making everything soggy and smelly. My stepbrothers played a trick on me when I first moved in.

We were in the backyard playing Frisbee one summer when my older stepbrother threw the Frisbee in the direction of the soggy cesspool. Not knowing what was in store, I chased after the errant disk and ended up sloshing in the most disgusting smelling water this city kid had ever been exposed to. My shoes were ruined (I had slipped and fallen into the poopy ooze) and my clothes stunk of that hell. For a hot minute, I thought these country mice had spread cow poop everywhere and hosed down the grass – until my stepdad yelled at us for playing in the "toilet." The injustice of it all. I was mortified and furious at the same time. No one likes a smelly, angry, embarrassed, fat kid.

That experience scarred me for life. I shudder at any septic-tank-like stench. Enter our current base. I assumed a couple septic tanks and evaporation pools served the place. That loathsome, rotten, septic smell emanated from the opposite side of base and permeated everything. We occasionally smelled it in the office, at the gym, near the basketball courts, in the motor pool, etc. Thankfully, it hadn't drifted into the DFAC or living quarters but it was only a matter of time. The worst location was the shower building.

The shower building... Imagine a gigantic shoebox. There was an entrance on the long wall at the north and south side of the building. Directly across from each entrance were two sinks and

113

mirrors. Between the sets of sinks were six individual showers. Across from the showers (between the entrance doors) hung shelves and a long wooden bench. Water was ever present on the floor between the bench and the showers, and the septic tank smell was everywhere.

That was why I felt nauseous during every shower. I was thankful for my strongly scented liquid soap. It helped disguise the thought of bathing in the septic tank of my past. Brush your teeth, and the smell was at the sink. Guess that's what living in India might be like.

The stench wasn't always around. Sometimes we didn't smell it at all. Those times we must've been upwind of the offensive odor. I was sure it could've been worse. The winds could've permanently shifted and we would've suffered. Or worse, we could've lived downwind of that unholy stench. Just imagine adding the Texas type heat to the mix! Come summer, we'll probably see people spontaneously barfing all over base. I can't wait.

"If I was deaf, I could read her lips!" I said regarding a woman's tight pants.

BOREDOM AND STRESS RELIEF

Warning: this section contains offensive material which some of you might find inappropriate. I, on the other hand, see it as an extension of the deployment and would suggest to those with a delicate constitution to skip this section. If you continue to read, please do not hold me responsible for any offense taken to this personal observation. I'll warn you when the descriptions become more personal in nature. It won't be totally shocking; I omitted some of the more scandalous anecdotes.

Just like family back home, those of us deployed to a war zone got stressed out, some more so than others. Stress in a war zone was more acute because of the long work hours and sense of being locked down – not just physically but also mentally and sometimes emotionally.

Back home, there was a plethora of options by which one could decompress. We had very few in Afghanistan. There were no bars, or alcohol in general, no loved ones from whom we could get a hug, no driving aimlessly around, no retail therapy because the PX, local bazaar, or even internet shopping just didn't cut it (PX because of the lack of options). There were no girlfriends you could cry with or buddies with whom you could shoot pool. There was no dinner and a movie (the DFAC and your computer didn't count), no trails to run, no fishing, hunting, or camping. You couldn't walk your dog, work in your back yard, go for a bike ride, etc. However, there were a few ways soldiers dealt with stress that deserve attention.

Lots of us got involved in religious services, played video games, took classes, lifted weights, or ran while deployed.

Unfortunately, a fair number of my comrades began to "eat" their way through the deployment either by gorging on too much food, eating ice cream with every meal, attacking the table of sweets too often, or overdosing on Mountain Dew or other sugary sodas. Again, we all dealt with stress our own way through church, food, working out, video games, and even sex.

Yes, dear readers, I heard that soldiers were now marginally allowed to have sex while deployed. No idea if that was true or not, nor did I care. Naturally some restrictions applied – one couldn't have sex with a supervisor or subordinate, married soldiers could have sex with only their spouses (some couples deploy together). One couldn't have sex with someone of the same gender, and officers couldn't have sex with enlisted members and vice versa. Were all these rules followed? Are you *kidding*? Of course not! Men are pigs and women to whom you wouldn't give a second glance stateside were suddenly "Combat 10s" (more on the rating scheme later).

Women as a gender, were often short changed in the military. However they were the fortunate ones when deployed. Not every guy was a horn dog and wanted to get laid, but enough were, so women on deployment usually had their pick or could sample as many men as they wanted, if they wanted to at all. And some of them did.

This was my third deployment so I think I spoke from experience – my own, personal, experience. Others might not have experienced the same situations and might disagree. I do not dispute their experiences. I just ask you to respect mine.

The Army is a multi-ethnic institution composed of men and women from several countries and ethnicities. As a matter of fact, today I met a U.S. soldier originally from Nigeria on his first deployment. On each of my deployments, I served with Latinos, Blacks, Caucasians, Indians, Asians, and a few others of undetermined race, creed, and origin. Each time I deployed, my organization (either my immediate group or the overall unit) had a few women and men who demanded special attention. I meant that in two ways – their sexual antics called attention to themselves, and the individuals were much easier to tolerate if they got laid. With

116

that being said, I'd like to introduce you to Carmen.

Warning – offensive material follows

Carmen was a Latina. Each of my deployments had a Latina who needed her "fill." She was nice enough to look at, even by stateside standards. She could be sweet and demure, loud and sassy, professional and respectful, easy-going and fun. Guys flocked to Carmen because she'd been around the block and knew how to use what she had to get what she wanted. And believe me, Carmen wanted a lot.

Carmen was one of those people whom you wanted to get aid because she was much more pleasant when her meat wallet was full.

Most guys in our organization were smart enough to avoid taking one for the team, and I heard of no one who strayed into her whore-hole, but I knew some had been invited. That was cool and all – honestly, I didn't care one bit with whom someone had sex, unless of course it was a supervisor/subordinate thing. That's not cool in any organization, military or civilian. But our dear sweet Carmen needed to find another venue through which she could work out stress. I feared her vagina would resemble tire tread from a backcountry Ford Ranger if she didn't slow down. Not that I cared what her poon resembled, but for the love of Mary! Carmen, if you don't want your uterus dragging behind you like a 1970s cirque crotchet purse by the time you're forty, you had better find a suitable alternative. Take up yoga or Sudoku, for crying out loud.

Don't get me wrong, I liked Carmen. She got her work done, was entertaining, and if you needed something that was nearly impossible to procure, nine times out of ten Carmen had the connection. If she had been a guy, she would've been a hero other guys would've tried to emulate, but with our societal double standard, let's just say she wasn't emulated. I, however, applauded her. If I had a "little girl" I would've fed her as much candy as she wanted, just so long as her teeth didn't rot.

In the interest of gender equality, let me introduce you to Jack. Jack was a guy I knew from a previous deployment (he wasn't on this deployment) – and his method of stress relief was similar to Carmen's. He was a typical young guy, with an abnormal amount of testosterone. There were enough women to hit on but he usually got no attention. With no bars to drink in, football to play, or trails to run, Jack worked out his aggression the most primitive way possible – he "jacked off."

Jack was a bit of a metro-sexual, which meant he cared about his appearance more than guys of past generations. Oh, he liked girls. The more the better, but I don't think Jack got that much play. He was plain looking and was the guy who goes to a bar and exudes the whole "I need to get laid" vibe. He usually went home empty-handed, but in Jack's case his hand was rarely empty. That guy beat his meat like it did him wrong.

Jack liked to masturbate and was not afraid to talk about it. His carefree descriptions were somewhat endearing – there was always Jack to tease. Nowhere was sacred to him – I bet he'd even toss off during church services if he could get away with it. Jack revealed some of his locations and I'm thankful because it let me know where and what to avoid. Port-a-Johns, shower stalls, bathroom stalls, guard tower, bunker (the thing we ran to when there was a mortar attack), in all of our Humvees, his sleeping bag, and lastly, out in the open during pitch black darkness. I don't think there was a place Jack hadn't sprayed his seed. He even told us how he was caught one time in the office late at night by a female supervisor and just kept at it. We had a thorough day of cleaning the office once that revelation came to light.

I guess ya gotta give the guy an "A" for concentration and perseverance. Good thing masturbation doesn't have an "exfoliating" side-affect. If it did, Jack would've returned home with a nub instead of a penis. The more Jack told us, the more concerned I was anytime I had to shake his hand or take anything from him. I made sure to keep a bottle of hand sanitizer on me at all times.

CHOW HALL CHARACTERS

In addition to the funny names from the chow hall, there were some constants, and by that I mean the characters we saw on a regular basis. The names we came up with for them were sometimes funny, sometimes mean, but always appropriate.

Take Cube for instance. This guy was as tall as he was wide and I'm not kidding. Cube was probably 5'3" tall, had a fifty-four inch waist. Whenever we saw him, his tray was loaded with nothing but fried foods (chicken, cheeseburgers, French fries, potato chips, cheese sticks, egg rolls, fried rice, etc.). No wonder his girth and height matched.

A new unit arrived, bringing Cube's cousin, Retarded Cube, or RC for short. RC was just slightly taller than Cube by maybe an inch, but his girth was probably sixty inches. I couldn't fathom how anyone could let himself degenerate into Jabba the Hut.

He got the name Retarded Cube when we heard him talking at a table behind us. The poor guy was quite unfortunate looking. Besides the layer of blubber that would make a walrus green with envy, RC had huge jowls, buck teeth, no chin, and an over bite. Oh, and don't forget, the unintelligible diction and thick accent – he was from Mississippi. It was obvious how he dealt with stress.

Muffin man: a dude who ate a regular breakfast (we saw his plate). On his way out M-M grabbed seven to eight Otis Spunk Meyer muffins, stuffing three to four per cargo pocket. This happened every day after breakfast. We always wondered where he worked and what he did with those muffins because he wasn't grossly obese like the Cousins Cube.

We all noticed the new crew of US Army Rangers that arrived about three weeks ago. It was funny, the guys arrived mostly skinny and departed mostly muscled monsters. The lucky bastards had such a great schedule they worked out twice a day if they wanted, or ran and worked out. It was frustrating for those of us who wanted to lift even occasionally. But whatev, we each had our distinct missions with individual responsibilities. Mary Danger

119

pointed out that many of the new Rangers had hairy legs and big noses. For some reason she insisted they were Jewish. I guess her concept of Jewish men included large noses and dark hair. I had no idea of their background, but I dubbed them "the Chosen ones."

A long time ago, we noticed this tall guy (at least 6'4") with an enormous belly and thick blond locks of hair that swoop down across his forehead. Mary Danger dubbed this one Hey Kool-Aid because he reminded her of the gigantic Kool-Aid pitcher in the commercials – I think it was his belly. Well, he developed a shadow – a smaller, darker-haired version of himself, whom I dubbed Crystal Lite.

The guy looked like Hey Kool-Aid, but he wasn't as big, tall, or blond. However, unlike the Cubes, these guys were in the gym daily and ate right, and as a result, had lost a lot of weight.

Sister Mary loved to compare herself to them and it reminded me of Tom & Jerry's size difference. At the gym, she'd purposefully make her way to the machine adjacent to theirs, stand right next them, arms crossed, chest puffed out and look back at us smiling. I think she liked the contrast of her diminutive self with these towering (fat) He-men. If only I had a camera.

Foe-Foe was this semi – attractive, female MP who always ate dinner with two Air Force guys. Like all women in the military, she had to wear her hair in a bun or cut it really short. Foe-Foe pulled her hair back into a tight bun, which caused her frontal lobe to resemble the Alien monster. She had less of a forehead, more like a five or six head. Made me ponder the size of her brain.

I'm sure you've noticed an oversized muscled guy once in your life. We had many meatheads on base – the civilian contractors whose jobs required very little of their time or the military guys who only worked an 8 to 5 job and had ample time to work out. There was a guy I called Tiny. He was probably 6'3" and weighed 250 lbs. Tiny was a black dude with a permanent mean look on his face. The first time he approached me in the gym asking to use the machine I was on, I told him to fuck off – that he wasn't big enough to lift with us (me and Mary were lifting). He looked shocked, then Mary, Tiny, and I laughed. He became an instant friend. Mary told Tiny he couldn't hang with us because he was too

120

weak. It was hilarious.

You should've seen Tiny's plate at the DFAC. He needed a cart to transport it because it was always teeming with healthy, protein-enriched food. He told me he quit ordering egg-white omelets for breakfast because the substance they used only contained a few grams of protein, not the regular amount, so he switched to chicken breast, steak, and other high-protein stuff. Must've been nice to have all that free time. I bet he crapped a lot.

Buttah was Tiny's military complement. The guy was young, probably twenty years old or thereabouts. He traveled off base often but always seemed to have time each day for the gym. Buttah was my height but must've been 200 lbs. of solid muscle, which would only get bigger. He ate enormous amounts at each meal, always healthy, well as healthy as you could get at our DFAC.

One morning, I watched him consume a huge veggie omelet, a big bowl of oatmeal, lots of fruit, and two bowls of cereal. Then he got a plate "to go." Jesus, another lucky one who worked out regularly. Oh, the reason we called him Buttah? He had a slammin' body, lean and not too big for his size – but his face would scare small children. Hence, Buttah, cuz he was butt ugly.

There was a chick we saw in the DFAC at least once a day. Turns out Layla and she grew up together. We called her Superstar because she looked like the Molly Shannon character from SNL. However, the girl was tragically stuck in her childhood, style wise.

Layla dropped her fork when she first saw Superstar, stating, "Oh My God, I think I went to elementary school with her."

After a short investigation, sure enough, Layla was right. Layla said the girl's style hadn't changed since kindergarten and that she couldn't wait to return to the small, Kansas town from whence she came – thinking it was the best place on earth. Good for her, poor thing.

Although I could describe many more people, I'll close with one of my favorites. She was a train wreck from which you couldn't avert your eyes. I called her Miss Titty. T, for short, was a light-skinned black woman who could've been marginally attractive except for the sour scowl she always wore. Yes, T was packin' much breasticles, but the reason for the Christian name I gave her

RIDICULOSITY

was the clothing.

      Hoochie Momma wore the lowest-cut, tightest, short-sleeve shirts possible, exposing both breasts nearly to the nipple. But why bother; the nipples fought for attention themselves, protruding through the gauzy fabric anyway. I can't remember ever seeing her wear anything but designer terrycloth-type sweat pants. My favorite was the brown ones with rhinestone studded "Juicy" embroidered across her ample ass. She was not fat per se, more like a fusion of J Lo's and Nicki Minaj booties that assault us from TV or magazines. I guess my issue with her was, yeah, you're packing a good body, but why walk around dressed like a prostitute? Didn't your employer have a dress code, of *any* kind? There were enough crazed, horny military guys on base already, why give them more reason to stalk you, honey? One thing was certain: Miss T wouldn't be the last – there'd be more nutjobs to describe before we left.

ONE FOR THE LADIES

Now you know of the various people we encountered on a daily basis. There were the DFAC workers – American management & Macedonian laborers who did a lot of the cooking and serving, and the Afghans who did most of the cleaning. There were contractors from FLUOR to KBR filling government requirements – all civilians. There were all kinds of military people – U.S. forces, a few western-coalition partners like Kiwis, and an occasional Brit or two. Within the U.S. military force is a highly trained special sub-group – the US Army Rangers.

Rangers were the supposed tough guys who conducted night missions, raiding insurgent compounds, confiscating weapons caches, attacking groups of insurgents, etc. They truly were the Billy BadAsses of our area. Because most of their work happened at night, the guys were free during the day, which meant they hit the gym during the day. The gym was always crowded with them in the mornings and somewhat less in the afternoon, but it was never a hassle having them around. They were usually well mannered, stuck to themselves, and did some crazy workouts, which invariably, people, including me, copied. I talked to one guy about his ab routine. He ripped it out of his notebook and handed it to me. I never expected that. Of course, the page was covered in his sweaty prints, but it will be used a lot when I get home.

As with the rest of the army, the Rangers had the same penchant toward tattoos. They certainly had the right canvas for them. I saw some interesting artwork on the guys' legs, arms, etc., but unlike the greater Army, I didn't see many neck or hand tattoos. I'm not saying those didn't exist, just that I didn't noticed them. I guess one could surmise the Rangers were a bit classier? Hard to imagine, but it could be true. Note: I didn't say intelligent, just not as prone to tacky ink jobs. Typical stain included flames and skulls, the occasional crucifix, and some killer shadowing. Whoever did their work must be a millionaire because I think in the nine months I spent on base, I only saw four or five Rangers without at least one tattoo (officers excluded).

When the Rangers conducted mission, they naturally wore uniforms and had all their Hoo-ah gear, night vision devices, etc. But whenever they were around base, eating in the DFAC, lifting in the gym, going to the PX, getting haircuts, the Rangers wore their standard PT gear – and this is why the ladies will appreciate this section. The most badass guys on base, who worked out the most and thus were mostly brawny or lean and buff, wore the skimpiest, tightest outfits of anyone.

Don't know how that came about, but for those who like to ogle a bunch of young, muscled, All-American men in tight black shorts and tan T-shirts strutting around base, oblivious to all the female and a few men's fantasies they were responsible for, any base with Rangers was a "must visit" destination. I only knew a few such places in my greater area of operations, but I bet Rangers were everywhere.

I worked with the guys on a professional level and knew a few from the gym. Some were brilliant strategists and understood the importance of integrating my line of work with theirs. Others were complete Neanderthals with the verbal skills and vocabulary of a chicken but bodies and occasional faces of Adonis. One guy in particular from this current group stood out. I called him Hans.

At roughly 6' tall and around 225 lbs. of solid, ripped muscle, Hans wasn't lean enough to be in one of those national muscle magazines, but he was no slouch. Hans had thick tree-trunk legs, the muscles of which were clearly defined, each distinct from the other. It was like something from an anatomy book. He could run too. I joined him for a lap around base once, until he picked up the pace and left me in the dust. The guy had a huge ass, clearly visible above the dust he created – it was so big it probably needed its own zip code, but it was in perfect proportion to the rest of his body. It reminded me of a bowling ball cut in half. Get the picture?

So, imagine a "Victoria's Secret Fashion Show" all day, every day, consisting of young, muscled, sometimes sweaty tattooed men of all sizes lolling about in what we refer to as Ranger panties (basically black onion-skin running shorts) and tight tan T-shirts. Ladies, for those of you who need a moment to yourselves after

124

this section, I suggest you close the door to whatever room you're sitting, turn down the lights, make it yours, and complete the fantasy. Then use it tonight on your spouse, bf, sig other, etc.

RIDICULOSITY

"What's a three-letter word for distant?" Mary Danger asked, stumped by a crossword puzzle again.

"If I wanted a mom, I would've asked Chip!" Woody, shouted in exasperation to Shaniese's motherly advice.

BANG! BANG!

Every once in a while you needed a break from the daily routine. We really couldn't work twelve-hour days, six days a week and keep our sanity for very long. Back home, one could go to the beach, go shopping, take a short trip, etc. We didn't have that option in Afghanistan, but we did have guns. Oh yeah, did we ever have guns. I mean, what was a deployment to a chaotic area in a shithole country without multiple types of weapons?

Our coworkers in another office did even more incredible stuff than us. They were always out "on mission" and had all kinds of guns: from machine guns, to regular M4s (short rifles), to hand guns, and even grenades – both the throwing and gun-launching kind. Although we didn't have the proper firing range to practice shooting or throwing grenades, we did have access to the local weapons range on base and were able to acquire some extra ammo. Oh, I need to explain that...

I didn't know this, but it turned out that when a soldier deployed to Afghanistan he was given a supply of ammo that wasn't actually his. Bullets were restricted and unless he got in a firefight, the soldier had to turn in everything before redeploying home. That made sense, I mean, who wanted to haul around heavy ammo, right? But every bullet had to be accounted for whether fired or returned. Shooting practice or qualification for most soldiers wasn't allowed or condoned in many places. Maybe it was the Army's way of controlling assets (bullets) and keeping costs down. But here's the thing, no matter where you went there was usually extra ammo up for grabs. So with that in mind, the kids were able to join the coworkers next door for some shooting practice.

RIDICULOSITY

The coworkers could use the shooting range because their job required they be proficient at shooting. And that required lots of practice. Chip and I manned the office so Shaniese, Woody, and Mary Danger could join Josh, Carmen, Mitchell, Don, and a few others at the range. They planned it for Sunday because that was always a slow day at the office, mainly because the U.S. soldiers were allowed time for religious services. So, the kids tromped off to the range while Chip and I enjoyed some peace and quiet.

Three hours later, the kids returned with stories of great shots, and laughter about complete misses. Plus, everyone talked about our girl. As expected, Sister Mary dominated the course (everything was a competition with her). She shot the most weapons and hit the most targets. She even tried to help Mitchell improve her shooting but that's like trying to teach a panda how to bake cookies. Danger got so frustrated, that she shot at Mitchell's targets when Mitchell kept missing. Everyone laughed at that, but Mitchell didn't mind. She wasn't going to hit anything anyway.

Naturally, Sister Mary volunteered to go "on mission" with the guys the next time they left base, and the guys really wanted her to join. Believe me, she was ready – no one could restrain her enthusiasm. It reminded me of Don and the rope-climbing incident. But no, we needed her for our mission, even if she was sullen and resentful. Instead, they took another female soldier who ended up crying when things got tough. I think her tears were more a result of frustration than actual heartache, but guys never want to see tears, especially in front of Rangers during a dangerous night mission in a hostile Afghan village.

I promised the kids they could shoot whenever they wanted to, provided the coworkers next door controlled the range. That quelled Danger's fidgety frustration for a while. But it wouldn't last long. Thankfully, she couldn't hear Chip and me making fun of her – the boneheads forgot to bring earplugs to the range but fired anyway. Their ears buzzed for two days, which came back to bite me and Chip in the ass because Shaniese, Woody and Danger were exceptionally loud. So, we had a three-hour block of peace when they were gone, but almost two days of shouting when they returned. Sometimes ya couldn't win for trying.

128

*"I can't concentrate and focus **at the same time**!" Sister Mary Danger yelled at us again.*

DIRT AND THE EXPERIMENT

Afghanistan is primarily an agricultural society with eighty-plus percent of its people making a living from the earth. While the soil must be different throughout the country (I mean, how could it not be?), I discovered there were a few standard characteristics that transcended location. Unlike the U.S. Plains, South, or Midwest, Afghanistan had no deep, rich soil in which to grow crops. Well, none that I saw anyway. Somehow, these poor souls eked out a living from some of the most tired, arid, dry, dusty land I had ever seen. And that particularly low-quality dirt was everywhere. I travelled all over the country, from Mazar-i-Sharif in the northwest to Taloqan in the north central, to Chah Ab in the northeast, to Bamiyan in the center, to Kandahar in the south, and finally to the southeast provinces. The common denominator was what we call moondust.

Moondust was just what you'd imagine it to be – dry powder. It was at every location. The stuff had the consistency of talcum powder or powdered sugar. It was an ever-present layer above the concrete-like earth on which we worked. Imagine a tan-colored flour and you have an idea of what we dealt with. It got into everything, through cracks in the window and doorframes, into the housing units, in the shower areas, in the vehicles, hell – no place was immune. And man, was it useless.

Lazy fuckers would often pour coffee pot dregs in the moondust just outside their office doors. They were lazy and avoided walking to the bathroom building to use the sink. What amazed me was the inability of moondust to absorb any liquid. It hit home one morning when I discovered the partially unabsorbed pee puddle I had left behind one night when I was in the middle of something and didn't want to trek to the bathroom. (Don't worry; it wasn't right outside the door. I do have some standards, ya know.) I wasn't alone in the office so I couldn't pee in a bottle, thus, a trek outside in the dark. Come on, we're guys, remember? The entire outdoors is a potential urinal.

Yeah, a residual puddle of pee. That possibility had never crossed my mind. Pee absorbs, right? It damn well better, in my reality. I mean, that was evidence, wasn't it? If I was on Bagram, there would've been a sergeant major snooping around with a DNA kit, taking samples to compare to the ones in our files in order to track me down for a reprimand. Thank God I wasn't there.

So, after a day or two of deliberation, I decided to embark on my experiment. An orchard of some kind was located almost directly behind our office building. Someone said there were oranges growing on base, but I never saw them in the trees behind us. Maybe it was an olive orchard. I've been to Greece and seen olive groves. Yeah, maybe they were olives. At any rate, no fruit of any kind grew on the trees. Maybe because it was the winter season? Whatev. The grove was pretty neglected and there were plenty of bone-dry weeds that sprouted from the bedrock soil in better (rainy) times.

I located a clump of three small weeds set back from the edge of the orchard. It was hidden enough that the casual observer shouldn't notice a guy standing there. It was open enough so that I could find it at night when the moon was at least half full. My experiment began in earnest four days ago, about mid-morning, when I had to get rid of my morning cuppa Joe. I purposefully walked over to my obscured clump-o-weeds, unzipped, and began watering. And sure enough, nothing really absorbed into the ground. I picked a site that had as little moondust as possible to (hopefully) ensure maximum absorption. Nothing doing. Yeah, the weeds absorbed some liquid, but the majority drained off and pooled in a small depression next to the clump (the clump was on higher ground).

Yuck! But I expected as much. Over the course of four days, I dutifully watered my charges as frequently as Mother Nature called. Believe me, they got enough water. However, the ground
130

around my precious experiment never became dry. It appeared to be in a perpetual state of semi-submersion by day's end. It was disappointing to say the least. I hit the weeds only a few times today, most recently about ten minutes ago. At 8 p.m., I had no idea what the ground looked like, but I was sure that come morning when I checked again, there'd still be liquid not quite fully absorbed. And to think this was an orchard! Amazing. I thought I'd continue until I saw the weeds turn green – unless of course my water was toxic and the weeds remain in their catatonic state of death. I'll keep you updated.

Lucky you, an update

Awhile passed since I first wrote about my experiment. Nothing changed that much, especially with the plant. It still looked desiccated and lifeless. However, we had some rain recently and it changed the ground everywhere. It rained for about eighteen hours starting January 27; not a torrential rain, more of a Seattle mist rain. Well, come February 2, there were still puddles on the ground in places where the water hadn't soaked in or evaporated. (The temps didn't promote evaporation just yet.)

Come February 7 and it rained off and on all day. Those puddles just got bigger and more puddles appeared. And my plant still hadn't changed form. I deduced that growth is less predicated on how much water something gets than the ambient temperature. I still wanted to water my plant, mainly because I thought it a worthwhile experiment. Well, sorta, I was bored.

RIDICULOSITY

"What kinda choice is that? It's like choosing between syphilis, herpes, and gonorrhea!" Shaniese angrily interjected, on having to pick one of the visiting battalion leadership team members to have dinner with.

MR. KNOW-IT-ALL

In every deployment, some people merit special attention. There were a few at my location whom I mentioned in previous dispatches. Well, a few more deserved recognition. One guy in particular was especially irritating from Day 1. I finally settled on a name for him – Wilbur. Do you remember that timeless children's classic, Charlotte's Web? Besides Charlotte, the other main character was Wilbur the pig. Very fitting for this guy because over the course of the deployment with his eating habits he became more porcine than human. Here's a visual – try not to vomit.

Wilbur was not a thin guy to begin with. At 5'8, he tipped the scales at 170-175, very little of which was muscle. He easily topped two bills before we departed Afghanistan. But why? Well, Wilbur enlisted in the military late in life, like at forty years old. Nothing wrong with that, but at that age the body's metabolism is slower than at twenty. Add to the mix Wilbur's profile against running – he could only walk during the PT test (An Army 'profile' is often a temporary exemption from physical activity.) Finally, there was his penchant for potato chips. Ole' piggy liked his deep-fried snacks. Oinkin' Wilbur got emotional fulfillment through four bags of cholesterol and sodium *after each meal*. The guy ate three squares a day, and snatched four bags of potato chips from the bin on his way out of the DFAC, which were consumed between feedings. It was disturbing. But that wasn't the half of it. He was addicted to Mountain Dew and drank it by the case – at least six to eight cans per day when available.

Piggy was a special case. No one would've cared if he wasn't such an insufferable boor. He was an arrogant, know-it-all, opinionated, condescending, entitled, obsequious to authority, incapable of giving yes or no answers. I found out much later that he had been passing information about our daily operations to another unit's First Sergeant whom he had befriended while at Bagram. Knowing his personality, I could see that happening because Wilbur would consider them equals despite the huge rank difference. That First Sergeant was equally unctuous around authority and a subordinate and friend of Molly's. In our unit, Wilbur was liked as much as Molly was.

With each passing month, his shirts got tighter around the waist, buttons expanding to near bursting. His moobs, or man-breasts, gradually reached pregnant woman proportions. But the best part, under his button-down uniform top, Wilbur wore spandex shirts. We all wondered what went through his mind. I mean, why accentuate the bulbous man-tits, the hefty blobular belly? He was delusional if he thought those shirts had a slimming effect.

Chip never liked Wilbur to begin with so his critiques were extremely biting, stating Wilbur sweated Crisco and his moobs leak butter, or that he was taking estrogen supplements in order to lactate and feed himself. There were more, but I think you got the point. Toward the end of the deployment we'll learn that although Wilbur volunteered to extend a few months longer to help out the new crew, he departed with the rest of us and we had the distinct pleasure of riding one row behind him on the plane, Under Armor shirt and all. At least we had unique entertainment. You should've seen the moobs and belly bounce when we hit turbulence.

"I think its Allah's will I chip a tooth here." Layla annoyingly said at the DFAC after biting down on something hard in her meal yet again.

"What? Is that a status symbol where you come from?" I asked.

"Thooth. Oops! I spelled tooth wrong." Mary Danger laughed, adding to the quote board in the office after lunch.

"Did you spell it 'toof'?" said Layla, laughing at Danger.

MARY'S METAMORPHOSIS

Y'all familiar with the saying "when Hell freezes over," right? Well folks, I can tell you with one hundred-percent certainty – Hell officially froze over. Yep, it was basically an iceberg for a spell. And how did I know that, you ask? Well, Sister Mary Danger, aka Betty Badass, had a complete make-over. I know, don't crap yourself. We were all astonished.

Danger was a tomboy through and through. She smoked like a chimney, swore like a sailor, was better at sports than any of the guys, and radiated the tough-girl persona like nobody's business. She wore flip-flops, basketball shorts, and a wife beater under her gown at high school graduation. That didn't surprise me at all. She probably drunkenly stumbled across the stage with a ciggie in her mouth. So, Mary had never worn make up before in her adult life, until the other day.

I don't know how we got her to put on the war paint, get her "hair-did," shellac the nails, and wear clean clothes, but we did. Remember Layla, the recent addition to our larger group and Danger's roommate? Layla was a total tough chick as well, but a girly one. Layla started hanging with us more often – going to chow, chillaxin in the office, watching the occasional movie, etc. She really wanted to makeover Mary, to which Mary vehemently objected. Of course, Mary was going to do that, and no one could imagine

Danger dressed as a girl, but it happened.

"No, I gotta do this before you leave!" Mary said emphatically at dinner one night. I suggested she get all dolled up for my return from R&R, but she wasn't having it.

"I'm gonna need to smoke a carton of cigarettes first." She said urgently, planning it out.

"You're going to inhale like a hundred cigarettes before the make over? WTF?" I reacted in surprise. Dude, this tough chick didn't bat an eye when it came to dangerous missions outside the wire, but suggest mascara and fingernail polish and she'd sweat bullets. Ha!

Danger made me promise to get her beer, not liquor, only beer. She wanted a six-pack before agreeing to the girl's day in. I said I would tap into my sources, fully expecting her to say No! (BTW, I had no connections on base to get beer, nor would I promote such debauchery – it was against the rules, remember? Wink wink). So, Danger thought I'd score her some brewski. She insisted no pictures or video (God, I was a bastard. Not only did I not get her beer, I snapped a full photo album like a Japanese tourist in Times Square).

"Okay, if we're going to do this right, you need to get up early to take a shower, and dry your hair." Layla instructed Danger.

"What, like 5 a.m.?" I joked.

"Fuck that!" Mary protested – a phrase that came out of her mouth more often than "Excuse me" and "Thank you" combined.

The day arrived. They had eventually settled on starting at 10 a.m. (it was Sunday after all). Danger sullenly left the office and the process began. She showered then returned to her room where Layla did her magic. And magic it was.

Nearly two hours passed. Woody, Chip, Shaniese and I had finished with chores and were eagerly waiting. There was a knock at the door. "Come in!" we all shout.

Layla cracks open the door and sticks her head in, a smile on her face like she's privy to an inside joke. "Okay, she's ready." she quietly said, obviously suppressing laughter.

"Let me in!" we heard from beyond the door. Mary was already more feisty and fussy than ever – trying to force the door
136

open. Maybe she didn't want to be seen in public?

Layla hadn't let Mary see a mirror – or Mary didn't want to. I don't know which was the case. Layla opened the office door but made us face the other way (I didn't). Not only were we eager to see the outcome, we were hungry and really wanted to eat.

"Hurry up, I'm *starving!*" Woody cared more about food and himself than anything else right then and yelled for them to hurry up.

In walked this complete stranger in big white sunglasses. Layla had straightened Danger's careless hair and pulled the top into a pouf, it looked great. Mary had changed into clean, unstained, unripped clothes and tucked in her shirt (I didn't know she had unstained, unripped clothes). Layla had painted Danger's nails a vibrant shade of lilac.

But the best part was the makeup. We could see the war paint even through the sunglasses, but when Mary finally took them off after much cajoling, I was speechless. Our caterpillar had turned into a butterfly, well at least a moth. No kidding.

"Oh my God!" Chip said. "Holy Shit, you're a goddamn Frieda Kahlo!" I whispered, feeling like I was in a trance. I would have said Picasso or Dali but that'd be mean, and anyway I didn't think Danger would get it. Hell, she didn't get the Kahlo reference either but at least it was a woman.

"STOP!" she yelled – leaping at me, eyes bulging, hands outstretched, frantically reaching for my camera as I snapped picture after hurried picture. I just ran away laughing. Being like 5'4", it was easy playing keep-away with her, ya just had to protect your balls. I know, what a bastard.

Mary's eyes looked smoky hot, with just enough makeup to highlight and deepen them. Stunning! Altogether, she was a knockout. I couldn't wait to see guys' reactions at lunch. But suddenly our sweet Sister Mary had lost her appetite and didn't want to go. Figured. It didn't help that as Mary took off her glasses Woody exclaimed, *"Oh my God! You look like a Girl!"* a complete look of joy and surprise on his face.

Mary chased him around the room throwing as many punches as she could and landing a few. Those smoky eyes revealed a nervous frustration of impending embarrassment at her 'big reveal.'

"Fuck you Woody!" she shouted thru gritted teeth. He just laughed out loud and dodged. Those two fought like siblings sometimes, it was funny to watch.

Arms crossed, staring at the floor, Mary plopped down at her desk and forcefully announced, "I'm not going, I lost my appetite."

Ha! Fat chance of that happening. We convinced her to go and it was great. Sooooooo many guys did a double take – some outright gawked. It was precious and Danger was miserable. That was the best part – not the fact that she was "Going against my morals!" as she so loudly and often proclaimed, but the fact she was absolutely miserable sitting there with all the dudes checking out her chili. I think she secretly liked the attention, but she'd never admit it. I got a few more pics there, and a lot of cuss words from her.

Later, Mary changed into her normal clothes: a T-shirt, basketball shorts, and boots, then sat in the office. Now that was juxtaposition from heaven. All dolled up but in trailer-park garb. I loved it. She'll probably never do it again in her life, but why should she? I had evidence that it happened once. I love blackmail.

"It's all about compromise and doing what I say." I
intoned to the team.

CANDY AND ME

I discovered something last night that I hadn't thought about
before. Candy and I aren't a good mix. I rarely eat candy in general
and had forgotten the effect it has on me. However, I made an
impulse buy at the PX yesterday when I saw boxes of Whoppers,
the malted milk balls. I used to love those as a youngin' – that's
probably why I was a "husky" kid.

There was an eye-catching display of king-size boxes (sure,
go ahead and make the bored, fat, lazy Americans even fatter – we
have no self-control). It stood right next to the aisle leading to the
checkout line. Could this get any easier? Suddenly reminded of
my childhood, I bought a box of Whoppers and some Corn Nuts. I
gorged on those in high school.

Due to our work schedule that day I had a late lunch and
lost my appetite in general because I stopped had working out. I
decided to eat the bag of Corn Nuts and Whoppers around 5 p.m.
as a substitute for dinner. By 7 p.m. the sugar high had worn off and
my energy level crashed. Work was slow and I was grumpy so I left
the office early. Dumbass me decided it'd be a good idea to go to
bed at 8 p.m., hoping that I'd sleep through the night.

Unfortunately, I woke around 11 p.m. when my mind sprang
into action with thoughts tumbling through my head like clothes in
a dryer, twisting and interrupting stories with the help of Cling Free.
I laid there for a good forty-five minutes, trying to get comfortable
through different sleeping positions. It was useless. All the relaxing
thoughts and techniques I had used in the past were for naught.
More and more thoughts busted into my noggin' fighting for
attention like a pack of boisterous first graders at Show & Tell. I
decided to get up. Since I hadn't yet showered (see experiment No.

RIDICULOSITY

2) I rambled off to the shower building. Thankfully, I had the stinky place to myself.

My roommate was in bed when I returned. He said he didn't mind if I kept my light on and typed on the computer. Don was a very reasonable guy and I was very respectful of his space and sleeping habits. I dinked around the Internet for a bit, then wrote a letter, finally crashing around 2:30 a.m. I woke at my regular time, 5:50 a.m., and had a surprisingly energetic day – even making it to the gym. That small success aside, I'll remember that candy + me = bad.

Experiment No. 2

The shower I took that night of sleepless frustration ended Experiment No. 2. Please allow me to provide the backstory and inspiration behind that experiment. I experimented not so much from inspiration, as from boredom.

It was a bit cold in my province. But other places have it much worse than us – Silas and his team in the adjoining province trekked 300 meters through twelve inches of snow, ice, and mud uphill both ways to get to their shower building. I had it good. My barracks was only about seventy strides from the shower building. I was never eager to make that short trek at midnight in the inky darkness and cold of winter. So, I decided to recreate Experiment No. 1.

Experiment No. 1 took place in San Antonio, Texas (SATX) one summer a few years prior. My battalion sponsored an Army Reserve wide training exercise in SATX. My office was the brain trust and operations gurus responsible for the success or failure of the 200 plus person exercise (it was a resounding success thanks to some great team work). However, it was a very stressful time. Trevor and I – a Captain in my section who was a former infantryman – decided to see how long we could go without showering. You might wanna plug your nose.

The showers at Camp Bullis, TX, where the exercise took place were nasty. They didn't stink like Afghanistan, but they weren't standard Army issue facilities either. The showers were in a square room with two shower heads evenly spaced on three

140

walls of the room. It was exposed to anyone outside the building when one opened the main entrance door so your "Johnson" or "Jane" was front and center for any passer-by to see. You were also completely exposed to anyone in the shower. Not the most ideal conditions for privacy – much worse than here. Deciding to go without a shower was an easy choice and something guys did.

Understand those conditions: San Antonio is hot in the summer with temps regularly hitting high, humid nineties, crappy showers, insane work schedule (hey, something akin to what we have here), and utter exhaustion at the end of the day. The easy decision to forego hygiene actually turned in to a competition. Trevor and I laid the ground rules – one could shave, wash the face and feet but nothing more. Whoever deviated first lost the bet. We didn't bet on anything, just dumb-guy braggin' rights.

By Day nine both Trevor and I threw in the proverbial towel for two reasons. First and foremost – on Day ten the battalion had a free day (it was a three-week exercise). Trevor had planned to see his kids and didn't want to be disowned. (Funny how that could happen, it's usually the other way around – but this is the twenty-first century.) But second and just as important, we had really started to stink. Although the rules allowed us to change our socks, T-shirts, and underwear, I still smelled horrid. In fact, by Day seven, I had taken to holding my breath or breathing through my mouth when I pulled my pants down to pee because the malodorous stench had started to make me gag. Neither of us paid much attention to the protests our roommates had lodged starting on Day three (they were pussies), but I couldn't refute the downright disgust my own body had started to register.

RIDICULOSITY

ENTER EXPERIMENT
NO. 2

Refer back to the paragraph about not wanting to trek to the shower at night in the cold of winter in Afghanistan. Well, at the end of an eighteen-hour work day when you were really tired, it was dark and cold outside and you had no one to impress (have you ever smelled an Afghan?), going without a shower wasn't a big deal. It'd be different if I were back home. The shower is inside my house, I could turn on the light to get to it, I wouldn't have to fight the elements, there's no ungodly septic stench (see previous portion), and I wouldn't have to jostle with a bunch of guys for a shower. But I wasn't back home, I was in lovely Asskrakistan, and the aforementioned factors were in play.

I figured I could easily go two or three weeks before I had to shower. It was February and rarely got above fifty-five degrees (downright balmy, I'd say). I'd not sweat as much this time as I did during that funky summer in San Antonio, unless I started going to the gym again. Woody didn't shower that often so I'd be in familiar company on the "stink" level. I was bored and wanted to see how far I could push my limits this time (the longest I'd gone without showering was nineteen days on my first deployment). Plus, I didn't care.

Well, my non-showering total had reached three days when the candy tragedy struck. I had thrashed about in bed for a good forty-five minutes before finally getting up. My head had begun to itch so much over those three days that I realized how often I was diggin' at the scabs, which were surely forming on my scalp. Thankfully, I had a habit of avoiding mirrors (unlike Woody) so I was oblivious to any mothball-size chunks of dandruff that had probably taken refuge in my hair. Hence, a trek to the shower wasn't out of the question. I was not a complete pig; mind you, just a lazy piglet at times.

The shower still stunk of "eau du septic tank" but my relief at being able to wash my scabby head far outweighed the none-too-familiar offensive smell. If my mind hadn't been racing like a crazed NASCAR driver I might not have showered or been inspired to compose this e-mail. See, we both benefited from it. Hope you've enjoyed.

*"You move like **Christmas**!" Shaniese, complained about how slow Woody moved when he was tired.*

CAN YOU BELIEVE? NAME UPDATE NO. 3

More transitions to and from base meant more soldiers, which naturally meant more interesting names. We added to Eagle and Pigeon (the noble and the nuisance from a previous e-mail), Hawk and Mallard (the hunter and the hunted). There was Houston and Lauderdale, Marsh and Pond, Hector and Camacho, Handy and Dandy, Little and Richard (no kidding – I laughed when I realized it), Foote and Locker, Cash and Register, Long and Short, Page and Story, Stout, Sass, Shank, and Stuck.

There was Solomon, but no Grundy. There was no one named Guy, but there was a Smiley. Guy Smiley – he was the Announcer on the original Muppet Show. Remember Tiffany, from a previous e-mail? He was a Captain – yeah, a man. Well, he wasn't the only guy cursed with a female name. We saw Vera, Carroll, and Beverly – all dudes.

Couldn't forget the "un" pairs – we had Liberty but no Valance, Cotton but no linen, rayon, or polyester, Presto but no Chango, Sheets without a Pillow, Singledecker but no double-decker, Coffin but no Nail, Cobb without a Corn, Coon but no Skin, Holdaway but no Castaway, Triplett but no Twins, Morse but no Code, Palm but no Pilot, Neece but no Nephew, and Jolly but no Rancher.

Then there was the group I called the politicians – Washington, Adams, Monroe, Jackson, Polk, Tyler, Grant, and Calhoun. I saw a couple of Bush(es) and more Johnson(s) than I'd care to admit to. Finally, don't forget Thatcher, Kerry, Fox, Kim, Hillary, Calderon, Kennedy, Nixon, Ford, Carter, Reagan, and Dole. Whew! I'm sure I missed a few but I didn't know many politicians.

145

RIDICULOSITY

Finally, there were some silly fun names: Spitter, Gamble, Saucier, Dang, Troll, Funzi – yeah, you read that correctly – Funzi (t'was worthy of a second mention), Comfort, Meek, Keys, Venable, Crisco, and Unterborn – which to me sounded both German and sinister. My time on deployment was far from over so there would be more names and spontaneous laughter.

"Even hookers don't get this many phone calls!"
Mahmud, our interpreter exclaimed in frustration.

"Sometimes, when I am tired, my balls just need holding"
Woody mumbled to Shaniese, when she asked why he
was cradling his nutsack.

CELLPHONE SYSTEMS

Don't you hate it when you've got spotty cell-phone coverage? Doesn't it annoy the crap outta ya when a person at the next table or on the bus or at work is practically yelling into his cell phone because of a bad connection or crappy speaker? Don't you want to throw your phone in disgust when you get nothing but static or there's a repetitive delay when you call a friend and hear your own voice echo?

Welcome to my Hell. Cell phone coverage in Afghanistan sucked ass at best. It made you want to kick a puppy at worst (yes, I heard people say that). But how could one complain? This Bronze Age culture was lucky to be connected at all. Their alternative was trekking from village to sad, dusty village on a donkey to speak to someone. Not that anyone would go to another village – different mountain villages were practically distinct individual societies and occasionally at war with one another. But cell-phone coverage might bridge that societal gap.

It did exist, but where I was (the capitol of a province bordering Pakistan), cell-phone coverage was horrendous. Having a phone call drop two to three times during a conversation was a normal. In fact, it was expected. Throw in any type of bad weather like wind, thick cloud cover, or heaven forbid, rain, and you practically lost the ability to communicate. In bad weather it was easier to text than to call because a call wouldn't go through, period. The text might've. If at my desk in the office or in the bathroom where the roof was corrugated metal, there was absolutely no connection. I had to walk outside to text, accept, or make a call. That was our Afghan standard.

Oh, I forgot to mention, I had it good at my location. My buddies at outlying FOBs and COPs had it worse, or maybe better, depending on your definition. Taliban controlled many cell-phone towers in the countryside. They forced people with a cell-phone tower on their property to cut power to the tower by 6 p.m. every night. That way, insurgents had free reign to do what they wanted under cover of darkness, without anyone reporting their illicit activities. That's how many IEDs were placed in roads everywhere. Taliban targeted U.S. and Coalition Forces, but innocent Afghans were blown up as well. If it sucked for us, it sucked for Afghans even more. They didn't have MRAPs.

Internet connection was similar to cell-phone service – abysmal and expensive. I can't remember how many times I went to my room after work, usually around 10:30-11 p.m., hoping to send off a few quick e-mails only to discover I couldn't connect. And I paid a Benjamin per month for this glorious service. Yeah, can you believe it? No complaints though, at least I had Internet access in my room – when I could get there and the weather held out. I tried downloading an album from iTunes once, just eight songs. It took all day. I had to restart my computer and reconnect to the Internet three times before I gave up. Only got six of the songs and honestly I didn't care anymore. Ya know, I'm looking forward to returning to the States for normal Internet and phone service if for anything at all.

"You need to start smoking again, I don't like this!" Chip snapped at Mary Danger, about her crabby behavior while trying to quit smoking

"Team Twelve, this is me," I answered the phone one particularly rough day.

THE MOUSE THAT ROARED!

The military is a unique institution with a set of rules and hierarchy through which one must carefully tread, that is, if one is smart. The restrictions inherent in the military system are usually absent in a civilian company. In the civilian world, if a worker has a suggestion, s/he can submit a proposal through a "process improvement" program and hopefully get the suggestion reviewed. If it's a beneficial suggestion and the worker is lucky, the suggestion could become the new standard and the company overall might benefit from the improvement. At least that's the theory. Sometimes that's the case. Submitting a recommendation or complaint with suggested improvements is an accepted practice in corporate America. Why? Because capitalism usually rewards the most efficient, most adept, and most innovative companies.

The military is not a company. It's an organization. And that strict hierarchical structure I mentioned occasionally impedes progress. One can get in trouble for going "above one's station" with a problem or suggestion because commanders at all levels are empowered to implement change and improvements at their respective levels. Plus, commanders don't want to draw undue attention to themselves by making waves.

The military is very conservative and often commanders are hesitant to speak out for fear of a bad evaluation or other, more subtle "punishment." Hurray for the troops who have a commander brave enough to buck the system for a worthy suggestion. Soldiers are often viewed as troublemakers for bucking the system, so

---

complaints are grumbled, suggestions are made, then paid lip service, nothing changes, and soldiers become disgruntled. But what's worse, the overall mission could suffer or be distorted and worse than that, soldiers might stop caring.

That whole process played out for me recently. My team collected information. We tried to find out what the bad guys were planning and stop them before they caused more chaos in this Neolithic, fractured society. I was like hundreds of others charged with the responsibility of getting the freshest, most complete information possible, passing it through the system where it eventually got to the battle space owner, or BSO (usually an infantry Lieutenant Colonel – LTC). The BSO could take action against the bad guys if he felt the information was correct, verified, and timely – and supported his overall mission. There were different outcomes of those actions with various levels of success. Some of you might recall hearing the horrible consequences of acting on bad information. Unfortunately, that outcome was a painful aspect of war.

Well, an indirect consequence of my job was to help the U.S. "win the hearts and minds" of the Afghan people, to foster faith in their government, trust in the Coalition Forces who fought insurgents, and get them to believe our mission of having their best interests at heart. Let me tell ya, everything we as foreigners did on deployment had an impact on Afghan impressions of us, from interacting with the elders in town, to attending town-hall meetings, building medical clinics/schools, repairing roads, delivering humanitarian aid, giving classes on crop rotation and animal husbandry, and taking bad guys off the street. Hell, even how we drove our vehicles in town made an impression. The trickiest part was how we dealt with bad guys, because that had the biggest impact on the innocents, whose hearts and minds we wanted to win.

Everyone wanted the shit bags off the street. They emplaced IEDs, which injured or killed U.S. soldiers and local Afghans. They shot mortars at U.S./Afghan bases, which injured or killed soldiers from both countries and might've killed locals working on base. They harassed and extorted bribes from local shop owners. They

150

did a lot of crazy stuff. So when Uncle Sugar (code name for U.S. Army or the military) incarcerated a shit bag, most villagers were happy. We "won the hearts and minds" of the locals, and insurgent activity decreased in that area for a while. That was the norm, unless the innate, cultural Afghan attribute of corruption distorted or negated our success.

Corruption within Afghan society was omnipresent. If someone was put in jail, a bribe could get him released. If someone wanted a coveted job, a bribe could get him hired. If someone wanted his kid in school, a bribe could guarantee a seat. If someone was gravely injured, a bribe could buy the medicine that was stolen from the hospitals and sold on the black market.

The entire country was like this from top to bottom, and it negatively impacted my job of building trust between the locals and U.S. forces and between locals and their government. It was this inherent corruption that ate at my psyche.

My fellow collectors at other locations experienced similar frustrations. We discussed our experiences with corruption and how it thwarted our big objective of "winning the hearts and minds." It hit home for the third time on this deployment when a furious Chip had to appease an irate local with whom we had been meeting because corruption not only ruined the work we had been doing with him, but also resulted in the deaths of innocent villagers in his area. I understood the guy's frustration. Why should he endanger his life by working with us if nothing came of it but dead innocent villagers? Why did we go from being the good guys to being the bad guys when Afghan corruption negated our success? Chip had lost the Afghan's cooperation, would I lose Chip?

I stewed on this and previous incidents for a couple days and when I stewed, thoughts boiled inside my head. The only way to get clarity and closure was to write, mainly so I could understand and put everything in perspective. That writing became a three-page discourse on how a lot of our work got jacked up because of Afghan corruption, thereby "losing the hearts and minds" of the people whom we were supposed to win over. Some of our national policies and goals for Afghanistan were consistently undermined by the widespread corruption at all levels of Afghan society and the

U.S. policy of working with and empowering Afghan leaders at the national, provincial and village levels.

At the local level, we did everything right. Commanders did good work. We followed guidance emanating from the highest levels of the military and yet, local Afghans often considered us the bad guys when things went wrong. With all this nonsense and frustration bubbling up inside me, affecting our work and morale, I decided to send those three pages of thoughts to General Stanley McChrystal, the ultimate military dude in charge in Afghanistan. Yeah, I e-mailed the king.

I had my reasons, which at the time I thought were relevant. I wished I could say I "drunk e-mailed" him, like what one does after a night out when one "drunk dials" friends. Not that I could drunk e-mail GEN McChrystal – we weren't allowed to drink on deployment. But on a more realistic note, the last thing I'd want to do when drunk is get behind the keyboard of my computer. Well, I wouldn't want to get behind the wheel of my car either, but that wasn't possible because my car was in Texas.

"But Chief, why did you e-mail *General McChrystal*?"

I can't tell you how many times I heard that question from everyone. I guess, maybe it was because I was dumb like that. Or maybe it was because the strain and pressure of the nonsense made me crack.

First, my team was designated general support (GS) to the big guys at HQ in Bagram (we worked for HQ and the local BSO) but we didn't report or belong to the local commander. I ensured we "paid the rent" by working our butts off for the local BSO – fulfilling his requirements. Being GS gave us a level of immunity from local control that we wouldn't enjoy if the team had been in a direct support (DS) role. Had we been DS, I might not have sent the e-mail, or I might've been court-martialed.

Second, fellow collectors throughout the country suffered from the same negative impact Afghan corruption had on "winning the hearts and minds," a policy GEN McChrystal promoted countrywide. The issues were not local, they were national. If we had to engage government at all levels, yet lose Afghan support and are seen as the bad guys when engagement worked against

152

us, then the issue of engagement had to be addressed at a much higher level than ours in just one province.

Third, I honestly didn't think I'd get much of a response, let alone a visit from "the Man." But he was like that, I discovered.

Fourth, I'd been associated with the military more than twenty years, was somewhat articulate, and pretty much an expert in my field. My team had done tremendous work, backed up by quantifiable results. We "paid the rent" here and then some. I spoke for many of us collectors.

And finally, the main reason I e-mailed the General directly, was because his e-mail address was in our global address book. Turned out, he answered his e-mail. Like I said, I was shocked, half expecting an aide or staffer assigned to answer the probable flood of e-mail a man of his stature and position received. But no, the General himself e-mailed me back.

I had detailed how we at the ground level worked to implement his policies and were coming up short because of pervasive corruption. The U.S. can't win against Afghan corruption in the long run and I said so, then added a few related topics. I even offered to arrange a meeting with him and the local Afghan who compelled me to write.

You know what he did? He came to visit us a few days later. No kidding. I nearly shat myself when I saw his response. He wanted to hear firsthand what kind of problems we were up against, how the average Afghan viewed our work, and how we'd address the problems if we could implement changes.

Well, let me tell ya, the days between telling my team what I did and the General's visit were a bit unusual to say the least. I felt like Pariah Carey for a while. Everyone freaked out when they learned that "the King was coming, the King was coming." Honestly, I was hesitant to send the e-mail in the first place, but as I hit send, I figured I could spend my retirement years breaking rocks and mowing lawns at Ft. Leavenworth just as easy as lounging on a beach in the Caribbean – and it'd cost me a lot less.

At first, the team was furiously incredulous. Imagine, you're a young, twenty-something junior enlisted soldier who's intimidated by your local company commander and your boss tells you he's invited the commander of all U.S. forces in Afghanistan for a visit and that guy wants to hear your opinion on the problems and issues you encounter doing your job. A bit daunting, wouldn't you say?

Woody and Sister Mary yelled loudly and cussed me for a good five minutes – they probably needed more. Poor Chip took a much longer and vociferous beating after I left the office. They rounded on him pretty severely. No one slept for a few nights, including me. I hadn't slept since hitting the send button. I was running on adrenaline.

I also had to tell my immediate boss, the company commander my junior soldiers avoided. He was actually a great guy and really understood our mission on the local and national level. He totally supported us every way he could, and no, he wasn't on my email distro list.

"Captain Lincoln, can I bend your ear for a few?" I approached and directly asked. He recognized the unusual tone, which was quite unlike my regular, jovial self. We made small talk as I drove our battered pick up over the dusty roads to our secluded tent where we met with Afghans. It was far enough away from main base, yet close enough to the combat hospital – just in case he shot me. "Okay, hear me out." I started as we sat on the dusty couches.

I explained the frustrating situation, Chip's demoralized anger, the Afghan's fury, and the repetitive helplessness of corruption. He sat quietly nodding, listening intently. Then told him of the e-mail and the General's visit in a few days' time.

Eyes bulging and face red, I half expected him to launch outta his chair and go for my throat. He sat upright and edged closer to me, but he sat there, waiting for more info, which I provided in copious detail.

"Why did you email McChrystal? What did the email say? Did you cc the BSO?" he peppered me with rapid-fire questions. As he started spinning up, I exhaled and calmed down. I handed him the printed version. I knew he wanted to see just what I had sent. Thankfully, he read and listened with an open mind, and most importantly, he understood the big picture issue I had tried to highlight. I got the impression he was excited, but honestly, only a corpse wouldn't have been. Whew, that was a relief. Now, the real

154

sweating began – telling the Battalion Commander.

It was so strange, sending e-mail to the King was the easy part: write, edit, and send. Dealing with the hysteria after the General says he's coming to visit was the hard part. The circus was coming to town and everybody wanted to know what I had said. My poor teammates were now under the microscope but we had nothing to hide, we did everything by the book. Who cared if they scrutinized us? They might've learned something. Members of my unit gave us sideways looks, the local bigwigs danced around me at the daily meetings (business as usual, right?) and those whom we supported thought I was trying to stab them in the back by e-mailing the General. (Local commanders were empowered to confront and address issues at their levels, remember?)

The senior commander for the three province area, who also owned the base on which we live, called me to his office.

"Yes, Sir! Yes Sir! Three bags full Sir!" I responded, and rushed to his castle. The last thing I had wanted to do was piss off the guy whose units and soldiers we support. Too late. His minions ushered me into the throne room.

"Chief, you're under no obligation to tell me the contents of the email you sent General McChrystal" he began in a serious tone. "My mission is to…blah, blah, blah" he droned on while my attention wandered. This guy can't be intimidated by me! He can't be treating me as an equal, I thought. He was trying to find out why the King was coming. Right then I guessed the General hadn't shared our correspondence with anyone locally.

"Sir, although we're GS, our team whole heartedly enjoys supporting your mission, doing all we can to maintain security in your battle space." I earnestly reassured him. I methodically rattled off the number and topics of the intelligence reports we filed on behalf of his mission and collection requirements. You know those big ego types – ya gotta let them know you recognize the supremacy of their authority.

"This problem is national in nature – my fellow collectors experience this in other provinces, therefore I had to raise this issue at the highest of echelons." I continued. I answered his every question and gave him a printed copy of the e-mail. I didn't want there to be any lingering doubts as to what I had sent. If General McChrystal is the King, this guy is at least a Duke. A few days passed.

The day of the meeting was sooooo surreal. The team had breakfast as usual and returned to the office – had to brush and floss; no one wanted bad breath. I gave a pep talk to the sweaty-palmed, anxious, unnaturally quiet, freshly washed-and-scrubbed team, and then we headed to the castle. Have ya seen the movie The Devil Wears Prada? Remember one of the opening scenes when the Meryl Streep character arrives at the office unexpectedly in the morning and everyone scurries around like rats, trying to get out of the way or in the right place, or whatever? Well, that was life in the castle that morning. I was a bit anxious myself.

Combat Barbie, our battalion commander, had flown in the night before and brought with her the lackey stand-in for Fudge Spice, our command sergeant major. I didn't know it at the time, but this was the dude Wilbur had been emailing information about activities on our base. Both were present as was my company commander and my team. I half expected the conference room to be full of all kinds of brass, ash, and trash but it was empty, except for us. The General wanted to speak only to the team, thankfully. I half expected to walk away a Private, but what the hell, it was show time.

The man bounded into the room. He was a tall one, General McChrystal. Look, all I knew about him before e-mailing was that he ate one meal a day and ran like eight miles every morning. He reminded me of a giant, thin Redwood tree, minus the moss and branches of course. He was like 6'5" and really lean.

General McChrystal brought with him Major General (MG) Flynn, the most senior person responsible for intelligence in Afghanistan. He was more manageable, probably 6' 2", but just as lean. I thought of how much I hate running.

"Where's Todd?" The General called out.

Of course I strode right up to him, hand outstretched, big ear-to-ear smile, hopefully masking my nervousness. "Good Morning Sir, that's me."

I lost another patch of hair on my head at that exact moment.

Thank God I didn't fart. We shook hands, he invited everyone to sit down, and he prefaced the meeting stating, "No one should be mad that Todd e-mailed me. People should be unafraid to e-mail someone... blah, blah, blah."

OMG, what a relief, maybe I will keep my rank. I exhaled.

We talked about everything I had sent in the e-mail and a few additional topics. We had spirited discussions, with Generals McChrystal and Flynn suggesting how organizations should be re-structured. That was a political question totally off subject, aimed at my reasoning for e-mailing. Thankfully two of my team members spoke up, offering very salient points to the topics at hand and adding perspective to our position.

Direct, engaging, sharp, intelligent, lively, pointed – all attributes I'd use to describe both Generals afterward. We may not have gained all we wanted from the meeting, but the team left the Generals with a better understanding of how we used everything at our disposal to implement their policies and what we thought would aid mission success from the micro-level, in spite of the policies and Afghan corruption which undermined collectors everywhere.

I finally had a decent night's rest. It was strange to think I e-mailed the King and he came to visit. It was almost as if it didn't happen but enough people brought it up, so I guess it did.

"Chief, your end-of-tour award should be a set of brass balls." Sergeant Winfield joked. Well, better than a noose, I thought.

In retrospect, the event was a bit embarrassing, and nothing I planned to do again (my boss made me promise to e-mail him first before I sent any errant email – yikes). But at least I highlighted something important that will hopefully get addressed and corrected. And of course, the team got to meet the General. That was a bonus – just another day in my insane life – the mouse that roared.

RIDICULOSITY

"Between the both of you, I feel like I live with two females!" Mary Danger said to Chip and me during an argument he and I were having about me going on R&R.

"Fuck you!" Chip roared.

REST & RELAXATION?

R&R – the highlight of any long deployment, what everyone looked forward to and planned from the minute they set foot in country. Just thinking about R&R was pure escapism. It was an opportunity to physically leave this shithole, and definitely important for our mental well-being. It was the same for all y'all back home, vacation – right?

Vacation! Yours could be a staycation at home or a trip to the beach, the slopes, or to a foreign country. Who cares what happened at work, right? It was time to relax. Not everyone could be out at the same time, unless your company shut down operations. My dad worked as a Tool & Dye maker for Ford Motor Company and they'd shut down operations a couple times a year for maintenance or the holidays or whatever. That was when we took our family vacations.

For the deployed soldier, it was a bit different. We created an order of merit list for people to pick their R&R dates. There had to be someone doing your job, unless your section had a lot of people. I let the kids collude and decide who'd go out when. Mary Danger left first, followed by Shaniese, Chip, me, and then Woody. Everyone actually got the general time frame they wanted – we were lucky. Enough of us remained to pick up the slack for the rest so we didn't need a replacement to do our collective mission.

Danger left first. She hated the cold. It was January and she was eager to trade the freezing temps of our small base near the mountains for the warmth of Miami's south beach. All we heard for weeks was how much beer she'd drink, how many clubs she'd party in, the miles of beaches she planned to visit, all the sex she expected to have. She was distracted, not focused on work, and her daily reminders were annoying. She even insisted we tell her what booze to drink in our honor. I suggested water. We were relieved when she left, and we picked up her slack. Poor thing, Mary expected to have typically warm south Florida weather.

That year I think the U.S. set a record. Mary Danger didn't need to unpack her bathing suit (basketball shorts and a wife beater) because it snowed in each of the fifty states during her time at home. Remember the record cold of the winter of 2009-10? The beaches were cold and the water was choppy, fewer people went out, but our girl made good on the promise to drink herself silly. I think she used the weeklong return trip to Afghanistan to sober up and dry out, but she still returned reeking of stale beer. So much for rest and relaxation.

Shaniese went home shortly after Mary Danger. She wanted to go on spring break with her friends from college. That girl had a good time. Again, it involved a beach, this time in South Padre Island, Texas and she returned refreshed. Chip also returned to the States, not wanting to spend too much cheddar on travelling abroad – besides his girlfriend insisted he come home. Whatev... I wonder how relaxing that trip was.

Woody was the last to go and had a brilliant time in Spain. He had always wanted to visit and decided to let Uncle Sugar pick up the tab for the flights. Smart guy. He finally settled on the Canary Islands and was partying his hairy butt off as Spain won the World Cup that year. Talk about excellent timing. I doubt he rested much, but would you?

Our team picked up the work for the absent member. The mission was identical for all of us. With enough preparation, anyone could and did step in. That contrasted with the time my high school math teacher left to have her baby. She was gone for much longer than two weeks, but the concept was similar. We had an actual substitute math instructor, not just a placeholder taking attendance and ensuring we didn't go wild. She was as good as our regular teacher and we definitely learned something. In the business world

160

someone might take over your responsibilities when you get away from the office – and sometimes that was no different for us on deployment.

My buddy, Tyler was at a small remote base in a really hostile area with two other soldiers. Our boss picked him for this austere location because of his background, more on that later. Tyler's three-man team couldn't really function with only two people so he needed temporary replacements as they rotated on R&R. Enter Wilbur.

Overall, I guess Wilbur was a value add, but he was someone you might want to strangle after working with for a while. I don't know how my boss/roommate Don did it – Wilbur worked for him. Wilbur was a lesson on how to piss off everyone in your organization. Every unit in our battalion had one of these asscrackers.

Wilbur was too smart for his own good. It was all book smarts; his common sense was in short supply. The guy wasted time philosophizing over inconsequential crap while ignoring work or the obvious hints to shut the fuck up. He had no friends because of his delusional self-confidence and smug attitude. He was an emotional eater and didn't exercise at all – getting ever bigger during the deployment. His worst habit was wearing the Under Armor style tight shirts. My God, he looked like the Michelin man. I had so many frustrating run-ins with this lower ranking bore that I forbade him from calling or visiting my office. Don or Mitchell would stop by instead.

Back home in Virginia, Wilbur owned something along the lines of a gun and ammo store. And as a result, he was what we called a Gear Queer. His uniform was festooned with all kinds of extraneous and unused knives, pouches, multi-tools, ammo holders, flashlights, etc. Even more appalling, he was able to entice junior enlisted soldiers into buying this crap from his store. WTF? One naïve jackass bought more than $700 worth of junk from Wilbur and considered himself a Billy Badass too. Good Christ.

So Wilbur was sent to Tyler's remote combat outpost to replace a soldier going on R&R. Wow, you should've heard the multiple hissy fits and witnessed the tears of rage our little porker shed trying to get out of that assignment. Tyler was happy. He hated Wilbur and although he'd be fair, Tyler was gonna show the little piglet how the big boys play Army, and Wilbur was terrified.

He had to trade a real bed, actual shower and toilet for a cot, baby wipes, and piss tube. Another benefit at Tyler's outpost: they burned their shit. Wilbur being a forty plus-year-old junior enlisted man would definitely get his turn at the burn pit. Tyler would see to that.

The schadenfreude was palpable! Everyone was giddy over Wilbur's perceived misfortune. Even the commander chuckled, knowing Wilbur was pissing himself silly with dread. The day Wilbur left, I ate an extra big bowl of ice cream in celebration. Everyone was relieved to be rid of the guy for a while. But all good things came to an end.

It wasn't all bad. Sure, Tyler put the screws to piggy, but no more so than to anyone else. He said Wilbur used his knowledge of reporting, computer systems, and main-base infrastructure to help their remote operation. That was good. Another plus was that Wilbur lost weight. He was still fat, but he trimmed down some. Unfortunately, his return meant easy access to Mountain Dew and potato chips. The weight quickly returned. And there was another, more unfortunate outcome.

Now that Wilbur had "operational experience" by actually doing the job instead of just reporting on it and keeping track of statistics, he affected this overwhelming arrogance of knowledge. Have you ever seen the self-important, conceited character from M*A*S*H*, Charles Emerson Winchester, III? That was the monster we had created, minus the pedigree and Boston accent. Wilbur became more than unbearable, he was intolerable.

Chip hated him even more now and went out of his way to make life miserable for Wilbur. It didn't matter; in the end Wilbur screwed himself where it counts, at home. I learned that the little maniac told his foreign-born wife he wasn't allowed to go on R&R. Oh, he was allowed and did leave, but went somewhere other than home.

Let's call her Charlotte. Char had been going to the Spousal Support Group meetings and wondered why her husband wasn't allowed to come home, while other husbands had enjoyed that privilege. She lodged a formal complaint with the commander, questioning the unfairness of his policy. Naturally, the commander was shocked, and that came full circle to Wilbur. The greedy little bastard got his in the end. I never discovered, nor did I care where Wilbur went for R&R, but I'm certain he got neither rest nor relaxation back home in Virginia when the deployment was over.

RIDICULOSITY

"I just saw one of those dog things!" Woody lazily drawled.
  "...a Ki-oat?" Mary Danger suggested.
  "Yeah." Woody slowly nodded.

ANIMALS

About three weeks into the deployment, when we had settled at the FOB, I heard something at dusk I had never heard before – the cry of a coyote. Maybe I shouldn't have been surprised – we were in an undeveloped land, full of wildlife and for that matter, wild peoples.

It was dusk and I stepped outside for one last trek to the latrine in daylight. I got about fifteen feet from the office when the wail/cry/yip of animals went off nearby. At first I didn't recognize the noise. Then it hit me. We had no dogs on base, (the guards shot the ones that skulked around – more on dogs later) so the noise must have come from coyotes. A buddy of mine told me about the coyotes, but I hadn't experienced them yet. It reminded me of a young dog yipping and wailing – not the deep, almost soulful howl of the German shepherd we had when I was a kid and the tornado siren would go off warning us of a possible Wizard of Oz experience. This was almost playful yet aggressive. I looked forward to hearing it. I made a mental note to spend some time outside at dusk.

Dogs – how should one correctly put this? Afghans had no history of domesticating dogs for human cohabitation like Americans. If an Afghan family had a dog, "Fido" always slept/lived/ate outside, no matter the weather, temperature, or danger. The dog was not a part of the family because it was an unclean, wild creature that was more than likely abused, kicked, ignored, or pelted with rocks.

It was common to see dogs wary of human interaction because of the systemic abuse Afghans inflicted upon them. At night, packs of dogs roamed villages, the countryside, and cities, attacking and scrounging anything they could find to eat. That was why guards shot dogs that made it onto base. It was for our safety really.

That being said, on my last mission to the provincial capitol I saw a guy with a lean, muscular dog – eyes predatorily glaring about, ears forward, straining at the leash he held tightly. The dog looked intent on getting away. My interpreter told me the dog was most likely vicious and would attack anything it could sink its teeth into. Some people kept such dogs in their qalats (compounds) for protection.

Cats – a different story altogether. Afghans had an entirely different opinion of cats. I saw one cat while in town. It looked healthy but kept a wary eye on us. According to Islamic legend, a cat approached and sat next to the Prophet Mohammed once during prayer. Henceforth, the cat has been viewed as an almost holy figure. Don't ask me why. I thought people valued cats more than dogs because cats catch mice/rats/etc., which eat grains and other foodstuffs. Either way, cats had it much easier in Afghanistan.

"Dude, you're gonna get cancer!" Chip yelled, trying to persuade Tyler to move into the shade.

"Dude, I'm smoking!" Tyler yelled back laughing, waving his cigarette in the air.

BOOM! GOES THE DYNAMITE

The dynamite phrase is something people at home say all the time. I didn't know its origin, but it was funny and I guess applicable in more than a few situations. It definitely applied to us in Afghanistan.

Ours had been a relatively quiet deployment in that our base wasn't attacked much, and thankfully those few attacks were underwhelming to say the least. As stated before, the base had been known as Rocket City, and hosted the Rocket City Cigar Club, which the kids and I joined. Things had died down just before we arrived, so we were lucky. A buddy of mine at a small outpost, maybe fifty miles away, was attacked all the time – dodging mortars and small arms fire about every two weeks. Often the outgoing artillery blasts that rocked our base were in support of their defense at his base. Occasionally, they'd find locals on base at night lurking about – talk about scary. Not a cool place to spend ten months, for sure.

However, our FOB wasn't always quiet. We suffered a couple mortar attacks, one of which really freaked me out. Late in the morning on a routine day, Chip and Mahmoud were talking to an Afghan in one of our tents. Ironically, turns out the guy came to tell us about an impending attack.

Sister Mary and I were at the office prepping for her meeting a few hours later when mortars landed and the incoming alarm sounded. Shaniese and Woody were driving to meet Chip at the tent. They heard the blast and watched people running for cover. Woody pulled over and they dove into a nearby concrete blast

167

bunker as Shaniese called to tell me they were safe. Thank God they were okay. I was both proud of their quick reactions and concerned about Chip and Mahmud. We hadn't heard from them yet.

I didn't want to freak out and I didn't need to because Danger was doing that for me. She and Chip were tight and she was trippin' that I couldn't reach him.

"We need to get over there *now!*" she yelled/pleaded with me.

We kept trying over and over but Chip wouldn't answer the phone. The attack siren blared, Chip wouldn't answer, Mary literally wanted to run across base to see what was up at the tent, and my boss was on the line wanting accountability of my troops. My day had turned into anything but routine.

Finally, Mahmud calls. They were safe. They had ducked into the safety bunker by the tent when the alarm sounded. As usual, Chip had turned off his phone and left it on the table inside. But Mahmud's phone was on. Those sons-a-bitches laughed at my concern, stating they were all right. Chip was especially ornery when they returned, yelling about having to crouch down in the tight bunker with the stinkin' Afghan whose information about the attack, although correct, was late. Mary stayed pissed at Chip for the rest of the day.

Thankfully no one was injured. The gym tent took a hit and a small chuck was torn from the roof, but little damage was done. If mortars had hit in the afternoon, we would've had a completely different outcome. This attack was in stark contrast to what Tyler dealt with at his base.

If Mary Danger had a male complement, it was Tyler. Think of an extra from the movie 300. Tyler was a burly He-man warrior at a nearby base. Both of us were team leaders but since he was a former infantryman and current police officer back home, our boss sent Tyler to a remote combat outpost to leverage his background and experience. He was a good guy, smart, funny, quick-witted, and a real alpha male. Mary loved hanging out with him and they were tight smoking buddies. Even Chip liked and respected Tyler. All three of 'em would chillax in the shade of the olive grove, smoking and telling war stories.

Tyler told us one that stunned even Chip. His combat outpost was often hit with mortars. They never had warning, just a boom and chaos. Tyler and a buddy were smoking at the end of the day. The sun was going down and they wanted to watch it set over the mountains. The oranges, pinks, blues, greys and sometimes reds and purples of sunset made a technicolor display that overwhelmed even the hardest souls. Clouds separated colors over the mountains, or sometimes blended them into a canvas even Van Gough would envy. It was magical. I rarely saw the sunrise, but imagined the display was similar.

So Tyler and another soldier were chilling near a bunker because that was the location of the designated smoke pit. It was their nightly ritual. The sky was awash with vibrant color and the constant buzz of generators filled the air. Tyler finished his cigarette and turned to leave when *BOOM!* a couple mortars hit nearby, shattering the otherwise peaceful dusk.

They were under attack! The alarm sounded. Tyler heard gunfire and would've rushed to get his flak vest but heard desperate screaming. His buddy had been hit and blood was everywhere. Tyler dragged him into the bunker where they waited out the attack, frantically phoning the local medic, then got help. The guy was evacuated to Bagram then Germany. It was incomprehensible chaos. Tyler was physically untouched, but his buddy was permanently blinded, having lost both eyes to shrapnel. The survivor's guilt must've been overwhelming but instead of quitting the ciggies, the attack prompted Tyler to smoke even more. He got through the remainder of the deployment normal enough but the PTSD emerged years later. I always joked with Mary Danger and Chip that smoking kills. Well, it blinds, if not kills.

What did I learn from this? I guess it really doesn't matter where you are: a war zone, school playground, or on a train – crazy shit can happen without warning. Hopefully, you're lucky. Don't freak out, and always keep your cellphone on and charged 'cuz ya just never know.

RIDICULOSITY

"That rock made my brain rattle!" Mary Danger shouted at Tyler, who hit her in the head with a stone.
    "Well, it's not hard when you have a pea-sized brain!" Tyler shouted back grinning.

LARRY THE LIZARD, OUR PSEUDO-MASCOT

When the weather warmed we noticed a few changes near the office. New buds sprang to life on the olive tree branches behind our buildings. Patches of green weeds and grass appeared on the ground. More songbirds came to nest in the trees, fighting with the loud, grey winged crows, and we encountered a new friend, Larry the Lizard.

I had heard about Larry from Marc, the supply sergeant. His office was a few doors down from ours, near the opposite end of the building. Marc had six metal connexes, similar in shape but shorter than the box part of a semi-truck. They sat in a line across from our building at the edge of the olive grove. They stored tons of military related stuff, and you could walk between two of them. Directly behind the connexes were piles of rocks, some big, some small. Woody hated those rocks 'cuz of the corrective training he did, remember that? The rock pile was where Marc first encountered Larry.

Word spread of Larry's presence. Everyone had heard of him but few had actually seen him. Shaniese screamed, eyes bulging, when she first encountered Larry and quickly ran into the office to alert us.

Finally, I saw Larry one day on my way to the watering experiment. He was tan, about four feet long from his head to the tip of his tail. He stood 'bout six inches off the ground and swaggered back and forth in typical lizard fashion. Larry liked hanging at the rocks, under the connexes, and in the olive grove.

RIDICULOSITY

One of the locals we meet regularly gave us baskets of fruit from his tree. The pieces were small, resembling lychee, and mildly sweet. They were really ripe and since many were left over after we all tried and ate some, I decided to see if Larry would eat them. I took the basket outside and placed it on the rocks at the edge of the olive grove where Larry sunbathed. I couldn't say I ever saw Larry eat the rotting fruit, but I expect the birds had a field day with them. They left typical bird evidence of their presence on the rocks all around the basket. I just hope Larry got his fill, too. Since we couldn't have a dog, Larry was the next best thing.

"I am going to be the most envied person in my neighborhood!" Woody proclaimed, boasting about his prowess at the video game Dragon Ball Z

"Yeah, by twelve-year-olds!" Sister Mary shot back.

AFGHAN DIP

Let me begin with an observation of tobacco use among U.S. soldiers. A lot of U.S. soldiers dipped. (A moment of self-disclosure – I used to dip. With as much as I harsh on tobacco and tobacco users, you'd think my entire family died of jaw cancer, and I worked in a retirement facility for soldiers who dipped. I stopped years ago.) Usually the closer one was to combat arms meaning infantry, artillery, military police, etc., the more apt one was to be a heavy dipper. Why? Who knows? But the motion of sticking a thick pinch of moist shredded tobacco between your cheek and gum – usually right in front of your lower front teeth – seemed to be a rite-of-passage, then tradition, and finally a habit for many soldiers.

My favorite part wasn't the deformed jaw outline, stained teeth, or even flecks of tobacco on someone's tongue. My favorite part was the constant spitting. It was revolting. Some delusional image of coolness must've existed for those morons because you'd often see instructors, or soldiers whose jobs put them in front of people, constantly spitting. I hated it and was shell-shocked when I learned that some guys swallowed that shit! Like I said, it was revolting, but it was even worse when someone spit into a cup (always while inside a building). The smell eventually permeated a room and there was always the potential for spillage, which eventually happened because some dippers can be lazy fucktards. Those who spit into a bottle weren't much better. With the constant screwing off and on of the cap, they must have had mad finger muscles. I never understood why people were allowed to dip inside a building. Smokers weren't allowed to smoke were they? Of

173

course not (and thank God for that), so why should dippers have been any different? Now, on to Afghani dip.

Naswar, the Afghan version of dip, was used just like ours but was exponentially more potent than American dip. Ours was fresh, clean, came in a sealed container, and was usually moist and flakey. We had a decent selection of dip, including the ubiquitous wintergreen, as well as spearmint, cherry, and the funny little tobacco-filled packets with which the dipping newbie sometimes started his journey to mouth cancer.

Naswar was a completely different animal. First, I'd only seen naswar in a plastic baggie – the crappy, low budget non-sealable sandwich baggies my mom used when I was a kid. I remember my sandwiches sliding out of those fold-over baggies if I didn't carry my lunch carefully. Ah, memories.

Naswar came in two varieties, green and black – tucked away in the baggie. The green was much more potent, and I bet that with regular use, one could bore a hole through one's lower jaw within a year if not careful. The black kind was equally harsh, but not as potent. It'd probably take two years to achieve the same result.

Anyway, naswar is addictive. I wouldn't touch it, but Afghans said it was almost a national pastime, like growing poppies, refining opium, beheading infidels, and swindling people for as much as you could. Naswar – a way of life. The stuff came in a thick clump and was made from the ground, crushed, treated, and pressed leaf residue of some kind of hellish plant. No one could describe its origins to me.

Afghans told me the first time they tried naswar they always vomited. What a lovely start to a life-long habit. In time, they became used to the stuff and then got addicted. But they never liked to say they're addicted… appearances, ya know. Well, to me, naswar looked like some clumpy, almost tar-like substance, but it wasn't sticky or gooey. It was similar to the thick, rich black soil farmers in the Midwest have to grow crops. Naswar had an almost earthy smell to it. Well, a chemically treated earthy smell. Unknown chemicals were used to treat the leaves that composed naswar and they imparted a serious after smell. Yet another reason not to try it.

174

A couple of my team members were brave enough to go there. Woody dipped anyway, Chip smoked but would try anything, and of course, you know Sister Mary Danger couldn't pass up the chance to stick some of that odious poison in her mouth. They all hurled within forty seconds. Served 'em right. Woody might've tried another taste of Hell but I don't think either of the others did. I discovered they kept quite a bit of questionable activity from me – and for good reason. I'd probably have lost my shit had I learned of their frequent miscreant adventures.

Afghans spit the residue of naswar just like Americans do but they didn't keep naswar in their mouths for nearly as long as Americans. When Afghans had enough, they pulled out the entire clump and tossed it in the street. It usually maintained its form. Here's the most retching and disturbing part – young entrepreneurs (very young kids) would collect the discarded clumps and resell it in the bazaar to unsuspecting addicts. I love Afghanistan. Everyone, even the youngest, was out to make a buck.

RIDICULOSITY

"Oops, I am so tired I can't even keep drool inside."
Woody said, in a typical mid-afternoon malaise,
drooling onto his shirt.

NAMBLA - AFGHAN STYLE

Have ya ever heard of NAMbLA? It's the North American Man-boy Love Association. Basically it's an organization for perverts who want to legalize corn holing young boys. Wonder how many priests are members, just a thought.

There was a similar disturbing practice of Man-boy love in Afghanistan but it was mainly isolated to Pashtuns, the ethnic majority. To my knowledge there was no chartered association in that country because homosexuality is/was officially punishable by death. Pashtuns compose around forty percent of the population and while not all older guys wanna anal dock young boys, enough of 'em do to give Pashtuns a reputation. I know, I know – it's their culture, but so is marrying off eight-year-old girls and that's not right either.

Anyway, y'all remember that with a full beard and long hair, our Woody could pass for an Afghan? He has the right skin tone and speaks Farsi, which is similar to Dari, an Afghan language. That was an asset so I sent Woods on a five-day support mission with another unit. He really wanted a change of pace and they certainly wanted him and our interpreter, Wahid. Yup, if I sent someone out, I definitely sent a mouthpiece with him.

Don't worry; I checked 'em out beforehand. The boss leading the five-day mission was a crusty sergeant, older than me, with previous deployments to Iraq and Afghanistan. I felt good about the mission and so did Woody. Wahid didn't care; he just wanted to get out. The team prior to us frequently went off base. Wahid always volunteered to go and saw much of the area.

The trip was successful in that no one was shot, they

didn't encounter IEDs, no one was kidnapped, and they actually accomplished more than expected. One thing happened, which Wahid told us about and Woody confirmed. Woody looks like a young man, not a boy. But this didn't stop some local Afghans from trying to buy him.

"Ha ha ha, he wanted to buy Woody so I told him the price was five sheep and a couple goats!" Wahid laughed through telling the story. Lucky for Woody, the Afghans thought the price was too high.

WTF was that? They probably liked Woody's pungent smell – he ate raw onions with everything. They had spent a few long afternoons sitting around drinking tea, and eating raisins and nuts before the elder broached the subject with Wahid. Woody was oblivious to the price haggling because it was in Pashto, not Dari. Wahid kept telling jokes to make Woody laugh, which he did, and that further excited the elder. Ha, ha, ha, poor bastard! But Woody's experience was nothing compared to Riley's.

Tyler had a three-man team and Riley was one of them. He and Woods were about the same age and they both had olive complexions but that's just about the extent of the similarities. Riley was good at soliciting information from Afghans because those pervs were in love with him. He had big bright blue eyes, bushy eyebrows, full cherry-red lips, and a lean athletic body. He could barely grow a beard and looked like a young boy, whereas Woody's beard was full after a week of not shaving.

Riley had a habit of hanging out with any local Afghan on his combat outpost. He even let one dude put henna all over his hands one boring Sunday afternoon. Henna use was very common in Afghanistan, with women painting intricate designs on their hands, and men using it to dye their hair and beards. Occasionally young men and boys applied henna like the women.

A local Afghan painted the tops of Riley's hands one Sunday afternoon. The intricate, curlicue designs of spirals, vines and leaves were quite impressive, with henna extending onto Riley's forearms. Unfortunately for Riley, Tyler wasn't a fan of that "girly shit," as he called it, and made Riley wash. Anyone who's used henna knows that once set, it takes a long time to fade away. Riley
178

was able to wash off some of it, but a definite pattern remained for weeks. Enter the problem...

Like us, Tyler's team met with locals to extract information. They were in a really tough hot spot, often getting mortared. His mission was critical for their very survival and he needed 110 percent from his guys. Riley's henna actually became an asset because Afghans already liked him for his sparkling blue eyes and boyish looks, and now a few seemed to fall in love with him because of the henna. Henna was most often used to decorate girls and women. Seeing it on a fair-skinned man-boy generated the same excitement a pedophile running wild in a kindergarten might experience. Poor Riley, the same physical attributes he used to score chicks back home would earn him the frustration and anger of his local outpost commander.

The henna took like three weeks to fade away during which time Tyler, Riley, and Jurgis (the other member of the team) met with more than a few locals both on and off base. Riley garnered quite a following among the Afghans, like a young Zac Efron did with High School Musical. He even got a stalker.

One of the more affluent elders in the area met with Tyler and Riley, and was smitten. Being an elder in that part of Afghanistan meant having clout, always getting what you wanted, making it rain. I was sure he knew U.S. soldiers weren't for sale, but it didn't stop him from trying to spend some quality alone time with our boy. Affluence in that small tribal area was much different from what we think. It could be as simple as owning a well, having a herd of sheep, controlling access to a bridge, or so on. This guy was powerful, he probably had all three.

Our job was quite sensitive and we had to balance the fine line between meeting with someone enough times to establish good rapport to collect valuable information, and keeping our distance to protect the locals. Taliban had spies everywhere. They watched us, and more importantly, they kept tabs on the locals. If some insurgent suspected a local of meeting with Americans, it could be serious trouble for the guy. So this elder's infatuation with Riley was bad for everyone involved.

Their 'terp Mo (interpreter Mohammad) took most of the

179

heat. We often distributed our numbers so locals could contact us on the DL and pass info, schedule a meeting, or whatnot. The elder pestered Mo for a couple weeks with phone calls throughout the day. When that didn't work, he started coming by the outpost to meet with Riley.

Maybe he expected his clout would protect him from Taliban threats. I doubt it. Some Taliban were savages, caring little for human life in spite of what the Koran preaches. His obsession with Riley pissed off Tyler and the outpost commander – an infantry officer with a short fuse. It didn't take much to get Tyler and the commander all over Riley's case. That meant pretty-boy was sent packing to hang with us for a week until everything blew over and the henna completely wore off. However, instead of helping my team, he kept a low profile and treated the incident like a staycation – the bastard.

I guess the unintended message here was that our actions, harmless and without forethought, had major implications for those around us. What appeared to be innocent fun could be a big ugly in disguise. In Afghanistan, ya might wanna bump uglies with someone, but I can guarantee it wouldn't be with a local.

"Hey Todd, your shirt does not agree with your mood." Woody said about the contrast between my bright pink shirt and surly disposition.

WATERING EXPERIMENT RESULTS

Remember the watering experiment I told you about way back when? It started one morning in February when I noticed the puddle of urine in the moondust I had left the night before. I tested the viability and absorption rate of some weeds in the olive grove behind our building. Weeks passed but nothing happened to the shriveled foliage; I think it was too far-gone. So I moved onto a bigger clump of weeds near the first location. Those were also dry, but since their root system was bigger, and it looked like they contained a bit of green, I expected the weeds might actually spring to life.

Weeks passed and my second clump remained unyielding – it wouldn't grow. So, I moved to an even bigger clump of live weeds. Surely these would benefit from my tender bi-hourly application of personal liquid ambrosia. I purposefully picked a mid-sized clump that was partially green. Don't know how they were alive while the others were not, but they were, so I concentrated all my efforts on them. No such luck. The desiccated weeds refused to grow in spite of all attempts at rejuvenation.

Woody even occasionally helped water the same green clump. I anticipated rapid growth or at least a change in color from bone-dry brown to lush green. The weather had changed since I started the experiment and the days were very warm. Well, I got a change, but it wasn't what I expected.

I discovered that my urine is a herbicide! That green cluster of hearty Afghan weeds turned dark yellow after a couple of weeks of my personal attention. Whereas I thought my liquid ambrosia

181

would bring the plant to its full potential, instead it had the opposite effect. My pee killed a plant! I was disappointed and elated. Disappointed because the experiment produced unanticipated results, but elated because I discovered I won't need to invest in expensive lawn treatments after I buy a house. I can pee on the weeds in the yard instead of using something from Lowe's. Serendipitous indeed.

"Don't ignore me! I am a person!" I exclaimed at the kids in frustration.

DEATH DOES NOT BECOME HIM

One morning, the kids (Woody, Shaniese, and Sister Mary Danger) were acting like they were mad at me for some reason. Most likely, I had asked them to do something they didn't want to do, or didn't think needed doing, so they were mad and ignored me, even for official business conversations. It was their playful, passive-aggressive way, acting as if they didn't hear me when I wanted them to do something. They often pulled that trick when they thought I was in a good mood.

We were standing outside, Chip was smoking, and Woody, Danger and Shaniese were sitting in the shade. I was talking to Chip about a project and said something to Woody and Mary Danger, who both continued to ignore me. I thought I'd get their attention by throwing some rocks at them – not trying to land any shots exactly, but more to get them to answer.

Mary looks at Woody while glancing at me and says, "What was that?"

To which Woody causally replies, "Looks like a rock, thrown by some pussy ghost or something." a surprised look on his face, knowing he "went there."

That did it. Everyone was shocked at Woody, but giggled none-the-less, including me – although I glared at him.

I started throwing more rocks to make Woody dance (he and Mary had leapt out of their chairs). Then I found a small boulder, probably weighted twenty pounds. No way could I possibly throw it, so I started chasing Woody around the corner of the building, the damn boulder held above my head. I had landed most of the other rocks on Woody's legs or feet so maybe he thought I was really

183

going to hit him with this monstrous thing, even though there was no way I possibly could. Woody had much to fear, as I had nailed him in the balls twice before from great distances, just by luck.

My shoulders ached from maintaining the rock overhead, Woody trotting/stumbling backward toward the street, half laughing, half shocked.

"Chief, you're gonna give yourself a hernia if you don't put that down!" he protested as I kept toward him, angry look on my face, threatening him with the boulder. I was more irritated than angry, as the scraggly-bearded kid in perpetually dirty pants and untucked shirt stumbled backward. He clutched his bottle of dip spit in one hand, the cap in the other. A Humvee came barreling down the road behind him.

Woody was the only one of us who didn't see or hear the Humvee. Have you ever heard a Humvee? They're loud, easy to recognize and certainly easy to hear, especially if you're moving toward one. Not Woody. He was in his own world, teasingly trying to outrun his tormentor. The closer I got to him the more I realized he didn't know what was coming.

Surely, he heard the Humvee in the street ten feet away! Nope, not this kid. I slowed down, now clutching the rock at my waist. The Humvee wasn't going to stop or change direction. I could hear the others shouting behind me. "Devon, Woody, *Stop*!" Hell, even I implored him to stop moving, but I'm still clutching the rock. Yet there was Woody, mischievously half laughing, half excitedly stumbling backward toward the road, now five feet from the oncoming Humvee.

I dropped the rock, threw out my arms, and yelled, *"WOODY! STOP!"* Woody had finally slowed down right where our parking lot meets the edge of the road. He thought everyone else had been cheering him on, reveling in the thrill of escaping the boss. He finally stops, puts down his arms, cocks his head and says, "What?" just as the Humvee drives by, not a foot away, the swoosh of air covering him in a fine coat of moondust.

Mouth agape, eyes wider than I'd ever seen, blood draining from his face, Woody was stunned when he realized he was nearly run over. We were nervously laughing but relieved the game was
184

over.

"You tried to *KILL* me!" Woody shouted in righteous indignation, arms outstretched, his palms facing up.

"Well, next time you better pay attention to me!" I said, picking up the huge rock and putting it away for the next act of mock insubordination.

Being chased around the parking lot by your rock-carrying boss, what a way to start the morning. It'll wake you up faster than a cuppa Joe.

RIDICULOSITY

"Not trusting your soldiers is taking care of them." Molly
said during a lecture to her subordinate commanders.

HEALTH & WELFARE

Few things were more personally violating and annoying
than a Health & Welfare inspection. Way back in the day, probably
the War of 1812, a Health & Welfare inspection was intended to
ensure lower enlisted soldiers kept their living quarters in a clean
state of readiness. Soldiers can be slobs, and it was common to
find piles of dirty clothes, overflowing trashcans, food residue, and
used dishes in soldiers' quarters. Naturally, all that filth attracts bugs
and vermin or what the Army calls disease vectors. It makes sense
to ensure quarters are not in a putrid state of unhealthy disorder, so
the senior leadership uses the Health & Welfare inspection.

I think the current regime of the H&W evolved as a result
of the Vietnam era. Early in my career, I met soldiers who, years
before, had served during the Vietnam era. Some told tales
of rampant drug and alcohol abuse. I bet our thorough H&W
inspection dates to that behavior. Nowadays, a H&W consists not
only of looking at the obvious state of cleanliness of a soldier's
living space, but also includes going through his possessions in
the pursuit of contraband. Nothing is sacred. This hit home after
Christmas. Battalion mandated a H&W inspection. Remember, a
micromanaging control freak led us.

Company commanders (our battalion consisted of four
companies) were instructed to conduct a H&W of their soldiers'
living conditions soon after Christmas. Good timing, because if
a friend, spouse, etc., had sent someone booze, porn, or other
contraband it probably would've arrived in the avalanche of
packages that surrounded the holidays. A post-holiday H&W
inspection would, and did, nail the offenders. But there were ways
to avoid getting caught.

RIDICULOSITY

Once the first person was inspected, word got out. Sometimes we had advance warning and soldiers went to great lengths to hide their stashes. Although someone told me about the impending H&W, I had nothing to hide so I didn't care when the inspection took place. The element of surprise meant nothing to me.

One morning the Commander and First Sergeant called me to their office and marched me to my room where I unlocked everything and stood aside for them to joyously rifle through my stuff. One started on the bags of military equipment under the bed while the other went through my wall locker.

I could tell they loved this, which was a bit annoying. I mean, come on, guys. I'm an adult, have worked with you for how many years back in the States, five? How about some professional courtesy, officer to officer? Ask me where my stuff is, if I have any, I respond, and you accept my answer. Nope, not this time.

I did have one bottle of Stolichnaya vodka used as an incentive for the locals I met. It was unopened, and as soon as I opened my wall locker I showed it to them and the receipt saying it came from our HQ in Bagram. Their faces lit up, suggesting either they intended to confiscate it (that didn't happen) or suggesting they had caught me with contraband (I had none). They took out their disappointment on the remainder of my things.

The commander found bottles of shampoo, mouthwash, liquid soap, etc., which he opened and sniffed. Yes, an ingenious location for alcohol, but I had none hiding there. They went through my junk box and discovered old medication from the previous room occupant that even I didn't know was there. Confiscated. Big deal, I don't want someone else's stuff. Then they found my bag of condoms and both smiled greedily. Well, folks, I was a Boy Scout for a short while and if I learned anything it was 'Be Prepared.'

Although I had a bag full of rubbers, I never used one in Afghanistan. Trust me, I wish I had used every last one of 'em and had more shipped from the States, but alas, no such luck. They left me with my skins, almost adding insult to injury. I offered them a few, something like a reverse trick-or-treat, but they laughed and quickly declined, too embarrassed to take anything or implicate

188

themselves by doing so.

With the H&W over, my room in disarray with stuff everywhere, I organized the chaos. Why was this even necessary? Who cared if someone had a bottle of booze or porn or whatever, if he did his job and didn't get in trouble otherwise? Why was every aspect of a soldier's life up for inspection? Because that's the way it was. But that's not the way it was everywhere.

My friends who are team leaders at other locations had to conduct their own H&W inspections, which of course, they did. Those team leaders 'inspected' their soldiers' quarters and miraculously found no contraband. Imagine, only soldiers unfortunate enough to be co-located with their command staff or who didn't get advance warning, end up getting caught. Others could have a nip of booze every night, or even brew beer, and be considered model soldiers. What an absurd disconnect.

RIDICULOSITY

OUT OF "T-O-U-C-H"

Wow, there are a bazillion ways to begin this topic. Y'all know that when military personnel deploy, much of our lives goes on hold. Enough of you have family, friends, or coworkers who have been to Iraq, Afghanistan, Korea, etc., to know that our time away from the States kinda puts us in a vacuum.

True, some have Internet and Skype, but not all TV shows are available and a lot of regular Internet sites are blocked. Sometimes when we do have connectivity, the Internet bandwidth sucks so badly we can't download anything – even those obligatory Microsoft updates that always pop up at the worst time.

We lose touch with those tertiary friends we see at the gym, the kids' sporting events, church on Sunday, etc. We miss birthdays, sports broadcasts, anniversaries, report cards, fender benders, work promotions, deaths, births, and even mundane Friday nights after a long, uneventful week. We miss changes in our local communities, road-construction delays, being connected to those feel-good stories one occasionally hears on the news. You could say that we are out of touch on many levels. But in my opinion, those are secondary to a greater loss. When deployed, we really – don't – T O U C H.

It's a weird concept and non-experience that burdened my psyche. Think about it for a second. At home, the kid/spouse/Sig-O goes off to school or work and you give her a hug or kiss goodbye. Or you curl up next to her on the couch at night to watch TV. You come home from work and might have an exuberant dog or even friendly cat anxiously awaiting your arrival and of course you shower him with love, petting, affection, and food. You see an old friend on the street or out shopping and you smile, give a hug, chat, and catch up. You go to visit relatives and always hug at Hello and Goodbye. You T-O-U-C-H someone.

The vast majority of us didn't experience that when deployed. You could say we were out of T-O-U-C-H.

Strange, isn't it? Something you completely take for granted back home – the simple act of touching another human being – was almost understandably forbidden in Afghanistan. Military general orders prohibit anything that would distract from good order and discipline, blah, blah, blah. I guess a basic human, dare I say fundamental need, was one of those forbidden elements. I found it barbaric, but I guess it made sense. I mean, who the heck was I gonna touch?

The simple act of placing your hand on someone's forearm for emphasis when speaking would not only raise eyebrows, it would seem so out of place. I could just imagine, "Who's the creepy perv with the fast hands?" But at times, I just knew that if I could get a couple nights of spooning (no forking) with someone it would've been very mentally regenerative.

Don't get me wrong; there were many who didn't suffer from the negative effects of this temporary monastic existence. Women were the power brokers when deployed because it was very easy for any of them to find a willing tactile participant. Guys, on the other hand, endured an entire ten-month deployment without experiencing one of our most foundational senses, that of being touched.

I almost felt hypersensitive to T-O-U-C-H. Touching someone even with a friendly pat on the back, shoulder punch, or wet-finger-in-the-ear would've seemed foreign. I erected this mental barrier where I couldn't let someone get close enough to risk the accidental brush of the arm against mine, or bump of a leg by my foot – didn't want to risk all those Spidey senses going crazy. It was so isolating and debilitating, yet my reality. I guess the trick was to not become permanently scarred by this jolting year-long physical denial. Wish me luck…

"I am so glad you guys aren't crazy, because if you guys were crazy, life would have been so much harder for Chip." I said to the team after returning from vacation.

GOING ON R&R

Finally, the day came when I departed for R&R. This should've been something everyone looked forward to – vacation. But it was a colossal pain in the ass for us. Everyone but Woody and me had experienced the arduous hassle, and now it was my turn. For the longest time I was on the fence, whether to leave at all. My R&R was scheduled for early June – the prime season for attacks. I wanted to be around for the excitement, and to help with the fight. The rest of the team would do a great job without me, and Chip was a very able and competent stand-in, but I didn't want to leave. However, *everyone* kept reminding me of my departure date and that I should go.

"Three more days until Chief leaves!" Woody announced at breakfast with a huge smile. It had become his routine dig. I didn't know whether he was excited to get me outta there or figured it would bother me, which it did. If I didn't go on leave, I could save for a down payment on the house I wanted to buy. But I'd probably lose my mind, which wasn't a fair trade-off considering the little I possessed, so I debated, then left.

The days leading up to R&R and my departure were normal enough. I only stopped in the office a few times the day before departing because I wanted to give Chip the chance of leading the team, yet be there for any emergencies. None came up. Usually a quick, efficient packer, I lollygagged that day and stayed up 'til almost midnight packing my one bag. My flight was early in the morning so I slept lightly. Turned out the early flight was cancelled so I was rescheduled to a later flight that same day. But first, the process....

RIDICULOSITY

When someone went on R&R, our HQ made the flight arrangements. If the flight was cancelled for any reason (weather, attacks, equipment issues, outdated inspections, etc.) the soldier was often rolled to the next flight, sometimes he wasn't. I was lucky to get rolled. The departure process was similar to the States – show up two hours before departure time. I think this was because of the uncertainty of flights. In a war zone, one should never expect people or things to be on time. So, I arrived three hours early. At one hour pre-departure, they weighed you and your baggage. Gotta ensure the plane had enough fuel, ya know. I only had my "flack vest" (now called an IOTV), Kevlar (formerly a helmet), a laptop, and one large backpack. I didn't want to schlep a lotta crap around.

The flight was great. We used a small mail plane run by civilian contractors. There were only four of us, yet eight seats, so no one was crunched in like sardines. That was how we flew into country – like sardines. The co-pilot briefed us on the normal stuff and we were off.

Wow, I had never been in the air before. It was cool. The cloudless sky afforded nearly unlimited visibility of the dry farm fields and gradual greenery. There was relatively no pollution or particulate matter in the air in the province. Gaining altitude, I was struck by the dusty feel of the sky. From the ground you often see blue skyward, but in the air, the dry dusty feel of the parched earth followed our ascent as if to say, 'You can't escape.'

Mini-mountains surrounded the base leading toward Pakistan, so the pilot quickly climbed to an altitude to get over them. Pockets of green fertile soil dotted the dry land. Enough water drained from the mountain snowpack to allow for various crops, which I saw growing in abundance around us. Trees were sparse, but that was probably because of the need for firewood – the destitute really don't care about conservation, it's all about survival.

One thing that immediately caught my attention was the vast difference between what one sees in the air while flying in the States versus here. Back home, you see cars, people, various-sized buildings, road networks like spider webs, the occasional lake, swimming pools, sometimes other planes, etc. In the air above

194

my base, it seemed as if I was an intruder from another world, catching glimpses of some ancient civilization.

The small villages composed of mud-colored buildings and retaining walls gradually transformed into tiny clusters of thatched-roof huts. Unlike back home, no metallic structures or glass reflected the sun or temporarily blinded me. The roads lacked motorized vehicles of any kind until we approached Bagram. I knew vehicles existed, but I didn't see them. Instead, I saw goats, donkeys, a few cows, sheep, kids playing, women working (in burkhas, of course), and the occasional smoke trail from a burn pit. Mostly it was mud huts, green fields, dry, mountainous land, trees here and there, wadis (that's the Afghan version of a wash in the south/southwest – dry or semi dry creek beds). The juxtaposition of a Super Power with all its might struggling to control a Neolithic country made me pause for thought. The change we expected won't come for a generation at the very best. The flight was about 65 minutes (Afghanistan is roughly the size of Texas) and I counted only four buildings with metal roofs. Nowhere else did I see any reflection of the sun's rays.

The ride was a bit bumpy because of our altitude, but they warned us. The pilots were nice, treating us like actual humans. That was so unlike the typical military demeanor. A lot of military people in charge of something were assholes, but that was understandable; everyone was constantly shit on.

We crested the jagged mountains surrounding Bagram. This area was truly like Denver, sitting in a bowl surrounded by snow-capped mountains even in early June. There was no wait to land, and no wait to taxi so we taxied to the terminal.

"Welcome to BAF!" the Air Force dude said, meeting us on the tarmac as we deplaned.

BAF = Bagram Air Field. Or as I called it BARF = Bagram Anal Retentive F**khole, a moniker quite appropriate, just ask any Bagramanian (Barfer) – who worked there.

BARF was a mini-city unto itself about 34,000 people strong, populated by military reps and civilians from all nations. The coalition of the money hungry – who do you really think paid the salaries of troops from Albania, Mongolia, Kyrgyzstan, etc.? It wasn't them. NATO and US civilian contractors, and local nationals worked on base too.

The continuous smell of a dirty metropolis, overcrowded, polluted, and populated by frustrated people – that's BARF. Officers darted between buildings, trying to avoid eye contact with enlisted members, irritated at having to salute, even in a war zone. Stupidity I tell ya. Seemed the higher the rank, the more uptight the Soldier. Jaw-clenched sergeants major ran amok with little to do but pounce on people seemingly breaking the rules. Check out what those jackasses focused on.

At BARF, a sergeant major always lurked about, like some creepy B-movie villain ready to skewer and chew some ass. What rules were they looking to strictly enforce? Soldiers in uniform had to wear a reflective belt at dusk/night. If you didn't have one, you couldn't go outside, not even to the bathroom. No one was allowed to walk and talk on a cell phone or smoke and walk at the same time. Listen up Army soldiers – don't get caught with your hands in your pockets, you better have a good haircut within regs, you better not walk on the main road during morning PT hours, and never, ever get caught wearing your headphones outside, ever, unless you want some rabid pit bull spitting at you, spinning around like the Tasmanian devil, shouting obscenities, and belittling you. Yeah, that really happened, so much for the "professional Army." Seems the higher the rank, the more infantile you could act with impunity. I was surprised there wasn't more soldier-on-soldier shooting at BARF. This wasn't exactly the easiest place to keep one's sanity. Just sayin'…

So, I got to BARF and checked in with my battalion HQ. It was great to see the friends I've not seen since moving to my base. I went straight to Mark's office.

I flung his office door open, yelling. "Where were you? You knew I was coming and there was no one to meet me at the tarmac! I can't believe the disrespect and disregard you have for our friendship! What's wrong with you?" So what that he outranks me a lot and was in a meeting.

"Dammit Chief, You just can't barge in here like you own the place! I'm in a meeting and you're not that special!" he yelled back,

196

surprised look on his face, laughing – we yelled over each other like brothers. His powwow coming to a halt, he kicked out the others, and we shared some laughs, complaints, wishes, etc., for about an hour.

Mark was one of my best friends. We had worked together before and constantly picked on each other. I'd do anything for the man and the feeling was mutual. Mark suggested I go see Magda, his immediate supervisor and someone with whom I had also worked.

Magda was a blast – one of the most professional and efficient officers I had ever worked for and a total (professional) riot to be around. Remember, Brainy Spice? We used to joke in her office when I worked with her, so I figured she was ripe for some Chief fun time.

Magda had a loft in her office – for storage. Mark helped me climb up there (he had to remove then replace the bric-a-brac she displayed on her steps/shelves). At 1:30 p.m. I ascended the steps as we both expected Magda to return from lunch soon.

Well, I woke up around 3 p.m. to the sound of her voice in the hallway outside. Just in time to sit up and be ready to spring into groggy action. Well, Einstein was in the hallway talking to her as she entered her office. Seeing the footprint on the chair – dumbass had forgotten to wipe it off – Magda craned her neck around, looks up, and asks, "Who's up there?"

"Chief! Uh-huh, I figured!" she said as both me and Mark started laughing.

I said something stupid, we laughed, and they helped me climb down. She knew something was up. Magda was a sharp one. I spent an hour in her office catching up before moving on to the main offices and checking in with Carrie, Ana, and the others. I won't bore you with more detail, because even I was bored. Let me just tell ya this – HQ insisted I fly to BARF five days before my departure from country, *five friggin' days!* Does this make any sense? Of course not! Why five days? Because our battalion was run by a stay-at-home mom control freak.

Part of getting outta here was sitting through some briefings, two of which were with Dizzy & Wheezy – the affectionate pet

197

names someone bestowed on the Battalion Commander and her Command Sergeant Major (CSM). Both women were completely out of their league on deployment, with the commander thinking this was a yearlong Girl Scout camping jamboree. But let me get back on point – I could write chapters on those two, but will spare you my insight, at least for now.

Even though I told the CSM, Rhonda I didn't drink and would take trains and other public transportation in Europe, she insisted on reading me the alcohol policy and driving-safety regulations. Bless her heart, she didn't know any better and was incapable of self-thought. Uh, honey, I've been drinking for over half my lifetime and driving longer than that. I've never had a DUI or moving violation. I'm older than you and have been in the military longer than you, yet you're preaching to me about being a responsible adult during my vacation. Sweetheart, you can't even qualify with your 9mm pistol and have some ridiculously unprofessional ghetto "up-doo" hairstyle that was way beyond regulation. You really need to look in the mirror, come to grips with your glaring shortcomings, go back home to your husband, and leave the adult Army games to the professionals.

Finishing that nonsense, I was ushered into the commander's office where I sat through an equally painful briefing, but somewhat pleasant discussion. It wasn't as long, thankfully. I think she was still scared of me because of the e-mail to the King and his visit. Oh, well.

I left the office for good and sat on my ass for days. Dig this, I got there late May and didn't actually depart until early June. Can you imagine this happening in the civilian world? You schedule your vacation to begin on Friday, but come Monday you must sit on your ass in HR so you can go to briefings that last an hour on Wednesday. Absurd, I tell ya. I wanted be with my team who experienced a unique version of crazy in my absence and I was missing out! But at least I bummed with friends I'd not seen in seven months, and witnessed the serious dysfunction of HQ that I'd only heard about. It was eye opening.

Finally, I reported to HQ at 830 a.m. to be escorted to the terminal at 9 a.m. No, this grown man wasn't allowed to go by himself. I waited all day in the terminal because the flight was scheduled for midnight or later but I had to check in. This process was managed by the mentally challenged. Finally crammed into a plane bound for Kuwait, I'd catch another flight to my final destination. Well, that's what I hoped for. Was it really worth all the hassle?

Kuwait – retarded hot, as Woody might say. Not only that, but there was nothing redeeming about that place. By 9 a.m., it was too hot to walk outside. A short fifty-meter trek to the latrine produced rivulets of sweat pouring from every part of your body. Although the A/C helped, even inside, one sweated abnormally more than one should.

I got there around noon. The temp was already 105 degrees and must've reached 118 that day. Although I had finished the in processing/out processing for vacation and could've departed for Europe, I was forced to spend the night and suffer through more briefings the next day at 3 p.m. Because my plans included non-U.S. travel, I was ushered into the customs office with the other non-U.S. bound soldiers for inspection. About two weeks ago, some genius tried taking a grenade with him to Europe so now everyone had to sit through customs before leaving the Kuwaiti air base. Thankfully, it didn't take long and we were on the bus headed to KIA – Kuwait International Airport.

I hung out with Cale, an Army lieutenant stationed near me in Afghanistan, heading home to his wife and kid in Vincenza. Cale was stationed in Italy. He was a cool guy and not annoying so we bummed around together. It's always good to have someone watch your stuff when you need to use the pisser, walk around, etc. The Kuwait International Airport…whoa, what a huge cultural difference from any airport in the States.

Obviously the airport itself was a destination of choice for Kuwaitis. Countless groups of men dressed in manjams milled about the lounge area, joking in a language I didn't understand. Fat boys, stomachs distended like African famine victims greedily lapped up huge drippy scoops of chocolate, pistachio, or rose flavored ice cream while other, more energetic kids chased each other around the food court.

RIDICULOSITY

I couldn't tell ya how many kids – I'm talking from stroller-age to late teenagers – I saw at the airport. Entire families were there, an extraordinary number of people. Clearly Kuwaitis know nothing of birth control. There were more kids than adults. It was ridiculous. So for you Christians afraid of losing the religious population race on earth, my suggestion to you is – *breed!*

The flight to Frankfurt was at 12:50 a.m., or 0050, in military time. That was where Cale and I parted company; him bound for Italy, me for Munich.

My buddy, Ryan, waited at the Munich arrival section to pick me up – something I never expected. It was great to see him. We'd been friends for nearly twenty years and no matter how much time between visits, we always fall right back into the antagonistically brotherly friendship we share. Ryan lived and worked in a quaint resort village in the Tyrolean Mountains on the border with Austria. It's been four days since I arrived in this idyllic place and will tell ya all about it in another e-mail. In short, it was pure bliss. Mine was certainly a restful and relaxing start to a well-needed vacation.

"How do those guys stay so fucking skinny?" I wondered out loud about the Indian Internet help-desk guys.

"I think they got worms," was Sister Mary Danger's astute analysis.

CHILLIN' - AFGHAN STYLE

Have you ever noticed the way people sit and/or relax? Some lean on one leg against a wall, or desk or chair. Others will sit relaxed, "cross-legged," especially in the park or back yard. Some will stand, feet firmly planted underneath, their weight evenly distributed on both legs. Well, my friends, not the Afghans. They have an entirely different concept of chillin'.

Whether in the city, in their compounds, on our FOB, or wherever I saw them, Afghans squatted. And man, do I mean squatted. They sat so low to the ground that their butts might've actually rested on the pavement. Kids, teenagers, adults, and old people – everyone squatted. Just seeing them in that unnatural position made my hip joints ache. Seriously, I can't even sit cross-legged without one of my legs going numb. It's been that way ever since I was a kid. I tried to squat like an Afghan – it was impossible, and I was in good shape.

Squatting high up on a ledge like a cat, the Afghans think 'the higher the better.' I stepped around a few crunched down on what passed as sidewalk curbs when in the provincial capitol, but their prized locations were always higher. It could've been anything – a boulder, jersey barrier, concrete block, or ledge, rest assured, there was an Afghan perched atop. Reminded me of pigeons. Thankfully, Afghans don't defecate like pigeons, at least not in public.

U.S. policy was to integrate our Coalition partners into operations. One of those partners was the host-nation forces (Afghans). Thus, Afghan National Army (ANA) Soldiers ate, worked (really, just learned to work), and lived on the FOB. The new Afghan arrivals slouched around base in groups, looking unsoldierly in our old, dark, camouflage BDUs. Beetle Baily would've been an improvement over these neophytes. But Beetle couldn't have perched effortlessly on the large boulders located at the four-way stop like our Coalition partners did. Smoking and squawking like a murder of crows, they sunned themselves, all the while grasping the rocks wearing what amounted to plastic slippers or flip-flops. They hadn't received their boots yet.

Sister Mary saw somebody – a U.S. Soldier, spreading birdseed all over the rocks on the corner. I'm sure the irony was lost on the Afghans. In fact, I bet ya they gathered up the birdseed and made a meal of it.

"The problem with tossing a salad is getting shit everywhere!" Woody said, completely oblivious of the innuendo while actually tossing his dinner salad.

BEWARE OF THE COURTESY FLUSH

How many times have you gone into a public bathroom and smelled the stench of someone else's efforts? Pretty gross, ain't it? I don't mind my own stink so much, but no way in hell do I want to smell someone else's. Sometimes when I'm at a party and I've got to crunch, or whenever I'm not comfortable with my own smell, I use the beauty of the courtesy flush. You know what I'm talking about – after the first round of "expulsion" you adeptly reach back and flush the toilet, sending the offensive effluent on its way. If you don't perform the accompanying courtesy wipe, the flush isn't as effective, so I try to do both before relaxing for round two. It doesn't kill the smell entirely, but the flush decreases it a lot.

The public toilets we used had a natural malodorous stench, which never quite dissipated, even after cleaning. It was a combination of poop and a month-old cat-litter-box smell – more on that later. There were four commodes and three urinals in the bathroom, always at some level of uncleanliness. The last time I ever performed the courtesy flush in Afghanistan was in one of those commodes.

I was sitting on the crapper one day, enjoying a short respite from the heat and getting rid of the latest experimental concoction from the chow hall. The smell wasn't unbearable, but I had a feeling in my bowels that I'd be sittin' there for a while so I did a quick courtesy wipe and flush – what a mistake. I quickly jumped, nearly falling off the porcelain throne as the cold, crap-infused toilet water quickly engulfed my agates, which had hitherto been innocently dangling below. I used a few of Sister Mary Danger's expletives –

she would've been proud.

Distress, frustration, anger, revulsion – emotions I experienced simultaneously as the poop water dripped from my stones and down my legs. Yuck! Those who know me understand how mentally debilitating the shockingly unexpected ball-washing experience was – I felt suddenly dirty and ashamed, all for wanting to pleasant up the stall. (My legs just now involuntarily clenched at the memory.) My team said I was OCD about cleanliness. I admit, I liked a clean office, desk, and living quarters so saggy, wet balls dripping with non-potable sewage water couldn't have been more revolting.

Thank Christ I carried individual wet wipes everywhere, especially to the bathroom. Even though I was able to clean myself with these heaven sent, anti-bacterial cloths from Jesus, I still felt polluted. So friends, my advice to you – before you "courtesy flush," I highly recommend you gauge the functionality of your toilet flusher and more importantly, the distance between your junk and the water surface. Otherwise your taint could be tainted for life.

*"WHY DO YOU HAVE TO TELL A STORY LIKE THAT? YOU KNOW IT GETS ME **EMOTIONAL**!!!" Chip bellowed, as I gave him some not-so-bad news*

"Dude, you need to jerk off more often!" I said.

ANGRY EEYORE

Do y'all have a relative, coworker, teammate who's almost not worth the hassle? Maybe he's well intentioned, but complains about stuff not going his way, even though he's not doing a lot to make anything happen? Here's the deal: the deployment would've been so much different without Chip. His regular snark and frothy attitude added a harsh, playful element to our mix and definitely kept me on my toes. The guy waited a year for a well-deserved promotion and complained about it weekly, but he let HR's administrative screw-up eat at him, and that didn't win him many friends.

I was lucky Chip worked for me. His stubborn personality was the perfect complement to my stubbornness and we traded ideas and debated things without either one of us getting butthurt. At first, Chip did everything with us, but then he started drifting away. I think it was because he became increasingly angry with everyone and everything around him – that's something many deployed soldiers experienced. It might've indicated he wasn't satisfied with himself, but what could I say, "Dude, get over yourself." Nah, I just let it slide. He was experienced and competent, but felt disrespected by our larger organization and he had zero respect for most of our leadership. I didn't try or want to analyze, I only wanted him to do his best for us. And he delivered every time.

Although he steadily gained weight during the deployment, Chip never reached Wilbur proportions. Maybe I should've forced everyone to do some kind of physical exercise, but I didn't. I didn't want to be a control freak like Molly and I figured people would look after themselves. Chip didn't. He was a workaholic and worked to the detriment of his physical fitness. Not good. I gave him opportunity to take off, but he'd never do anything to break a sweat except shit out his Sriracha-infused meals. Oh, for the love of Sriracha.

Chip carried a bottle of 'cock sauce' around with him everywhere. Each meal was coated in that red chili paste. That dude's butthole must've been permanently ablaze. He never went to breakfast with us, but Mary'd usually bring him a plate of something and he'd quickly squirt cock sauce everywhere then shovel it down.

During the Molly-directed H&W inspection, our boss discovered an empty whiskey-smelling mouthwash container in Chip's wall locker. Oh man, he was pissed and was punished for having it, but dude, WTF? Why would you keep an empty bottle? The dumbass never offered an explanation but I know he regretted keeping it, or at least regretted getting caught.

If Woody and Mary Danger were competitive twins, Chip was their older competitive sibling. He wanted to win at Jeopardy! so bad and would angrily denounce others when they got the right answer, especially when his was close. The dude was always good for a laugh.

Chip was the one to tell me about the olive grove when I returned from R&R. It was heartbreaking, and I knew I'd not easily recover from that shortsighted, disappointing Army decision. He recognized how important the grove was to me, to all of us.

Chip also knew the mood of the interpreters – when they were pissed, what they actually thought, how much they complained about the workload. That was invaluable; we couldn't do anything without our Afghan 'terps. Half of this job is managing relationships and expectations. Chip helped us succeed at that.

Despite his snark, anger, frustration, and smoking, I'm really glad I got to work with Chip. I learned from him and thankfully it wouldn't be the last time we'd be in contact. I'd have an opportunity to work with him during his subsequent deployment to Afghanistan, but that's another story for another time in the future.

"I'm about to be an O6 (one step below a General).

You should be doing everything you can to please me!"
Molly shouted at her staff during another angry outburst
when no one volunteered to carry her bags.

A BRIGADE TEMPER TANTRUM

Something very interesting happened the other day. But first, let me introduce the characters involved. The brigade commander (Bde Cmdr) was the most powerful local commander of U.S. forces in my three-province region (the Duke from the Mouse That Roared story). He provided guidance on his priorities to the lower-ranking battle space owners (BSO) throughout the provinces (He had five or six subordinate BSOs). His word was law. Unfortunately, we worked on the same base as the Bde Cmdr – which meant we lived at the "flagpole". Hence, our FOB was very uptight. There was no fudging the rules and regulations because someone of higher rank would freak out and bring unnecessary attention and chaos to an otherwise mundane existence. See previous sections for context.

This was war, so rules and regulations must be followed. I was all for that, depending on the rule. We had some very brainless rules, even by numbskull standards, but the Bde Cmdr and his minions were active duty soldiers from 3rd Bde, 101st Division – known Army-wide for being backassward. Don't get me wrong, there were some incredibly talented soldiers in 3/101 (as they're called) but some soldiers in positions of leadership were career and ego-driven more than mission-driven. Right or wrong, I came to understand those bad leaders as "Ego/Career first, Mission second." It was like they picked leaders from a pool of candidates who had inbred with family members for generations and were a few genes short on the DNA strand. They meant well and could talk a good game, but they weren't playing with a full deck and that reflected in their behavior and decisions.

Case in point. Everyone was critically short of soldiers to do our missions. There were plenty of ground pounder infantry types, but if you haven't guessed by now, I worked in the intelligence field. There were never enough of us in any deployment to do our job. Recently, one of the intel guys was kicked off the base because he wasn't following the rules. Was he walking around with his weapon in hand, round chambered, ready to shoot? No. Was he speeding on base or driving around recklessly? No, he had no access to a vehicle. Was he harassing female soldiers or local Afghan interpreters? No. His egregious sin – he didn't want to tuck in his t-shirt while working out at the gym.

His sin boiled down to a t-shirt. The soldier had a special skill that required hundreds of hours to learn over many months of training. All units clamored for soldiers with his skill set but he couldn't stay – almost.

The soldier was working out at the gym at 11 p.m. one night. Whatever he was doing caused his t-shirt to come untucked. Understand – a military PT uniform is still a uniform. I've heard guys get yelled at and kicked off the basketball court because their t-shirt became untucked from their shorts while playing ball. Are you shocked? It's almost comical how small-minded people with a little bit of power will over react to perceived minor infractions. Anyway, back to our story.

The soldier was working out, dare I say rebelling, with his t-shirt untucked. The Bde Cmdr, also in uniform, t-shirt securely constrained by the tight elastic waistband of his shorts, approached and instructed the soldier to tuck in his t-shirt. Soldier explained it was easier to do the exercise without the shirt tucked in, because the shirt 'untucked' after every set. There was more to the conversation than what I heard second-hand, but the end result was the Bde Cmdr had a hissy fit, stormed out of the gym with the soldier in tow, marched the soldier to the MP station, called and woke up the soldier's commander, and ordered the soldier to not only leave the base immediately, but kicked him out of the entire three-province area. Oh, it got better.

Prior to the t-shirt incident, we experienced three days of rain. Our base had a gravel runway that closed whenever it rained. So, this criminal soldier packed up his stuff, and sat at

208

the passenger terminal in the dead of night, waiting for a flight. Naturally, he was still there in the morning because everything was cancelled and remained so for the foreseeable future due to the non-stop rain. (Today is the fifth day of rain.)

The fact that there were no flights was not an excuse to the Bde Cmdr and his bootlicking subordinates. Mighty Mouse was incensed that the criminal soldier and his vital intelligence skillset, which, again, were in desperate need in our area of operations, was still on his base. Mouse sent some lackey to yell at the soldier and the soldier's commander.

I never discovered the outcome of the t-shirt incident and I never learned where the soldier went, but I ask you: Is this the type of person you want responsible for thousands of soldiers in one of the most dangerous areas of Afghanistan? I certainly wouldn't trust him with my dog overnight, let alone with the precious lives of our fine men and women in uniform. Whether their shirts were tucked in or not. Yet this behavior was our normal.

RIDICULOSITY

CRAZY CIRCUS HAIR COLOR

A couple of months ago the circus came to town. No, I don't mean the time General McChrystal (now retired) came to the base. I'm talking about the new civilians who came to work at the DFAC (the dining facility for those of you who didn't read that e-mail). Couldn't tell ya where these women came from or what their value system consisted of but good Christ, the hairstyles were entertaining to say the least. I actually looked forward to seeing them at meals.

Two women immediately caught my attention, Miss Shorty and Miss Biggie. Shorty was about 5'2", dark skinned, African-American with a very prominent gold-capped front tooth in the shape of a spade. She was interesting enough for that grill and her beautiful eyes; seriously, they were captivating – like dark, liquid gold. But the most striking part of Shorty was her hair. From day one, I was spellbound by her two-toned (natural) dark brown and (unnatural) daffodil-colored coiffure. Could the contrast have been any starker? Doubt it.

Shorty must've had a footlocker of hair extensions because sometimes her head was blonde in front and brown in back, sometimes one side was brown on bottom with long sweeping blonde hair stretching from one ear, over her head, and down the other ear. I saw all blonde one week and once it was blonde on top and brown underneath. I had no idea how that was even possible, but it certainly was entertaining. Just imagine the entertainment if the DFAC employees wore civilian clothes. The options and combinations for clothing would've been endless.

Biggie was much more predictable. First, she was about 5'8", thickly built, dark-skinned, African-American, who wore a disinterested frown on her enormous face. Biggie had one hairstyle the entire time and it was two-toned like Shorty's. Biggie had longish dark brown hair, short on one side but extending to the shoulder on the other. The longer side had a four-inch wide purple streak extending from the crown of her head to the tips. It

211

was bordered by dark brown on either side. Eye catching to say the least. Biggie didn't have a gold tooth, but she didn't smile very much anyway so the grill never caught my attention. Naturally, the two women were inseparable.

One day at breakfast, Shorty's hair was entirely brown. It stopped me in my tracks. I mean, I hadn't really paid much attention to women's hair in general, but I was both shocked and dismayed that the one certainly in my life – the walking, breathing Dali-esqe coiffed DFAC worker, was just another normal, plain Jane, albeit with a styling gold-plated front tooth. It took me a hot minute to regain my composure. Meals were never the same after that.

I can't leave this section without mentioning our Macedonian Madonna. Suddenly the base was inundated with DFAC workers from Macedonia. There was a 5'0", sassy, loud, boisterous chick from Macedonia who bossed everyone around. She was no more than a regular worker, but she wasn't bad looking and reveled in the attention that ninety percent of the male population showered on her. I imagined her walking the Promenade in some desultory eastern European country (pre-Warsaw Pact implosion), strutting around in tortuous four inch high heels, a tight, sheer blouse and a gaudy mini-skirt that showed her hairy growler if you looked close enough (they didn't know about Brazilians in Soviet times).

In the DFAC, she wore a thick layer of make-up, which gave her face a papier-mâché look, goopy black eyeliner, blood-red lipstick, and my favorite, the distressed and teased bleached-blonde hair that looked like it might fall off her head in clumps each night the minute she took off the obligatory hair net. So, with these three ladies and other colorful individuals, meals at the DFAC were entertaining, if not appetizing.

"Whah he said waaas..." Abdul enunciated, slowly trying to recall what an Afghan said during a meeting.

THE INTERPRETERS

Our job was impossible without the cultural and linguistic support of interpreters. Unless you knew dialects of each Afghan language, you were lost. Not only did our 'terps speak the general language, they told nuances specific to the different groups we met, what might motivate them, how we could leverage information, etc. And most importantly, they helped us cut through the bullshit.

Some Afghans who met with Americans tried to get as much as they could from us. It was more like "the enemy of my enemy is my friend," and I wouldn't trust one to have my back if it came down to that. Their society and culture were quite different from ours, and I didn't hold their societal mores against them, but I never expected to be treated fairly. It was just the nature of the game.

It was obvious when dudes tried to extract money, fuel, and food staples from us, yet give absolutely nothing of value in return. Those were the easy assclowns to deal with. However, the interpreters pre-dated my team arriving in Afghanistan and they were probably around long after we departed. They had operational history in their back pockets.

Wahid and Mahmud could and did tell us when a local was trying to pawn old information as new. Usually, I'd call out the asscracker and deal with the situation, embarrassing him in the process. Afghans didn't like to be embarrassed. I'd try not to get pissed. They treated Uncle Sam like an ATM. You had to see things from their perspective. So dealing with Afghans was an art form that 'terps greatly helped with, but sometimes dealing with the interpreters was just as hard.

Because we had a very robust mission and were incredibly busy all the time, our team had the benefit of not one, but three interpreters. Sometimes we only had one or two because of their vacations, but we still stayed busy. Wahid, Mahmud, Abdul, and Serena added to our flavor and family, each by bringing something to the table.

Wahid and Abdul were legacy guys – inherited from the previous team. Wahid grew up in an adjacent province and really knew the area. I asked if his working for the U.S. could have a negative impact on his family but nearly all had moved to the States in waves, starting in 1979 with the Soviet invasion, continuing until everyone was out. He wasn't concerned. Chip and Wahid were tight and through Chip, I learned a few things. The most important was that Abdul was worthless.

Abdul, that ol' some-bitch! He'd been with the team for a while. Working with the sixty-plus year-old senior man had always been a problem. It took a couple months to figure out why. I didn't have an issue with him, but nearly the entire team complained of his slow interpreting and attempts to run the meetings. I chalked it up to a generational disconnect. Eventually, a local complained to Wahid that Abdul didn't make any sense.

Turns out, Abdul was from Kabul and didn't speak any of our local dialects. He tried to use Dari – one of two official languages – to get his point across. Problem was Dari is the language for government officials and the educated elite, not the local Joes with whom we met. Also, his Dari wasn't that great. Abdul had left the country when he was like five years old and only knew the kitchen Dari his parents spoke at home. To get around all those complaints and ingratiate himself with the locals, Abdul had been passing soft-core porn magazines to them. You know the ones – Maxim, FHM, Victoria's Secret catalogues, etc. He was too embarrassed to admit it at first, but revealed this trick to me thinking I'd want to keep him. Oh, those Afghans were crafty. We replaced him with Mahmud.

Mahmud, what a joker. Great energy, fun guy, had lived in Afghanistan until high school then moved to California. His knowledge of English was flawless and he could easily convey subtleties. Mahmud liked to brag and joke and did so constantly.

"Yeah dude, I'm impressed that you worked with Spec Ops, but yer here with me now. Just bump yer gums and get my point across. You can tell me another war story later." I said to him the umpteenth time he tried to take over one of my meetings with action stories from a past assignment.

He and Chip became friends yet he joked with everyone. Mahmud found a squirt gun in a care package one day, filled it up, and began drive-by squirting us in the office. I was so incensed when he shot me in the neck that I chased him around the office with an open bottle of water, dousing him when I could, but also hitting a few computers. That rat bastard ducked out the door wet but laughing.

Wahid constantly complained about being burned out and threatened to quit. At first I'm like, "Nooooo! You're too important to the mission!" But then it was like "OMG! Shut it and leave already!"

I think he might've felt underappreciated but he was hardly overworked. Each interpreter sat in a tent interpreting maybe four hours a day, max. Their phone could and did ring whenever, but I knew damn well they didn't put in the twelve to eighteen hours we did and they were very well compensated for their time. So my point was, Whatev. You just want to complain.

We got Serena on a trial basis late in the deployment. She had been at Bagram and became a problem child, disappearing from work and spending too much time at the bazaar on-base. See what I mean about us getting all the "challenges?" Turns out, Serena had a huge personality conflict with her supervisor and that was the root of the problem. She became our third 'terp.

Nervous at first, Serena fit right in, Mahmud and Wahid saw to that. American-Afghans treat each other like family even if their tribes hated each other in the old country. I knew she'd get a good welcome from the local interpreter community. She didn't spend a lot of time at our local bazaar mainly because it was a sad set up. However, Serena developed and then promoted what the 'terps had been doing among themselves – she organized Friday dinners.

Most of the 'terps lived in one or two buildings where they reconfigured the inside of their living quarters to create a big living room/kitchen, if you will. Every Friday (the Muslim Sabbath), they prepared a feast of mutton, Afghan-spiced rice, chopped vegetables, and desserts. Everyone sat around a small table festooned with raisins, nuts, candies, etc., drinking chai, chatting, and waiting for the aromatic homemade dinner to be served, complete with warm local bread. Afghan or Indian music played in the background. Lord knows where they got the ingredients, I didn't care nor did I ask. It was awesome. As Americans, we were the guests of honor and our plates were never empty.

A lot of our job was based on networking. Sure, the interpreters weren't the movers and shakers, but they worked for them, and they might share a tidbit or two over a meal, if we were lucky. I learned why a certain officer on base was a complete jackass (his wife was having an affair back home that had become public knowledge), the car wreck a fellow soldier had while on R&R (drunk driving), and the new son a platoon sergeant had last week (he watched the birth via Skype).

In spite of the headaches they might've caused and their occasional whining or empty threats, spending time with the interpreters was real living. In retrospect, it helped me appreciate the 'ordinary' in life. We needed them to do our jobs, but more importantly, these guys taught me how to appreciate the mundane as well as the exciting.

We left them in Afghanistan at the end of our deployment. Chip remained in contact with Wahid and Mahmud, exchanging the occasional e-mail. Although not military, they were and continue to be, part of my extended family, having had such a huge impact on that deployment.

"The Taliban is bad…" Molly slowly said, pausing to think, while chairing her first staff meeting in Afghanistan.

ARMED FORCES NETWORK (AFN)

AFN – the omnipresent viewing staple of our dining facility. Like most large installations, our dining facility had a couple of televisions. The only thing playing on TV, day and night, was AFN.

AFN had a few channels pre-approved by the government, so no HBO shows, nothing risqué or controversial. Most everything was re-broadcast so instead of commercials, we got military-themed infomercials. These were usually lame attempts to influence us to recycle, cut our lawns, turn off the lights, etc. Sometimes the messages were worthy, like reporting people to the suicide hotline, don't take stress out on your family, save money for an emergency, or stop smoking for the benefit of yourself as well as others. There were also pitiful testimonials by high-ranking persons in command. They stood at attention like mannequins, reading something into the camera with zero emotion, inflection, or facial movement. If they only realized how stupid they actually looked they'd be mortified. I'm sure their kids got teased at school for their parents' talking, cadaver-esque performances.

In the DFAC you better like sports because that's aaaaaaaalllll they showed. College and professional football and basketball (I dread baseball season) played over and over. Unfortunately, the re-broadcast rights for college sports must preclude AFN from benefiting. We saw college games only once but were subjected to pro games all day. I remember watching Dallas in various stages of beating New Orleans at breakfast, lunch, and dinner. I mean, come on! Play something else! How about the news? Why couldn't we watch the news? Just for one meal a day? Don't you think it's important to know what's happening in the world? Even the Neanderthal army rangers and infantry guys would've fixated on the hot female newscasters and might've absorb some morsel of information about stuff back home. But no, sports it was. I never liked AFN, but found myself staring zombie-like at it while shoveling in the grub. Oh, to be home where I could eat in solitude.

"I like to keep my legs together, but one time I split them apart." Leigh naively stated, discussing weight lifting with her girlfriends at Bagram.

OLIVE GROVE AFTER R&R

I returned from R&R a while back, and the frustration at returning to the office not only remained, it intensified. Recall the olive grove I lovingly described in previous updates? It was where I conducted my watering experiment, where we hid from the scorching sun, where we corralled our goats until distributing them to locals, etc. The olive grove became a sort of refuge for our team and others. It was also a sanctuary for the wildlife on base. Mornings, you'd hear the incredible symphony of birds as they greeted the sunrise. Their songs continued all day. At midday, the rocks bordering the olive grove became a basking ground for Larry and other small reptiles. And evenings, the grove camouflaged the movements of coyotes that roamed base at dusk as the birds returned to their roosts for the night. I referred to the olive grove in past tense because it is no more. The Army bulldozed it.

Foliage was precious in Afghanistan, particularly trees. They represented wealth and status, provided income and labor, and when past their usefulness, they became firewood. Trees were a natural treasure in a rugged, barren, hopeless land. To the Army, the trees were excess and stood in the way of progress. It was sad to consider, because the U.S. will eventually leave this country and regrettably, we'll leave many places worse for the wear.

The olive grove behind our building was actually a remnant of what was once an expansive collection of fruit trees covering the valley. In addition to the olive grove, there were orange groves and date trees. Some eucalyptus and mulberry trees still existed on parts of the base, hopefully safe from destruction because they either provided shade to nearby buildings or they lined the streets, out of the way of construction. Although not a surveyor, I guesstimated the olive-grove remnant was about fifty acres in size. It stretched far from our building in two directions. Watering pump-stations sat within the grove and a paved road ran through it. Surely, this was a means of income for its owners before the U.S. occupation. It was part of my deployment history.

I returned from R&R to see the trees bulldozed, lying on their sides. No one had any idea how, when, or by whom it happened. Chip noticed them a couple days before my return. One morning the team woke to destruction. Birds still perched on the limbs but their songs were sad and muted. It was more than heartbreaking. My touchstone to a reminder of life back home was destroyed.

I recalled the conservation commercial I saw as a kid – an American-Indian standing on a rock surveying a vast expanse of ruined, polluted landscape, a tear slowly falling down one cheek. Senseless. There were other locations for buildings. All for the sake of space, the Army had razed a living grove, not just a home to animals, but also a respite of tranquility in an often-shitty place. I was too saddened to be angry, and besides, anger would've been a futile waste of energy when I had a month of work to address. I had to let it go.

This wasn't my first experience with the Army's insatiable appetite for land. During my Iraq deployment, the Army destroyed an incredible orchard of peach, orange, and apricot trees to make way for a chow hall. I was working at a former palace in Ramadi situated along the Tigris River. Maybe it was the Euphrates, I don't remember. But the military wanted to expand, and instead of using empty land somewhere else in the compound, it bulldozed a nearby productive orchard to make way for a slop shop. It was disheartening and shortsighted, like many military decisions.

Back to now, the reason for losing our olive grove was 'the surge' of troops, which we hadn't yet experienced. No one knew exactly how many additional soldiers the base needed to support. True, housing was at a premium and there was little to spare. But instead of building barracks on newly reclaimed land on the far side of base where they planned to build a new chow hall, the geniuses in charge decided to tear down trees near our area and put up more
220

barracks, which meant more noise, trash, shitters, traffic, etc. No more quiet sanctuary, no more idyllic songbirds, no more Larry the Lizard, and no more furtive peeing in the trees.

It was time to go home.

RIDICULOSITY

"They did keep you in a crib, didn't they? Or did they just tether you to something?" I asked an annoyingly, overly energetic Mary Danger.

A "DANGEROUS"
BATTLE OF WILLS

As you've probably guessed, Sister Mary Danger had a mind of her own. She did what I asked of her because I practiced what I preached and always helped out, but it usually had to be "her" way. Because she was a great soldier, good at her job, and always willing to lend a hand, I let her steely free will run loose.

I mean, if I had tried to control everything about my teammates' lives, not only would they be miserable, the mission would've suffered. I think there should be a healthy level of freedom of thought and action in order to succeed. I gave them a task and let them figure out the best way to do it. Naturally, I provided guidance, and you'd be surprised at the results from those who feel empowered and a part of the solution, instead of robots fulfilling orders from above.

Sometimes my requests were completely normal and made perfect sense. Sometimes they didn't. Well, I was the boss and they liked or at least tolerated me so I usually got my way eventually, even if it required much persuasion and a few guilt trips. But not always.

Mary and I had such an encounter not too long after Easter. Someone back home sent a cute Easter basket filled with goodies. The teeth-rotting candy wasn't the interesting part; it was the basket in which the goodies had arrived.

The basket was actually some small, cloth-covered bucket with a sturdy handle. The entire thing was covered in old Army camouflage material and had neon pink grass. It was hilariously adorable – the ideal gift a mother or grandmother would send her deployed child. I wanted to say someone sent it to Mary, but I wasn't entirely sure. Anyway, I placed that cute, innocuous basket on Mary's desk, knowing that she loathed anything cute, or pink.

"What the hell is this doing here?" Mary hollered the first time she saw it, moving it off her desk and onto the shelf. I kept sneaking it back on her desk when she wasn't around.

"What the fuck?" Mary bellowed her usual, articulate response each time the basket appeared on her desk. He! he! he!, Chip and I giggled to each other, with a knowing wink and nod. Even Woody snickered at my surreptitiously fuckin with Mary.

About this time, Tyler was visiting. Tyler was a team leader from another location in the province. He was a great guy, full of personality, dead set in his stubborn ways, and a smoking buddy to Mary. Those two and Chip were always outside puffing on the cancer sticks. Tyler liked the basket, too, but didn't know that I tormented Mary with it until he heard one of her outbursts for the millionth time I replaced the Army camo basket with the pink grass on her desk in her absence.

"What? It's *cute!*" he said, breaking conversation with me. Mary glared at him.

"Why are you torturing me with this thing!" she bellowed to no one in particular, putting us on high 'hilarity' alert. I had to turn around and face my desk so she wouldn't see me laughing. Chip grinned into his computer screen.

Regaining my composure I said matter-of-factly, "Tell you what – put it on your arm like a purse, walk around the room like a runway model, and I'll throw it away."

"Fuck that! It's against my morals!"

As I said before, I wasn't convinced Mary understood what that meant or knew what her morals were. Needless to say, she didn't budge.

"Come on Danger, put it on, it's cute!" Tyler pestered her about wearing it, to no avail. She wouldn't do it for anyone. You see, once Mary got it in her head to not do something, it was nearly impossible to change her mind.

That didn't prevent us from tormenting her all at once. "I think it'd look good on you. Pink is your color." Shaniese quipped.

"She won't do it, she doesn't have the balls." Chip added, trying reverse psychology.

"At least give me the candy. Don't throw 'em away!" Woody remarked to an increasingly irritated Sister Mary.

"Just prance around with the damn thing already and be done with it." I loudly harangued. Nothing. It was futile.

Mary was in a good mood a few days later when all the nagging to carry the basket started anew. Of course, she wouldn't carry the damn thing for me, but she did for Tyler.

I took off to water my plants in the orchard when Tyler kicks in the psychological twist. "I don't see why this is so hard." he said, basket firmly in place on his muscular arm, prancing around the office like Dorothy from the Wizard of Oz while staring and smiling at Mary, egging her on. That did it.

Mary took the challenge and the basket, skipping up and down the room once.

"What the fuck is going on?" I said astonished, walking through the door just as she quickly sat down. Grinning – no laughing, quickly snatched the basket off her arm – knowing she got one over on me. Everyone laughing but the boss.

"Dude, you missed the funniest fuckin' thing! She put the basket on her arm and skipped all over the place." Tyler joyously exclaimed while everyone laughed and nodded in agreement. I was livid.

I didn't know why I was mad. Maybe because Tyler got Mary to do something I couldn't, or because Mary wore it for Tyler but not me, or because everyone was laughing and enjoying the toughest chick skip around like a little girl, or because maybe if I had held back watering for a few minutes I would've witnessed her Follow the Yellow Brick Road routine.

"You mean like this?" I snapped, anger boiling in my soul. I snatched that stupid ugly camo-colored Easter basket with the neon pink shredded straw from the table, firmly placed it on my arm and skipped around the office. I was so pissed, extending the length between skips as much as I could – really pushing it. They just stared. I threw it down, bolted from the room and slammed the door.

RIDICULOSITY

What kind of role model was I, to skip around the room like a crazed lunatic, doing something I ordered a trooper to do? Let me tell ya, deployments make people do strange things, and when a person is strange to begin with, well, strange takes on a whole new meaning. That damn basket incident still pisses me off, even today.

"We are like a big family, Chip is the mom and Todd is the dad." Mary Danger said, explaining our team dynamic.

DON'T ASK, SHHHH! DON'T TELL

(This email was sent years before the military's policy on gays was changed)

If you haven't heard, there was a debate raging in Congress, and to a lesser extent, in living rooms, at dinner tables, in locker rooms, in classrooms, in barbershops, at churches, and yes, within the military itself. The topic – the concept of gay men and women openly serving in the military. Contentious? Certainly. Already existing? Definitely. A certainty? Probably. And my thoughts – oh yeah, you're gonna get 'em.

For those who've been living in a cave for the past couple decades, former President Clinton emplaced the Don't Ask, Don't Tell, Don't Pursue (DADT) policy back when he ruled the world. I always thought it was weird why and how he chose to tackle the gays in the military thing when he did because his actions seemed to draw attention to a group of people who had been quietly serving in the military for years. In fact, I think more soldiers got thrown out after the policy was in place than before, but I could be wrong. I frequently am.

There are now and have always been gay men and women serving in the military. A joke I've heard more than once: Question, What's the difference between a straight marine and a gay marine? Answer, a six pack. Alcohol-influenced decisions aside, negative reactions will always exist to something foreign, feared, misunderstood, or ingrained in one's head as being immoral, unethical, or wrong. That, my friends, is human nature. But the

227

issue of gays openly serving in the military is something that provokes reaction at a visceral level.

All the yahoos in Congress (specifically the esteemed gentleman from Arizona) and the babbling wonkheads on TV have it slightly wrong. DADT will change to allow openly gay men and women to serve in the military. If you openly and vehemently oppose a policy change, then you are out of touch with a majority of the constituents you serve and detached from the people the policy will mostly affect – the junior enlisted soldiers who make up the bulk of the military and are generally younger and more open to the idea. I don't care if you served before. I'm serving now and have experienced change.

I've never been a fan of Dick Cheney for all the warped bile and vitriol that spewed from his mouth, but he came close to a decent explanation when he said it's a generational thing. I would go a few steps further, Dick. Yes, younger soldiers are probably more likely to be open and accepting of a gay member within the ranks, but there will always be resistance. I've discovered a few things that factor into someone's opinion on the gay thing: age, education, gender, political identity, rural vs. urban, a gay relative, geographical location in the states, religious upbringing, and the field in which one works. Then there's the nebulous psychological part, which definitely factors into the equation, but I'm no brain doc and won't offer much of an explanation from that angle.

Most military women I've talked to seem to have fewer issues with gays openly serving. Oh sure, I know exceptions, both of whom are very educated. One baffles me in her opposition, the other is a complete head case so her opposition was a given. Guys on the other hand are harder to predict. I always expect some opinionated argument against policy change and am rarely disappointed. However, one can never really tell who will be pro or anti-change or ambivalent all together.

Your stereotypical status-quo supporter – either more senior ranking (sergeant first class and higher for enlisted, major and higher for officers), or a high school/GED-educated young male from a rural area who is somewhat to very religious, self-identifies with the conservative movement, has no gay family or friends,

228

serves in a combat arms unit, and suffers insecurities of some type. Again, I've been surprised by some people on the whole policy-change thing but usually if you're from a rural area, especially a Southern rural area, are Republican and religious, you're a hater. But why? I've tried to figure that out. Let's look at this in some detail.

I think the first thing most heterosexual soldiers (aka breeders) associate with gay and lesbian soldiers isn't the work ethic, or the man's quick wit and dapper sense of style, or the woman's ability to change a tire and skillfully handle power tools. And it's not how they excel at Soldier-of-the-Month competitions or promotion boards. It's the stereotypical behavior associated with gay men and lesbians seen in the media whenever a gay-pride parade or similar event gets coverage. Again, it's this foreign, sometimes over the top, one could say flamboyant behavior that breeders unequivocally assume will come out of the woodwork once the DADT policy changes. But it's more than just behavior.

How should the military implement changes? Will someone be reprimanded for saying, "This is gay!" whenever a stupid rule is imposed? Or could someone get yelled at for saying, "Don't be a fag!" while trying to pressure someone into doing something they'd rather not? Where will gay soldiers sleep, shower, live, etc.? Probably in the same place they sleep, shower, and live right now. But how does one decide who lives with whom and where? Should a commander ascertain the sexual orientation of a new soldier during in-processing to a unit before assigning him a room? I can imagine the interview going something like this: What's your date of birth, home of record, next of kin, license plate number, do you suck dick?

Will there be separate living quarters for benders (gays) and breeders? Could one house a bender dude with a breeder chick or vice versa? Why not, they're both sexually interested in the same thing? Come on folks, it shouldn't boil down to with whom someone has sex. But I think that's the biggest fear and misconception behind resistance. Well, almost.

There's also the whole showering together thing. Hey, currently I shower in a building equipped with six separate stalls.

RIDICULOSITY

There's a modicum of privacy. However, at Camp Bullis, TX, the showers were together in a square room, six spigots total. That honestly sucked – but not because some gay dude could've been checking out my baby-maker. Hell, breeders – the guys anyway – always check out each other's junk with a quick, furtive glance. It's a guy thing – ya know, comparing. And if your boyfriend, husband, son, or brother tell you otherwise he's bullshittin' ya. Checking out another dude's junk doesn't make you gay. Ladies, if that were the case, ninety-five percent of you would never get laid. The shower at Bullis sucked because they suck and guys do a junk check for comparative reasons.

The more vociferous the opposition to changing the policy, usually the more mentally unstable or insecure the originator of the rant. My favorite is the wanna-be-macho guy, the one who constantly tries to impress other guys, who is marginally ugly – in an ugly way, who's got no game with the ladies, is insecure on so many levels, emotionally unstable, and almost needy. He's probably a closet bender but doesn't know it yet and he loudly proclaims how he doesn't "want no faggot checking me out in the shower."

Those guys are funny. I mean, come on dude, you're repulsive to look at, are a mental wreck, have the intellectual capacity of a caterpillar, you're hung like a gnat, and you've got no muscle tone and pallid skin. Even Jeffrey Dahlmer would pass, and you're worried about a gay dude checking you out in the shower. Whaaaaaatever…. You probably have to pay for sex.

I've served with gays and lesbians for years, some of them obvious, some undetectable. Just like breeders, these benders were cut from many cloths. Some were outstanding soldiers – role models for others. One in particular was a female first sergeant of mine (that's the most senior enlisted person in a company usually responsible for one hundred plus soldiers). Angela was incredibly proficient at her job, very approachable, tough as nails, exuded professionalism and the warrior ethos, and you could always get a fair shake with her. I've served with others who unfortunately were the exact opposite. All I ask and demand is that, gay or straight, you do your job and do it well.

The argument that allowing benders to serve openly in the

230

military (with two on-going wars, oh no!) will disrupt good order and discipline and compel soldiers to get out of the military or prevent new ones from signing up, is ludicrous.

Let's face it; there will always be a conflict going on. Say it together – military industrial complex. Insisting that the U.S. must wait until we're at peace is saying, "Hell no, we ain't changing, ever." How many of you have family members trying to get a job in this economy? Employers aren't going door-to-door looking to hire bigots strenuously opposed to working with gays. Hell, in this economy you're lucky if you have a stable job. Therefore, I highly doubt there will be a mass exodus from each of the services when the policy changes.

If worse comes to worst, I'm certain someone will choose a steady paycheck and a gay coworker over no paycheck or uncertain employment status. Layoffs, anyone? And if they don't, if they choose to leave the service, then I say good riddance. I'd rather serve with a hard working, effeminate fag or butch dyke than a bigoted breeder any day.

RIDICULOSITY

TRUCKING

The U.S. military and contractors are very much governed by thousands of regulations. If you need to drive a tactical vehicle, you must wear a helmet, seatbelt, use your headlights – even during the day – and have someone act as a ground guide while backing up. If you need to sign out tools or use some types of equipment, you must first take a class, get a license, and wear safety glasses. If you need to go to the shooting range, you must have a medic on hand, wear ear and eye protection, have multiple levels of instruction and "guards," and only then, can you shoot a bullet at a target twenty-five meters away. Sometimes all this was overkill, sometimes not. So why in the world was the movement of cargo not affected by these safety rules?

First, what is considered safe? You'd be amazed at what passed for safe in Afghanistan – all manner of pickup trucks chock full of Afghans, some in various stages of tumbling out of the truck bed, smiles on their faces as they travelled at twenty KPH to and from the front gate. The way Afghans crapped, perilously perched on the seats of the port-a-johns, squatting over the hole while doing their business. At any time one could slip and end up with a leg squishing about in the blue liquid.

Then there were the flatbed trucks that hauled our cargo everywhere in the country, most unusual of all.

Those flatbed trucks vexed me the most. I was all for the transportation of goods, trust me. If it weren't for those brave Afghan drivers and their flatbeds, the majority of our troops would not get resupplied at all. Believe me, drivers had a huge impact on the war effort. However, safety as I knew it was not a concern for them, or for the military who entrusted them with connexes of supplies.

When a shipping container is placed on a flatbed truck in the States, it is locked down at each corner by heavy-duty bolts. The bolts themselves are locked in place, preventing items from moving at all. In Afghanistan, truckers used something totally different.

233

RIDICULOSITY

There, the truckers used straps. Scary, right? A huge twenty-five to forty-five foot long metal connex was secured to a flatbed with the kind of straps you might see holding down a tarp. I saw straps like this used in the States, but not for such an important job.

At any time the truck could lean, slide, hit a huge pothole – of which there were many – thereby shifting its immense cargo container. Do you think some woven, synthetic-material strap at each corner was going to prevent disaster? Surely, they helped and were better than nothing, but come on, for a military overly cautious and safety conscious, how could one reconcile transporting our supplies in such an unsecure, careless manner?

Oh, I forgot, it was Afghan standards. Insha'Allah – it's God's will. Ever heard that saying? We heard it often. Well, when it came to my mail, equipment, supplies, food, or other shit moving from one place to another, I preferred a heavy-duty bolt to God's will, thank you very much.

*"Does anyone want to argue intelligence with me?"
Molly snapped, furiously looking at a room full of staff
advisors, all of whom presented her data that didn't
support the outcome she demanded.*

YOU DON'T WANT TO KNOW

Every military commander from the company on up can
ascertain the level of satisfaction within his organization. Civilian
companies use internal surveys or might hire an outside agency
to conduct an assessment of worker satisfaction and morale. The
Army has something called the Command Climate Survey, or
CCS. It's the perfect tool for a new commander who assumes the
helm of a unit. A properly administered CCS can help a new leader
gauge the morale and level of faith and trust workers have in the
leadership and organization.

The CCS isn't a tool only for the new commander. Any
commander can administer it at any time. In extreme situations, a
higher-level commander might direct a subordinate to conduct a
CCS when whispers of acute dissatisfaction reach his level. That's
what happened to us.

Molly's vice-like grip on every element of managerial
freedom stifled innovation, flexibility, initiative, and soldier morale.
I heard there were more Congressional investigations on her
decisions and leadership than on any of her peers in the entire
intelligence community of the Army reserves. No idea if it was true,
but leadership at all levels in Afghanistan and back home knew of
our battalion's rock-bottom morale and frustration. Enter the CCS.

Roughly three-fourths of the way through the deployment,
Molly's immediate boss in Afghanistan directed her to conduct the
CCS. The soldiers were ecstatic! It was both a chance to voice
our frustrations and a slap in the face of the command leadership
team. Although our identities were supposed to be shielded, the
analytical mind might deduce which group or individual provided

which comments and responses. There was still a fair amount of anonymity, but at this point soldiers were willing to put their names, social security numbers, and selfies on any critique of the leadership. Things had gotten that bad.

The electronic survey took a week to conduct and the answers took a week to collate. And then the results arrived. Our participation rate was over ninety-eight percent. Imagine if we could get American voters to care that much about local, state or national elections. One thing was certain, Molly and Rhonda had united the battalion. Everyone wanted to know the results.

Since Molly was forced to conduct the CSS, only she received the results. When they finally arrived, she trudged over to her boss's office, results in hand, for consultation. He had ordered her to conduct the CSS, and he wanted to know the outcome. It wasn't pretty.

Molly hiked the short trek to HQ alone. That was unheard of – she was terrified of getting raped, even in broad daylight on a busy street. She didn't go anywhere without some kind of escort. When she begrudgingly did battlefield circulation to visit the troops, she surrounded herself with subordinates who served as her bodyguards. This woman shouldn't have left her neighborhood back home, let alone been sent to a war zone.

It was brutal. The results were overwhelmingly negative on every aspect of the survey. But Molly never shared the exact data, not even with Rhonda. Those at battalion saw a change though. Molly morosely sulked around the office for three whole days, barely eating, with puffy eyes and tear-stained cheeks on display for everyone to see. While a few pitied her, most felt vindicated. But we weren't out of the water yet. She still held sway over our awards and evaluations; revenge might've been in the making.

Truth be told, I wanted her and Rhonda to melt into a fleshy puddle of tears and regret for the hysterical Hell they had put us through. I couldn't imagine working in the Orwellian dysfunction she created and fostered at HQ. But bless her soul, she didn't know any better.

No doubt Molly's heart was in the right place, but her brain and common sense never deployed. She wanted the mission to succeed, but more importantly she vainly wanted success by forcing her twisted version of perfection onto a group of highly intelligent, creative people. With that mindset, she could only fail, and fail she did. The CCS was proof. Did Molly and/or Rhonda learn anything from the deployment, especially about leadership? I hoped so, but I doubted it, because nothing changed. More importantly, I hoped no organization ever put either of them in leadership positions ever again.

The stomach-knotting work atmosphere gradually returned at HQ and we finished the deployment a few months later. Only time would tell what was in store for the Dynamic Duo. For our soldiers specifically and the army reserve intelligence field in general, the damage was done.

RIDICULOSITY

*"If it weren't for Wheat Thins, I wouldn't be here today."
Woody said, lovingly looking at a box of Wheat Thins
he found in a care package.*

LETTERS FROM HOME

You really have no idea what a little piece of home could do for a soldier's morale. Not everyone had easy access to the Internet when deployed, nor could everyone make phone calls. The sports page of a local paper or a graduation announcement for the high school could and often did have a huge impact. My mom sent clips from her local newspaper, even though I moved from that small town long ago. Those clips still resonated and provoked twinges of nostalgia, admiration, sadness, or more. When gone for an entire year, any chance to feel connected to our lives back home was very much welcomed.

I can't thank you enough for sending care packages to us overseas. We got them from our families and friends, but also from elementary schools, church groups, little league teams, Girl Scout troops, coworkers, veterans, and many other dedicated and concerned people. The comforts of home tucked inside those boxes always brought a smile to our hearts and helped make any deployment just a bit more bearable. Care packages were especially prevalent around the holidays like Christmas, Thanksgiving, and New Year's.

The notes that accompany boxes from grade-school classes were simply precious. One could envision a group of third graders gluing pictures from magazines onto construction-paper cards, writing notes, or sharing a box of crayons to complete that project for the soldiers. They're kids, and some of the well meaning missives were hilarious, like: "My daddy is in the whor to." Or, "Thank you for killing peeple to make us safe." I loved that stuff.

Equally impressive were the drawings. One drawing stood

out from all the rest. A friend's five-year-old daughter sent a rendering of her dad (a friend and fellow deployed soldier) and mom standing next to each other. Normal enough, right? Well, Mom had one bloody Cyclops eye, dad's hair was on fire and his throat was cut, and neither one had arms. They had been chopped off and were falling to the ground along with other bloody stump-arms. I suggested he get his family to a therapist, now.

As a single man with no kids and little contact with my family, I didn't suffer the pain of separation many colleagues experienced. More than one friend regretted missing his son's football game or daughter's soccer match. I didn't relate, but was occasionally exposed to that personal emotion when a Dad Skyped at the Internet café, or teared up when viewing pictures on Facebook.

Keith, a soldier at another base, set the standard for care-package response. He forced his entire five-man team to compose Thank You notes to each of the little misspelled cards in the care packages his team received. No card went unanswered. Each kid got a hand-written response. He grew in my eyes for that action alone. Compassion for another is powerful, especially among warriors.

I'm not a religious man, but God bless those who sent packages to people serving overseas. You might not always hear back from us, but believe me; your actions are greatly appreciated. So to everyone who sent something to someone deployed, I say thanks.

"It's about fuckin' time! I thought I might die of old age here!" Mary Danger declared with hostility when our redeployment orders were published.

GOING HOME

When you first get notice of your impending deployment to Afghanistan, many thoughts race through your head. The first few are usually about how it will jack-up your current civilian job, family relationships, school schedule, health, etc. You worry what the boss will say or whether you'll have a job when you return. You wonder how the spouse or boyfriend/girlfriend will take the news, what the kids will do, and how much you'll miss the dog. You think about backburner projects you always put off, or the fitness routine you wanted to start, the repairs on the house that needed doing, or that strange car noise. Yeah, the deployment was a good excuse to keep putting off some things or prod you into fixing a few others.

You also think about what you'll miss – birthdays, recitals, ball games, anniversaries, births, deaths, etc. It's tough. You might consider all the mandatory pre-deployment training or the new people you'll work with, and your role and responsibility down range. What you'll probably not consider right away is your return.

Few understood that arriving at the final in-country location meant you'd eventually leave. Few thought that far ahead. Some focused on their departures the entire time, some on their R&R plans, but many threw themselves into the strange new situation in order to discover and master the factors of success. The departure date was far off and almost seemed unreal. For some, it didn't arrive as planned because they flew back home due to a family emergency. Others might leave early – in a box, now immune to the hassles of redeployment and joys of life.

Although we were heavily vested in the success of our mission and eager to see that success continue, only Sister Mary

RIDICULOSITY

Danger and I volunteered to extend our deployment for a few months. I wanted to set our replacements up for success, help them get accustomed to life in our province, and maintain the relationships needed to keep our local intel collection running. Mary wanted to continue doing the job and train the newbies. However, neither of us was allowed to stay.

It was weird – one moment you were an integral part of the success of a mission and the resulting safety and security in the area, and the next you were unwanted, more like a relic of the soon-to-be former crew. The new team wanted the help, especially since they were short-staffed, but their battalion leadership thought the new team could do the job just as well without us. My pride said, I doubt it. (Turned out I was right.) But we had to learn to let go.

After a few hits to my pride, letting go became easy. At first, I was frustrated and angry – those two emotions are everywhere at the end of any deployment. I felt I owed the Afghans because they were responsible for some of our success. But instead of festering on something I had no control over, the team and I started the return process.

Woody took a really late R&R – he was in the Canary Islands dancing at foam parties, drinking sangria, and watching Spain win the World Cup. What an incredible time.

Shaniese and about a dozen other soldiers re-deployed home before the rest of us did. Their job was to set up the reintegration systems and help process the main group arrival a few weeks later. She would return to college, so getting home early helped her get things ready for classes. It was such a simple gesture –helping a soldier-student prepare for the future, but that often didn't happen. Why help the future when the present was at hand?

That left Chip, Sister Mary, and me to take care of everything else. Chip packed up Woody's things (Woody only had 18 hours to pack and clean before our return). We met with each Afghan contact both on and off base to let them know what was happening. We said goodbye to our extended team, who returned to Bagram to gather with the rest of the battalion. Then we waited.
242

"Over adversity…, a lot…, our battalion has." Molly blurted out, trying to explain the daily challenges we faced.

THE RIPTOA

The guts of the deployment were complete and we were coming full circle. If your department, section, or office has experienced personnel turnover, you'll understand the concept of RIPTOA – Relief in Place, Transfer of Authority. It's the beautiful acronym meaning you're either entering a war zone and earnestly learning from your predecessors, or you're imparting wisdom to your successors and preparing to leave.

The standard Army turnover time is about seven to ten days, during which you establish computer accounts, read the local policies, learn the case histories of "projects" you'll work on, familiarize yourself with the base, and introduce your successors to all the important people, places, and meetings they'll need for success. You show them how it's done for a couple days, then watch and help them the remainder of the time until you leave. Finch was my predecessor – he chaperoned our team everywhere and answered every question.

Great guy, that Finch. He was so relaxed and ready to leave, knowing that he didn't have to deal with anything that might pop up. We even got to meet a few of the local Afghans his team had been meeting with. That was key for a smooth transition – gaining the trust of the people whom we might continue to see. He stuck around for seven days. The alternative was departing for that shithole Bagram, so I could see why he was happy to help. No responsibilities and no supervisor lurking about. Hell, sign me up.

Now it was our time. As we got ready to depart, Chip ensured that all project files and bio folders were up to date. We wanted to leave the operation in much better condition than we inherited. We transferred over as much to the new team as possible. Mary Danger and I volunteered to extend through the end of the year for a couple of reasons. First, the incoming team was short-staffed and wanted the help, and we wanted to ensure the transition between the teams went well. Second and more importantly, we wanted to avoid as much of the ridiculous redeployment circus with our parent organization. There was a lot of anger and animosity toward the leadership. Well, we couldn't stay.

I guessed it – Molly, aka Combat Barbie, had told her successor about our meeting with General McChrystal. That didn't sit well with him, and I learned he considered me an uncontrollable live wire. It was the standard Army kneejerk reaction – don't draw attention, don't think outside the box, and by all means, don't make the command look bad. Weasels are more concerned with surface than substance – one of the systemic problems with the military. See what I mean about small-minded egomaniacs? Or was that me? Whatev, you chickenshit.

I wish I could say at least the RIPTOA went well. It didn't. Their leadership decided when our replacements came from Bagram. That standard seven-to-ten-day learning curve was reduced to eight hours. We were stunned.

During the deployment, my team had the most robust operations, meeting with the largest number of Afghans, and generating the largest number of high quality intelligence reports than any team in our battalion. Our stats and analysis were fantastic. This team had paid the bills, kept our local area safer, and helped make our frenzied, insecure battalion commander look good. You'd think an incoming leader would want to capitalize on that success. Nope, eight hours. I picked up the confident, cocky newbies from the helicopter terminal; let them drink from the fire hose, then left. I forced myself to relax, exhale and let go. The yearlong work was over and another team was running the show. It was time to say goodbye.

You've often heard that we've not been fighting a fourteen-year war in Afghanistan. We've been fighting fourteen, one-year wars. At the time, I couldn't fathom why leadership was so narrow-

244

minded, focused only on its time overseas, unconcerned with history and how our operations directly impact Afghans. It's the Army way. Sure, there was a four-star General in charge of overall operations for a couple years at a time, but we needed War Czars at every level, staying in place for a couple years at a stretch. Give them more R&R, make life more pleasant for them, keep them connected to their families, but instill a continuity of mission. Nah, neither Congress nor the American public would stand for that. So, eight hours, and then it was someone else's fight.

A "RIP" is supposed to be a happy, joyous time. You get to enthusiastically show the newbies all the hard work and results of a year's worth of your life. I felt like a proud parent – eager introduce the new guys to the 'baby' my team had produced and watch them take their first toddler steps in our place.

Instead, the RIP was depressing, realizing that by sending our replacements only eight hours before we had to leave, the incoming battalion commander subtly said 'Fuck you.' He didn't give a shit or value our work. It was time to go, buh bye.

Looking back, the RIPTOA fiasco was the seminal event that crystalized my opinion of the war. Instead of replacement soldiers arriving seven days out from redeployment, my friends, anger and frustration reappeared. They befriended many of us early on.

That wouldn't be the last I'd see them on this deployment. Getting together with everyone else was an ugly, unwanted eye opener. We swapped stories, talked over each other, lamented the time in Afghanistan, and boasted about the first things we'd do when finally home, all of it usually involving alcohol, sex, food, and sleep. I was so angry and my head was so messed up that I stopped writing about my experiences. It took a long time to unwind and get normal. That was a typical reaction of people who deployed, no matter where they went, what they did, or how long they were gone. Each returned with a personal form of PTSD. Please be patient with us, we need it.

RIDICULOSITY

"I can spell a word: D-I-C-K!" Sister Mary snapped, when I complained about all the spelling mistakes in her report.

LAST NAMES UPDATE

We departed Afghanistan, made our way from Kyrgyzstan to El Paso, and are now home. Along the way I saw a few more noteworthy names, some that made me laugh, and some that made me cringe. Two guys in particular had funny names when you say them with their rank. Major Comfort and Major Biggie are officers I saw during the last few weeks of the deployment. Ridiculous, ain't it? I wonder how long they'll remain at that rank before making Lieutenant Colonel. I hope its forever.

There were more guys with chick names and ya couldn't help but feel sorry for them. Add Shelly, Leslie, and Shirley to Beverly, Carroll, Tiffany, and Vera. How much shit did those guys take growing up? More pair names to mention: Harry & Potter (also Dobby – the house elf), Richy & Rich, Traylor & Park, Cherry & Bacon (they have nothing in common but being food items), Ruff & Tumble, Weekly & Payment, So & Sweet, and Bird & Falcon.

Some made me laugh out loud when I saw them. Namm was a Soldier I saw on my base – and ya gotta expect the worldly kids who read anything besides comic books in elementary school called him Viet-Namm. Why wouldn't they? Hopefully, the guy had a witty retort.

In my unit we had an Asian soldier who always made fun of being Asian. He purposefully switched his L's and R's, trying to make us laugh. Once, he jumped out from behind a door and yelled, "Suh-plies!" It was cute and you couldn't help but chuckle.

I was standing in line at the chow hall at lunch, a few days before leaving our base. You naturally read the back of soldiers' hats – they have name tapes now. Can you guess what I saw?

Supplice! I nearly wet myself as images of Asians jumping out from hidden places bubbled up in my head. Sister Mary and I looked at each other and openly laughed at length.

Chip was with us, too; he's half Japanese. "Oh yeah, make fun of the Asians again!" he quietly said as he giggled along. I don't even think the guy was Asian.

Other names are just funny: Cruell, Shy, Stretch, Stuck, Six, Swimm, Lafairy, Heist, Humble, Quirk, Fair, Hemp, Rebl, Dickey, Beard, Booz, Bobb, Exile, McCool (no kidding, how awesome would that be), Obey (how strange?), Formal, Dues, and Eden. The combo names were interesting: Shortridge, Loveland, Musselman, Graypiece, and Showdown.

I confirmed every suspicion I ever had about being off balance when I saw this last name. We were in the chow hall in Kyrgyzstan (great place for observing stupid names) when a couple of soldiers sat at a table across from us. Looking over, I started humming a tune from my childhood about the dog, and you take away a letter of his name with each verse. Remember him, Bingo? One of the dudes sitting across from us was Ngo. I wanted to jump up, clapping my hands like a kid with Downs syndrome, pure joy on my face, yelling at the top of my lungs, "B-I-N-G-O!" I just started laughing and told my friends of my mental meltdown. They firmly suggested I get professional treatment. I can't totally disagree, but I'd rather have a massage.

"I can't believe this gym does not have punching bags..." Woody wondered out loud during a workout.

I yelled, "MARY!"

A MINI-REUNION

How many of you attend family or class reunions? My grandmother came from a big extended family so every summer we'd have a picnic by the lake where I'd meet cousins I'd never seen before. It was common to have up to 250 people. The annual family Christmas party was even bigger. There was a band composed of distant relatives, games, and entertainment for the kids, drinking, smoking, and card games for the adults, and the highlight of the evening – Santa Claus, usually drunk and reeking of cigarettes. The gifts always sucked and were never as cool as the gift you brought in exchange, but every kid got something that night, just like nearly every adult got a hangover. Oh, the carefree days of childhood – and those biannual events.

Our battalion returned from deployment in September. It was a painful process of reintegration training, demobilization paperwork, awards and recognition ceremonies, then a furious sprint to our separate homes. It was good to be back on American soil, but after a week at home with my new 'normal,' I began to miss the people with whom I spent an entire year. Normal didn't seem normal if I wasn't sharing it with my military family. Enter the reunion.

There's a huge annual Renaissance festival near Houston. I'd been once and loved it – it was a great setting for a reunion. I invited everyone to Austin, but Woody and Shaniese had started school, Josh wasn't interested, and Chip refused to return to Texas saying he hated everything about the state. But Sister Mary Danger and Layla came. My God, we had a great time.

I reserved a hotel room on 6th Street in Austin. If you're

unfamiliar with the Austin nightlife, 6th Street is the main attraction for bars, clubs, some restaurants, and basic debauchery. It's roped off on the weekends so the drunks don't get hit by cars while stumbling from bar to bar. It was a perfect place for us.

A few things happened that weekend – both Layla and Mary Danger decided they didn't like my ex, who had accompanied us to the Ren Fest. I understood their sentiments. It wasn't a healthy relationship and in their words I 'could do better.' During a late-night trip to the hospital, we discovered our dear Sister Mary is allergic to gluten – as evidenced by her weekend-long throwing up from all the gluten-laced tacos and beer. And most importantly, we realized just how strong our bonds of friendship had become and how much we missed each other. We decided to make this an annual event like the reunions of my childhood. I couldn't wait!

Fast-forward seven months.

REUNION, PART II

Much can change in a short time. Woody and Shaniese were still in school. Chip had broken up with his girlfriend and taken a job in D.C. Layla moved with her boyfriend to Virginia for work and Mary Danger had returned to Afghanistan as a civilian contractor. She was making good money this time, in direct contrast to her deployment as a low paid enlisted soldier. Yearning to reconnect with her old friends during a vacation home, she offered to rent a beach house in Ft. Lauderdale for all of us to party at. What a time that was.

But Chip would be absent again. I had the feeling he was still processing the return home and dealing with some demons. I e-mailed and called but couldn't reach him. He assured me things were going well and I took him at his word. Layla brought her boyfriend, Mark. Caitlin, a fellow soldier and mutual friend, showed up. Mary Danger's parents and sister were there and finally, me. It was an interesting group and a weird dynamic.

Our strong-willed, stubborn Sister Mary had fallen under the spell of her younger sister who generated and thrived on pointless drama. I had left my adult world in Austin and entered junior high girl-drama in Florida. Layla, Caitlin, and I thought we could booze or reminisce away the immaturity with some drinking games, war stories, and existential discussions, but our unholy Sister Mary wasn't biting. Turned out, Mary's contract job in Helmand province was surprisingly dangerous, and one day she stepped on a landmine on base. She only broke her foot and was knocked unconscious. This was earth-shattering news. One of our own could've been a statistic!

Danger, freely and almost nonchalantly, told us the story but we sensed the deep emotional and psychological scars. Our gun-slinging tomboy was a precious wounded lamb, who wouldn't accept our help. Caitlin and Layla tried getting into her head. I made many unsuccessful attempts to get her to open up and talk to me – nothing doing. I couldn't compete with her sister's familiar girl

251

drama instilled during adolescence and now overpowering. I wasn't her boss. I was a friend whose advice she could dismiss. And she did.

Layla, Caitlin, and I did our best to rekindle the original tight bonds we had developed with Mary, but it wasn't the same. She wouldn't let us. Like many people who served in a war zone, Danger was dealing with demons. Some were lingering problems from childhood, exacerbated by the strain of deployment. Others were new, yet just as debilitating.

We said our goodbyes at the airport on Sunday and went our separate ways. The fun times of easy laughter were over. One of our own was hurting and we tried in vain to help, but she refused. Thankfully, this wouldn't be the last time I saw Sister Mary Danger but our relationship and the relationships she had with everyone else would never be the same.

READJUSTMENT TO THE REAL WORLD - FOOD

Everyone goes through a period of adjustment when returning from an overseas deployment. I was no different. My experiences were unique to me just as other soldiers' were unique to them. Naturally, an adjustment to home life depended on the soldier's personality, sanity, deployment location, hardships, experiences, etc. And although unique, there were a few experiences I had in common with my buddies. Where to begin? There were so many. How about one of the basics – food?

If you read my previous updates about the DFAC (chow hall for those who've forgotten) you might recall the quantity and quality of food available. There was never a lack of decent food at my chow hall. Understand, some soldiers didn't have that luxury and instead, suffered through microwave pizza bites, chicken nuggets, tater tots, or the like, when they had hot food at all. That might be fun on a Saturday night when you were a kid, but an entire deployment of that shit would make MREs appetizing (caveat – I actually like MREs but wouldn't want them for an entire year either). So, the soldiers on our base had pretty decent grub.

While deployed, my system became unaccustomed to whatever preservatives, poison, or additives are commonly used in the States. I guess when stateside eating different foods, be it home-cooked, restaurant, fast food, deli, etc. our bodies are assaulted by organisms absent in Afghanistan. I thought I'd have a problem with the food over there. I didn't. But I was surprised to discover that when I returned, my digestive and excretory systems rebelled.

It was ugly at first. Initially, my appetite was pretty much gone. I didn't need or want to eat much. My stomach had shrunk and I required less fuel – probably because I hadn't worked out in forever and didn't need the energy. I'm sure it happened to many of us. But the more disturbing thing was what food did to my body.

253

RIDICULOSITY

Food in the U.S., at the chow hall at Ft. Bliss, at the fast-food joints at the mall, hell, even at decent restaurants, gave me bubbly guts. You know bubbly guts, right? It's different for everyone.

My bubbly guts were uncomfortable but not disgusting. I often felt a bloated, sometimes gurgling sensation in my stomach and intestines. It usually passed, depending on the food. But some of my favorites were absolutely off limits for a while. When I tried them anyway, I made sure I was close to a toilet.

I went on a date last Friday and had Indian food. It was great, I really enjoyed it, but my insides gurgled like I had swallowed cyanide.

Another time, during a blind date, I was in mighty pain and had some egregiously wrong gas – and if you know me, you know I think it's nice to share. I dropped dirty bombs all night – feeling like Saddam Hussein and my date was a Kurd. What a tragic way to return to the dating scene. BTW, I did get a thank you text but I doubt if I'll get another date.

A favorite of mine is Chipotle – you know, the Mexican fast-food chain created by McDonalds. Great stuff actually and a staple of my pre-deployment diet. Well, that delectable sustenance is currently off limits. I had it twice since returning home, mainly because it was the only eating venue near my storage unit since Quiznos closed. And although I relished the intense flavors and vivid memories of past burrito bowls, my guts exploded about two hours later and I destroyed two different public toilets.

Why do I tell you this? Well, mainly because some of you know returning soldiers. If and when you invite them to dinner, the bar, or over for a home-cooked meal, be sure to ask them what foods are off limits. I might speak for a few recent returning veterans when I say we certainly appreciate the offer of a meal, wherever that may be, but we definitely don't want to offend our hosts with what may follow.

READJUSTMENT TO THE REAL WORLD THAT'S NOT ME

If you watch TV, you've seen commercials with returning military members who surprised their families by coming home unexpectedly. The most emotive ones involve the uniform-wearing war vet surprising kids at school, who often shout "Daddy!" or "Mommy!" and burst into tears. Those commercials are pure marketing genius and always make my heart swell. However, that wasn't me. Not only am I childless, I wasn't in a relationship when I returned. My friends greeted me like good friends do with hugs and promises of beers, but I needed more.

My two-year relationship ended just prior to deployment and although I expected little from my ex when I returned, I was hoping I might get some compassion, even just a heartfelt, simple hug. I didn't. I'd been away about fifteen months total with the pre-deployment training and subsequent trip to Afghanistan. The entire time, I was focused on my soldiers, the mission, and staying alive. I never processed the break up – I couldn't afford that luxury.

The ex had moved on and was probably hesitant to show any emotion for fear of giving the wrong impression. I guess that makes sense, and believe me, getting back together was the last thing I wanted. But I hoped for more. If I learned anything during the deployment, it was that if someone isn't going to make you a priority, then you're only opening yourself to heartache. I had enough heartache while away. I became frustrated and angry that life had continued in my absence and friends, family, and yes, my ex, had experienced things I missed, or had moved on entirely.

I called Mark, my Army friend to catch up. We were deployed to different locations but talked and e-mailed a lot. He was like my kid brother and we're really tight. I told him how I got angry at the dumbest things, not like the typical stuff we all experienced – road rage, dogs peeing on the floor, a big zit right in the middle of your forehead, not being near a toilet when ya really gotta shit – no, not that stuff. I was mad about dumb crap that doesn't matter. He told me how he became enraged over his inability to make a meatball sandwich in his own kitchen. He was fuming about it when his wife walked in and asked him why he was yelling so much, and he laughed because he didn't know why. That's our normal redeployment integration in a nutshell.

I guess we were used to living in a small bubble with few of the freedoms and accompanying demands of home. Sure, things were crazy, but it was a limited, familiar crazy and we had mechanisms to cope. At least the army forced us to cope. However, back home many things were dependent on outside unfamiliar influences over which we had little control. We had to manage our own expectations as well as those of our friends and loved ones. We had to become dads, moms, brothers, etc. with the accompanying responsibilities – and that's hard when you're still adjusting.

It was hard to go from being a very strong, effective, productive person in control of only a small portion of one's life to being a regular Joe back home, responsible for and sometimes temporarily overwhelmed by everything for everyone. Especially when people treat you like you're stupid. Or maybe it's that we think people treat us like we are stupid. Yes, I returned from a year in Afghanistan, but I'm not retarded and I wasn't born two hours ago. Give me some credit. Now I know how blondes feel – considered a novelty or some kind of trophy. Uh yeah, I may look pretty, but there's a brain in here, too. I don't have rabid PTSD, even if I might be prone to angry outbursts. You're safe, I can be trusted.

Another thing I noticed about myself upon returning from deployment was that I enjoyed my time alone. I'd always been a people person, enjoying the company of others but completely content spending time by myself. Friends wanted to go to crowded bars, concerts, or sporting events (Rah! College football) and I'd go but usually only for a while. My tolerance for the juvenile games, noise, obnoxious behavior, and drunkenness was pretty low. I did miss going out in general, but I guess now I see things through a different lens. Maybe who's playing at the bar on Friday night isn't as important as it used to be because my focus for months had been finding bad guys and keeping people alive.

When one steps back and considers what is truly important, it wasn't how many numbers you got at the bar, which team won the game, or how much you benched at the gym. All that stuff was important, yet inconsequential. What mattered was whether or not the yearlong contribution and time in the deployment Twilight Zone mattered at all.

Many of my fellow soldiers were frustrated because it seemed our efforts were wasted. We risked our lives and the lives of Afghans to meet, develop relationships, and obtain information on the bad guys, only to have the actioning element (an infantry, armor, military police, engineer unit) disregard our data and our work. Instead of going after the bad guys, weapons caches, smugglers, etc., those units didn't do anything with our hard work – constrained by the rules that govern our conduct in Afghanistan. The rules the U.S. helped draft with our Afghan counterparts. Many of the rules sucked.

One thing I consciously didn't want to become was 'that guy,' the one desperate to talk about his experiences like it's the only important thing in the world. I observed 'that guy' at an airport awhile back. He was in uniform, young son in tow, acting like a minion sent to see the terrible ruler. The pleading eyes, his overly polite interaction with strangers, the hunched shoulders, all revealed an emasculated, impotent man. I couldn't approach. I couldn't make contact for fear of being sucked into his mental dysfunction and thereby threatening my own fragile, methodical reintegration.

Instead, I watched from afar, ready to step in if he devolved into a non-functioning being. I wondered how his eight-year-old son was coping. Daddy was supposed to be the guiding force in his life. Perhaps the roles were reversed, unbeknownst to him. So I watched and continued my self-prescribed therapy, thankful for being me.

VA counseling options were already overwhelmed and I wasn't distraught or affected enough to warrant taking an appointment away from the vet who witnessed a friend die, or lost an arm in a firefight, or suffered a traumatic brain injury from an IED. As a country, we've learned in retrospect that it was easy to build up our forces and eventually equip them with armor-plating, protective vests, etc. But the glaring oversight was what to do with us after the wars ended and we came home. Nobody planned for that.

The VA medical system needed an equal build up and restructuring. Instead, new veterans joined the long roster of previous ones suffering because of partisan bickering, budget cuts, and a lack of political foresight or will to address the problem. It should never have gotten this bad in the first place. But the average veteran doesn't contribute great amounts of cash or time to political campaigns, thus we don't matter – like much of the population. It's a fact, no sense gettin' bitter. We go on with life the best we can, coping and healing somewhat like our grandfathers did after WWII or our dads after Vietnam. If they can survive the horrors of war, we can survive this.

BACK TO OUR "NORMAL"?

To each his own. I discovered that despite the military's best efforts to help Army Reserve and National Guard soldiers transition from a military deployment to civilian life, there was no one-size-fits-all reintegration program. Each deployment was personal and unique; therefore the transition journeys were also unique. In general, it might've helped if you had something to which to return. What happened to my team?

Shaniese returned to college, she always wanted to be a nurse. Eventually, the beaming naïve girl let go of the military entirely. She would remain in touch with her friends from the army, but her life took a new, exciting direction.

Woody did what he intended to do – enroll at a four-year university. The genius transitioned from military to student life effortlessly and seriously kicked ass, graduating with a GPA of 3.97. Naturally, that one 'A' minus still vexes him.

Chip traveled the country visiting friends and spending much time with his brother in South Carolina. His untested relationship with Mikaela prior to and during the deployment ended amicably. He wasn't ready to put down roots in Mikaela's hometown so he moved to D.C. I'd hear more from Chip in the near future – both of us working through our individual PTSD.

Silas relocated to Belgium with his family to work at NATO headquarters. He leads an exciting life, full of adventure. Silas easily transitioned to success.

Don had a few hiccups getting back to normal after the deployment. The Army reserve finally awarded him a well-deserved promotion and he resumed teaching high school classes and the normal life to which we all aspire.

Like many women, Layla suffered from two things – first, she didn't recognize how awesome she was and the power she had over men. Must've been the insecurity demons that afflict many of us, or maybe she was comfortable, when she should've strived for better. Layla moved to Virginia with the toxic boyfriend in tow, but jealousy and manipulation characterized the end of their relationship. She's moved on, literally and figuratively. Layla founded a successful company and married a fantastic guy. He has yet to prove to me that he's her equal, but honestly, I don't know if any man could. She's just that incredible.

The person with whom I formed the tightest bond was Sister Mary Danger. Our friendship would experience quite a few bumps. Mary was mentally and emotionally lost, and felt compelled to erase the void our return from Afghanistan created in her immediate life. The IED incident really F'd with her head.

It's always tough transitioning from a value-add role to the daily grind, especially when the grind is mundane or worse, non-existent. Danger needed the camaraderie and immediate sense of purpose a war zone provides. She never fully transitioned to civilian life from the military mindset. Thus, multiple contractor positions were in her near future. We'd be in contact, but it would be very different. There'd be lots of drama, bouts of near black out drinking, scathing email, horrific, mean statements and deep sadness. I learned the extent of how Mary's demons controlled her behavior, and I'd endure the brunt of her vitriol. But I'd never give up. We will always be family.

I came to appreciate each team member and the goofy family dynamic we built and fostered during the deployment, which for me, was a hybrid of leadership and friendship. In retrospect, I think each learned a bit about himself, the mission in Afghanistan, and the personal effects of stress. I entered pre-deployment training confident in my skillset but wondering how to best motivate a team of strangers to succeed.

I left Afghanistan dispirited by the callous disregard for all we had accomplished, but grateful for the experience, the friendships and home. Did we leave the area better off than when we arrived? Meh, who knows, that wasn't my concern anymore.

The fifteen-month 'pause' in my normal life was over and I resumed those Friday night Happy Hours, the morning weekend runs at the lake, and easy phone calls to family and friends. But Afghanistan, now a part of my psyche and personal history, still lingered, as it always will. This wasn't my first deployment to

Asskrakistan, nor would it be my last.

Working for the defense industry is never a sure bet, no matter how much experience or education you have. Nine months after returning to that normal life I would find myself unemployed. And five months after being laid off, I found myself back in Afghanistan, but this time as a civilian contractor. I applied the lessons from the military deployment to my staff-advisor position in Kabul. Instead of one team, I eventually worked for three separate casts of military supervisors, a plethora of civilians, and countless NATO Soldiers. It would be an experience like no other.

But had I mentally returned to normal from the military deployment? In retrospect, no, not entirely. It takes longer for a citizen soldier to deprogram himself from a deployment than it does an active-duty member. Nah, I wasn't crazy, but I hadn't learned to completely relax and let my mental guard down. Maybe that was influenced by the layoff. Who knows? What I did and could look forward to, was another opportunity to experience and share military ridiculosity. Thus, I'm about three quarters of the way done with the sequel to this book. I hope you enjoy reading about those experiences as much as I enjoyed living them.

RIDICULOSITY

EPILOGUE

The U.S. has a long history of going to war, reflected in various movies and books that detail some of the struggles our Soldiers, Sailors, Airmen and Marines experience. I wrote this book for a few reasons: to educate my family and friends on our daily life in Afghanistan and to entertain them with stories of the ridiculous assclownery we created or were affected by. I also put pen to paper as a way of processing the dysfunction or hilarity that ruled our life for over a year. My hope is that it inspires veterans to do the same. Writing was my way of dealing with the effects of deployment-related PTSD.

There's an army saying you often hear – Train as you fight. In my military profession you can only train. Medics, supply techs, computer nerds – they can actually do their 'war time' job because it's the same as a non-wartime job. As an intelligence professional, I'm bound by regulations against collecting information when not in a war zone or on a specific mission. Thus, wars, police actions, conflicts – you name it – are what we live for. Therefore, I was and will always be thankful for that deployment experience. Would I feel the same had I suffered some horrific loss? Maybe not, who knows.

Friends asked – what about the Afghan war in general? What are my thoughts? I felt the 2001 Afghan invasion was justified. Those asscrackers came to our house and gut punched us. I lost my job because of them. I was elated to dish out some pain. Like everyone else, I wanted revenge. But then the national focus shifted. Less attention was paid to Al Qaeda where it should've been, the Taliban regrouped, and the Haqqanni network became stronger. I'd find myself back in Afghanistan eight years later, fighting a resilient set of enemies that should've been vanquished long before. It was another chance to gain more of that experience we only get from war, but I would've rather been eight years into a great civilian career. I'm nobody, so my opinion holds zero weight in the big picture.

Yet with each passing year, I reflect fondly on that last

deployment to Afghanistan and what we endured. It was frustrating and challenging, but maybe I'm one of the lucky ones. I tried to recognize the positives in the experience. There were many. And when no laughter existed, I tried to insert it. As Bruce Springsteen suggested – maybe I'll always reflect on those Glory Days.

ACRONYMS

ACU	Army Combat Uniform – the green/grey pixilated duty uniform for soldiers
BAF	Bagram Airfield, the central point in/out of Afghanistan, also known as BARF
BC	Battalion Commander
COP	Combat Outpost: a smaller base with fewer people/ amenities, usually in a more kinetic (dangerous) area
CSM	Command Sergeant Major – the senior enlisted advisor to a battalion (or higher) commander
DFAC	Dining Facility, aka Chow Hall, or gut hut
FOB	Forward Operating Base: a larger, better-equipped base with more people and amenities
Fobbit	A derogatory term for soldiers or civilians that never leave a FOB
Haji	An innocent (but deemed derogatory) term US soldiers use for an Afghan. Or, an honorary title for a Muslim who's attended the Haj.
HMMWV	High Mobility Multipurpose Wheeled Vehicle, aka Humvee or Hummer
HQ	Headquarters – where any organization staff is located
HUD	Housing & Urban Development

RIDICULOSITY

IED   Improvised Explosive Device – insurgents emplaced them in roads

M-4   A standard issue weapon, similar to the M-16, but shorter in length

Manjams   Typical male Afghan clothing which resemble pajamas

MRAP   Mine-Resistant Ambush Protected: one of those huge metal behemoth vehicles the military uses to transport soldiers and go on mission

MWR   Morale Welfare & Recreation – can mean a building or activities where soldiers/civilians can relax and let their hair down

NCO   Non-Commissioned Officer (Sergeant, Corporal, Staff Sergeant, etc.), responsible for training and looking after soldiers

PT(s)   Physical Training – Army exercising, or the uniform soldiers wear when exercising

PX   Post Exchange – the on-base store where we shop, if available

QC   Quality Control – editing intelligence and/or analytical reports

RIPTOA   Relief in Place/Transition of Authority – the overlapping transition period when one military organization replaces another in a combat zone

SPC   Specialist, an Army rank the same pay grade as Corporal, below a Sergeant but above a Private First Class

VBIED   A vehicle-borne IED (car bomb)

XO   Executive Officer – the second most senior officer, after
         a unit commander

RIDICULOSITY

ABOUT THE AUTHOR

Todd Campau is a successful project manager, business analyst, writer, and a long-serving intelligence collection professional with the U.S. Army. He is an astute observer and analyst of human nature and interaction. Todd deployed to Afghanistan in 2001 and to Iraq in 2003. His latest deployment, on which Ridiculosity – a Deployment to Afghanistan is based, was in 2010. Todd has served under five Commanders-in-Chief, working at various levels in the US Army Military Intelligence community to include the coalition joint forces (NATO) level. Todd received a B.A. in Slavic Studies from the University of Michigan and an M.B.A from the University of Texas. He is currently a member of the U.S. Army Reserves and lives in Austin, Texas. Learn more at: www.SoldierTodd.com

CPSIA information can be obtained
at www.ICGtesting.com
Printed in the USA
BVOW06s2134130217
476104BV00009B/240/P